"The writing in *Glas* offers startling evidence that the great Russian literary tradition lives on." —
AMERICAN BOOKSELLER

"GLAS gives us a sense of Russian literature in motion. If it cannot — perhaps mercifully — convey fully what it is like to live in Russia at present, GLAS at least gives us a taste of what it is to be a reader there." — *Times Literary Supplement*

"GLAS provides a fascinating picture of Russian letters today, and an absorbing, if somewhat disturbing psychological portrait of a society in disarray... It is indispensable for anyone interested in contemporary Russian fiction. If it is sometimes distressing reading, we should bear in mind the times it is reflecting, and not blame the mirror for the image it produces." — *Moscow Times*

"These stories, which are amusing and unique, act like a playground swing, each one flinging itself into a direction different from the others..." —
Boston Book Review

"A whimsical quality runs through these stories... To some extent the book is an attempt to come to grips with the chaos of the present through an examination of the formative past... Inevitably, Gogol makes his influence felt in many of these stories." —
Moscow Times

GLAS NEW RUSSIAN WRITING

contemporary Russian literature

in English translation

Volume 38

CONTEMPORARY RUSSIAN STORIES

glas

PY
3286 GLAS Publishers
.C37 tel./fax: +7(095)441-9157
2005 perova@glas.msk.su
www.russianpress.com/glas

Glas is distributed in North America by
NORTHWESTERN UNIVERSITY PRESS
Chicago Distribution Center,
tel: 1-800-621-2736 or (773) 702-7000
fax: 1-800-621-8476 or (773)-702-7212
pubnet@202-5280
www.nupress.northwestern.edu

in the UK and Europe by
INPRESS LIMITED
Tel: 020 8832 7464
Fax: 020 8832 7465
stephanie@inpressbooks.co.uk
www.inpressbooks.co.uk

Edited by Natasha Perova and Joanne Turnbull
Cover design by Anastasia Perova
Camera-ready copy by Tatiana Shaposhnikova

ISBN 5-7172-0072-2

CONTENTS

THE PERESTROIKA CHAOS

REMEMBERING THE SOVIET PAST

We're All Captives...

We are all in some sense captives in today's world: captives of a political system, of circumstances, of our obligations or our illusions, to say nothing of those who are captives in a literal sense. The world seems to be full of misplaced people trapped in captivity of one kind or another, sometimes self-imposed, but feeling nonetheless alienated from a hostile world around them.

These stories from earlier issues of Glas have long been classics in Russian literature while their themes have become even more relevant today due to the changed situation in Russia in favor of bureaucratic totalitarianism and the unending war in the Caucasus. "More now than ever before, precisely because hopes on their native ground are again precarious," to quote Georges Steiner who noticed the tendency already some years ago.

For the sake of our new readers who have missed those earlier Glas issues we decided to reprint selected stories from them. The stories have been grouped in two sections: "The Perestroika Confusion" and "Remembering the Soviet Past". The first group of stories, often verging on the absurd, conveys the chaos in the lives and minds of simple Russians in the face of unfamiliar market problems. The second part is a reminder of the Soviet past, which so many Russians are nostalgic for today forgetting its inhuman essence as they are coping with the present-day difficulties.

Vladimir Makanin's "The Captive of the Caucasus", which gives this collection its name, captures the gist of the Russo-Chechen conflict in the Caucasus in one episode from the daily warfare going on there. It is one vivid example of the illusory nature of man's freedom: here Russian troops find that they are the captives of the land they think they have conquered.

In "The Tambourine for the Upper World" Victor Pelevin, the idol of Russia's young readers, depicts a group of enterprising girls who resuscitate foreign corpses from the battlefields of the Second World War so as to marry them and get themselves out of the perestroika-ravaged Russia.

Vassily Aksyonov, an internationally known author, turns to the funny side of the Russo-American cultural gaps in the confusion of the early post-Soviet years in his "Palmer's First Flight." With his characteristic wit he describes the misunderstandings on both sides of the cultural and political divide.

Alexander Terekhov, a young and vital writer with a distinctive and individual intonation, is known for his figurative language and wholesome realism. He paints a satirical picture of a small provincial town in the throes of a local fight for power ("The Rat-killer").

Vyacheslav Rybakov's fantastic story "Hassle" paints a weird picture of the post-Soviet excesses and the epidemic of emigration, which the author depicts literally as a grave disease.

Georgy Vladimov's Booker-prize-winning novel looks back at the less-known aspects of the Second World War. The episode we offer here illustrates the all-pervading atmosphere of shadowing and spying in which practically all of the soldiers were involved (*The General and his Army*).

Vassily Grossman, the world-famous 20th century classic, looks at the Civil War in the 1920s Russia from an unusual angle: a woman commissar happens to give birth in a Jewish home and then she leaves the baby behind for the Jewish family to raise.

An undisputed master of realist prose, Friedrich Gorenstein has a wicked sense of humor reminiscent of Ivan Bunin. His "Bag in Hand" is both a funny and frightening portrait of the small person under socialism when the chronic shortages of the basic consumer goods and foodstuffs reduced people's lives to constant queuing leaving little time and energy for any loftier occupations.

Yevgeny Popov's story reverberates with laughter and teasing humor that sometimes verges on the lyrical. Popov insists that "literature of the absurd is the realism of the 20th century." His "Pork Kebabs" is set in the 1960s but could have taken place today.

The collection is concluded with a series of short stories about the communal living in Russia, a phenomenon that no Westerner can understand.

The Editors

The Perestroika
Chaos

Vladimir
MAKANIN

The Captive of the Caucasus

Translated by Arch Tait

"**B**eauty will save the world."[*] Most likely the soldiers had not heard that, but what beauty was they both had a fair idea. Among the mountains they were only too aware of it, and found it daunting. A stream leaping without warning out of a crevice. Right now an open clearing, dazzlingly yellow in the sun, testing their nerves. Rubakhin, more experienced, led the way.

The mountains were suddenly gone. The sun-drenched expanse ahead spoke to Rubakhin of a happy childhood he had never had. Proud southern trees whose names he did not know rose up in isolation above the grass, but what most stirred his plainsman's soul was the tall grass, rustling, breathing in the slight breeze.

"Hold back, Vovka. No hurry," he warned softly.

Cross an open place you're unfamiliar with and you can bet you're in someone's sights. Before emerging from the dense scrub Hot Shot Vovka raised his rifle and made a leisurely sweep with it from left to right using the telescopic sight as binoculars. He held his breath, surveying this expanse so generously flooded with sunlight. He noticed a small transistor radio by a hillock.

"Aha!" Hot Shot Vovka exclaimed in a whisper. (The glass on the little radio had glinted in the sun.)

In short bursts the two soldiers raced in their camouflage tunics to the half dug (and long abandoned) trench of a gas pipeline and the gingery hillock with its autumn colouring. They turned the radio over in their hands, already recognizing it. When Corporal Boiarkov was drunk he liked to go off and lie down somewhere on his own, cradling this antiquated transistor radio in his arms. Parting the tall grass they looked for the body and found it nearby. Boiarkov's corpse was weighed down

---

[*] A quote from Dostoyevsky.

by two rocks. Death had found him. He had been shot at point blank range, most likely before he even had time to rub his drunken eyes. His cheeks were sunken. It had been decided in the unit that he must have done a runner. His documents were missing. That would have to be reported. But why hadn't the fighters taken the radio? Because it could incriminate them? More likely it was too old and tinny for them. Not worth taking. The irrevocability of what had happened (death is one thing that is plainly irrevocable) made them move, made them want to get it over with. Dredging with flat stones, they hastily dug a grave for the murdered man, equally hastily shaped the mound of earth above him into a conspicuous man-made hill, and continued on their way.

Again they are coming out of a defile, again there is tall grass which hasn't shrivelled at all. It sways gently and birds call joyously to each other in the sky above the trees and above the two soldiers. Perhaps beauty is already saving the world, a reminder from another place, which keeps a man on the right path (walking not far away, admonishing him). Keeping him on his toes, beauty also keeps him mindful.

This time, however, the sunny open space is familiar and not dangerous. The mountains recede and ahead the path is level. Slightly further on is a dusty fork in a road much driven over by military vehicles where their unit is stationed. The soldiers unwittingly march faster.

Lieutenant-Colonel Gurov is not in the unit but at home. They will need to see him there. Without pausing to recover their breath the soldiers get themselves over to where Gurov lives, the undisputed ruler of these parts, and of all the beautiful sun-soaked adjacent parts of this earth. He lives with his wife in a fine wooden house with a vine-draped veranda on which to relax. A smallholding adjoins the house. It is noon, the hottest time of the day. Lieutenant-Colonel Gurov and a local man,

13

Alibek, are sitting out on the open veranda. Somnolent after lunch, they are dozing in light cane chairs and waiting for tea to be brought. Rubakhin, faltering and nervous, makes his report. Gurov looks dozily at these two dust-covered privates who have landed in on him and whose faces, another minus, are unfamiliar to him. For a moment he is young again. Suddenly raising his voice he shouts at them that nobody will be receiving reinforcements, for Christ's sake what do they take him for! He will be sending none of his soldiers out to rescue trucks up shit creek as a result of their own stupidity!

Worse, he is not going to let them off that easily. Angry now, he orders the two soldiers to get to work shifting sand. They can do some honest hard work on his smallholding. About turn! Quick march! Spread that pile of sand by the gate on all the paths leading to the house and the vegetable garden. There is so much frigging mud everywhere, you can't walk down them... The lieutenant-colonel's wife is pleased, as any smallholder would be, to have unpaid soldierly labour. Anna Fedorovna promptly appears with cries of joy in the vegetable garden with her sleeves rolled up, wearing muddy, broken men's boots, and urges that they should also help her on the vegetable beds.

The soldiers wheel the sand out by the barrow load and shovel it over the paths. It is hot, and the sand is damp, evidently brought from down by the river.

Vovka perches the radio of the murdered corporal on a pile of sand and finds music with a good beat to lighten the work, but not too loud. He does not want to upset Gurov and Alibek who are talking away on the veranda. Judging by what reaches them of Alibek's drawl, he is negotiating for guns, a serious matter.

The radio on its sandy eminence reminds Rubakhin of what a beautiful spot Boiarkov chose to get killed in. The witless drunk had been scared to sleep in the wood, so instead he had gone out into the clearing, and even on to a hillock. When the fighters came for him he pushed the little radio (his one true friend) aside so that it should slide downhill into the grass. He didn't want to lose it. He himself could take his chances. No. It was hardly likely. He had simply been drunk, fallen asleep, and the radio had fallen from his hands and rolled away down the slope.

They had shot him point blank. Youngsters, no doubt, who wanted to get their first kill in as soon as possible, to get the taste for it, even if the guy was asleep. Now here was his radio perched on this pile of sand, and Rubakhin saw again the reddish, sun-drenched mound with two bushes growing tenaciously on its northern slope. The beauty of the place had been breathtaking, and Rubakhin would not let it go from his memory. He drank it in more and more, the slope Boiarkov fell asleep on, the hillock, the grass, the golden leaves on the bushes, and all of it one more invaluable lesson in survival. Beauty strives constantly to save us, calling to a man through memory, reminding him.

At first they tried to force the wheelbarrows through the muddy soil, then had the sense to put boards down on the paths. Vovka came first, chirpily pushing his barrow along, and behind him Rubakhin shoving an enormous barrow with a mountain of sand in it. He had stripped to the waist. Wet with sweat, his muscular body gleamed in the sun.

2

"I'll let you have ten Kalashnikovs. I can give you five crates of ammunition. Hear that, Alibek? Not three, five crates."

"I hear."

"But I must have those provisions by the first of the month..."

"My dear Colonel, I like to have a little nap after lunch. You too, as I know. I do hope Anna Fedorovna has not forgotten our tea."

"No need to worry about that."

"What do you mean, no need to worry?" his guest laughed. "Tea is not the same as war. Tea gets cold."

Gurov and Alibek return gradually to their conversation, which shows no sign of concluding, but the sluggishness with which they talk and certain laziness in their arguing are deceptive. Alibek has come to get weapons, and Gurov, his officers and men, are in desperate need of provisions. What they have to barter is, of course, arms, sometimes petrol.

"I want the food by the first. And cut out those idiotic ambushes in the mountains. I'm not bothered about wine, but we must have at least some vodka."

"There is no vodka."

"Find some, Alibek, find some. I'm finding ammunition for you."

The lieutenant-colonel calls his wife. "How's the tea coming along?" "Ah, I'll just be getting you some good strong tea this very moment."

"Anna, what are you saying? I thought you called to us from the garden that you had made it already!"

While they wait for the tea the two of them unhurriedly light up, basking in postprandial torpor. The smoke trails indolently over the cool veranda to the vine, wafting thence towards the vegetable garden.

Vovka signals to Rubakhin that he is going to try to get them a bottle of something (to make the best of a bad job), and edges towards the wattle fence. He has an infinite repertoire of ingenious signals and gestures. On the other side of the fence is a young woman with her child. Vovka gives her a wink. He jumps over the fence and gets talking. Well, good luck to him! Rubakhin gets on with pushing his barrow full of sand. Each to his own. Vovka is one of those impetuous soldiers who cannot stand slogging away at a dull job (or any other job, come to that).

Already they are on the best of terms. Amazing, the way she came round, as if all she was waiting for was a soldier to come along and say a kind word to her. Of course, Vovka is a likeable guy who smiles a lot and puts down roots in an instant.

Vovka puts his arms round her. She smacks his hands. The usual stuff. They can be seen, and Vovka understands he needs to get her into the darkness of the house. He tries sweet-talking her, tries dragging her in. The young woman resists. "Not so fast, you!" she laughs, but step by step they are both moving towards the house with its door half-open because of the heat. Now they are there, and not far from the door her toddler goes on playing with the cat.

Rubakhin meanwhile is labouring away with his barrow. Where the path is too muddy he moves boards from where they were before and lays them end-to-end in the new position. He wheels the barrow over them carefully, balancing the heavy sand.

Lieutenant-Colonel Gurov continues his unhurried dealing with Alibek. His wife (after washing her hands and putting on a red blouse) has served each of them tea in a separate elegant little oriental teapot.

"Anna Fedorovna brews a fine cup of tea," Alibek compliments her.

Gurov says, "Why are you being so pig-headed, Alibek! To an outsider you could seem to be our captive. You need to remember where you are: right in the middle of my territory."

"What do you mean, your territory?"

"I mean just that: the lowlands here are in our hands."

"The lowlands are yours, but the mountains are ours."

Alibek laughs. "What sort of a captive am I? It is you who are the captive here." He points laughingly at Rubakhin, busily wheeling his barrow. "He is the captive. You are the captive. Every last one of your soldiers is the captive." He laughs once more. "But I, I am not a captive."

He starts right in again.

"Twelve Kalashnikovs, and seven crates of ammunition."

Now it is Gurov's turn to laugh.

"Twelve, ha-ha! What sort of a number do you call that? Twelve! Where do you get a number like that from? Ten I can understand. Ten is a proper number, one you can remember. Right then, ten rifles."

"Twelve!"

"Ten...!"

Alibek sighs with delight.

"What an evening it is going to be. My goodness!"

"It's a long time yet till evening."

They slowly sip their tea, two people talking unhurriedly who have known and respected each other for a very long time. (Rubakhin is wheeling another barrow load of sand. He tips it out, spreads it level with the soil.)

"You know, Colonel, what our old men are saying? We have some wise old men in our villages."

"Well, what are they saying?"

"They are saying it is time for another campaign against Europe. It is time to fight there again."

"You certainly think big, Alibek. Europe, eh?!"

"Why not? Europe is only Europe. The old men say it is not so far away. They are not happy. The old men say, where the Russians go we should go too, and how is it we are shooting at each other?"

"You'd better ask your own people that!" Gurov exclaims, irritated.

"Oh, oh you are offended. Let us drink tea and our hearts grow kinder..."

They are silent for a time. Alibek returns to his theme, unhurriedly topping up his cup from the little teapot.

"It's not so far away. Every now and again you need to invade Europe. The old men say it will immediately bring peace to us and life will get back to normal."

"Some chance, Alibek. Don't hold your breath!"

"The tea is truly excellent. Oh, Anna Fedorovna, please make us some more. I beg you."

Gurov sighs.

"It really is going to be a lovely evening. You're right, there."

"I am always right, dear Colonel. Okay, ten Kalashnikovs. I agree. But seven crates of ammunition."

"You're at it again. Where do you pluck these numbers from? There is no such number as seven!"

The mistress of the house brings out the leftovers from lunch (in two white saucepans) to feed to her fortuitous soldiers. Rubakhin is keenly appreciative. "Oh yes, thank you very much!" When did a soldier ever refuse food? "But where is your mate?" The inarticulate Rubakhin lies cloddishly that he thinks his mate has an upset stomach. As an afterthought he adds, only marginally more convincingly, "Really going through it he is, poor guy." "Perhaps he ate too much greens or fruit?" the lieutenant-colonel's wife asks solicitously.

The cold kvass soup is really good, with egg and pieces of sausage. Rubakhin gets stuck in to the first saucepan, rattling out a signal with his spoon.

It is a signal which Vovka hears and, of course, correctly interprets, but eating is not the biological function presently uppermost in his mind. The young woman in turn hears (and also correctly interprets) the hysterical miaowing coming from the yard, to be followed by the wail of her toddler ("Mu-um!"), evidently scratched in return for pulling the cat's tail. She is in thrall to her senses. She has languished for want of love and now clings ecstatically to Vovka, not wishing to miss this chance of happiness. As for Hot Shot Vovka, he is in his element, every inch a soldier. The child's petulant shriek is heard again, "Mu-u-um..."

The woman tears herself from the bed, sticks her head out the door, shushes the little pest, and shuts the door again more firmly. Padding across the floor in her bare feet she returns to her soldier and bursts into flames all over again. "Wow, you're hot! You really put out," Vovka tells her in delight, but she closes his mouth: "Shhh..."

Vovka explains his simple errand to her in a whisper, asking the young woman to pop down to the shop and buy him some of their terrible fortified wine. They won't sell it to a soldier in uniform, but it's no problem for her.

He shares his main worry with her too: right now they could do with not just a bottle but a whole crate of wine.

"What for?"

"To buy ourselves out of trouble. We're stuck at a roadblock."

"Well, if you need to buy wine what did you come to the colonel for?"

"Because we're idiots."

The young woman is suddenly crying. She tells Vovka she lost her way recently and got gang raped. Vovka gives a whistle of amazement. Having expressed proper sympathy, he asks (with considerable curiosity) how many of them there were. "Four," she sobs, wiping her eyes with a corner of the sheet. He is eager for more detail but she doesn't want to talk about it. She nuzzles her head in his chest, kissing it, hungry for words of comfort. A simple wish.

They talk some more. Yes, of course she will buy him the bottle of wine, but only if he comes to the shop with her so she can hand it straight over to him. She can't be seen coming home with a bottle after what happened to her. People know all about it. They will get ideas.

There is a lot of food in the second saucepan too, barley porridge with beef. Rubakhin polishes off the lot, but without indecent haste. He washes it down with two mugs of cold water. This leaves him feeling slightly chilled, and he puts his shirt back on.

"Time for a little nap," he says to himself and retires to the fence.

He lies down and soon drifts off. Through the nearby open window of the house, into which Vovka disappeared, a murmured conversation carries to him.

Vovka: "I'll give you a present, a nice headscarf, or I'll get you a shawl somewhere."

She: "But you're just now leaving." Weeping.

Vovka: "Well, I'll send you it, then. Course I will!"

For a long time Vovka tries to get her to bend over. He is a bit stocky and has never made any secret of the fact that he likes to screw large women doggy fashion. He has readily described it to the other soldiers. Can she really not see what he's on about? It's such fun with a big woman. She fends him off coyly. To the sound of their incessant torrid whispering (he can no longer make out the words) Rubakhin falls asleep.

Outside the shop, the moment his girl handed over the bottle of wine, Hot Shot Vovka shoved it deep into a good strong pocket in his soldier's trousers and ran for all he was worth back to the deserted Rubakhin. The young woman had done him more than one favour and now shouted reproachfully after him, apprehensive about raising her voice in the street, but Vovka just waved. "Bye. See you around." Now he had

21

other fish to fry. He ran off down the narrow street, taking a short cut between the wicker fences, back to Lieutenant-Colonel Gurov's house. He had news for Rubakhin (and what news!) While he was hanging around minding his own business outside their dismal little shop (and also waiting for his bottle of wine) he had overheard some soldiers walking past.

Jumping over the fence, he found Rubakhin asleep and gave him a shake.

"Rubakhin, listen. This is straight. Savkin is taking a posse into the woods to disarm the competition."

"Eh?" Rubakhin looked at him blearily.

Trying to wake him up, Vovka blustered,

"They're going disarming. Let's get in on it. Nab a cloth-head and we've got it made. You said yourself..."

Rubakhin was now wide awake. Yes, he got the point. Yes, it was just what they needed. Ye-es, they would more than likely strike it lucky. They should move. The soldiers quietly absented themselves from the lieutenant-colonel's estate, carefully collecting their knapsacks and the guns they had left by the well. They climbed over the fence and left by someone else's gate so as not to be seen and called back.

The two men on the veranda did not see them, and did not call them back. They carried on sitting where they were.

It was hot, it was still, and Alibek was quietly singing "Midnights in Moscow" to himself. He had a clear voice.

It was still.

"People do not change, Alibek."

"You believe this?"

"They just grow older."

"Hah! Like you and me." Alibek refilled his cup with a thin stream of tea from his teapot. He no longer felt like haggling. He felt sad. He had in any case already said all he had to say, and now his words would (with their own unhurried logic) find their way to the heart of his old friend Gurov. There was no need to say them aloud.

"Good tea has completely disappeared. You can't get it any more."

"Too bad."

"Tea is getting more expensive, food is getting more expensive, but the times are not a-changing," Alibek drawled.

Gurov's wife was just at this moment bringing another two pots of tea. It was true. Tea was getting more expensive. "But whether the times are changing or not, you will bring us those provisions, my friend," Gurov thought and also, for the moment, did not bother to say the words out loud.

Gurov knew that Alibek was brighter and craftier than he was. Against that his own thoughts, if not numerous, were solid and had been thought through over a period of many years to such a degree of clarity that they were no longer mere thoughts, but as much a part of his body as his hands and feet.

In the good old days (of the Soviet Union) if there was any disruption of the army supplies, or even if the soldiers' rations were merely delayed, Gurov would promptly don his dress uniform. He would pin on his medals. In the Gaz army jeep (the dust! the draught!) he would hurtle along the twisting mountain roads to the regional administrative centre, finally drawing up at a colonnaded building, sweeping in at full speed, looking neither at the visitors nor the petitioners worn down by long waiting, straight in to see the man at the top. If it wasn't the regional Party committee, it was the local Soviet. Gurov knew how to get what he needed. When necessary he would drive over to the warehouse himself, grease a few palms, and even sometimes persuade someone in power to see things his way by presenting them with a distinctive pistol. "Could come in handy: this is the Orient, you know!" he would say, little dreaming that one day his joke would become deadly earnest.

Except that nowadays one pistol counted for nothing. Nowadays ten rifles got you nowhere, they wanted twelve. Gurov had soldiers to feed. As a man grows older he grows more resistant to change but, in compensation, more tolerant of human weakness. It keeps him on an even keel. He had himself to feed, come to that. Life was moving on, and Lieutenant-Colonel Gurov was giving it a helping hand, no more than that. Bartering weapons with the local fighters, he gave no thought to the use they would make of them. What was that to do with him? Life had moved on into a world of dealing (trade anything you like for anything you like) and Gurov was dealing. Life had moved on into a world where wars were fought (ghastly wars, neither one thing nor the other!), and Gurov, naturally, was there to fight in those wars. He was there to fight, but there was no shooting. Only from time to time he would disarm the competition when ordered to do so. Or shoot if the order came from the top. He could handle even this period. He was up to his job but... of course he missed the old times. He missed the old times when you knew where you stood, when you jumped into your jeep, swept into that office, could turn the air blue with oaths and then, condescending to make peace, flop down in a leather armchair and smoke with the regional official as if he were an old friend. While the petitioners waited their turn outside the door. One time he didn't find the Party boss in his office or at home. He was away on a business trip, but his wife wasn't. She was sitting there at home when Gurov arrived, and he got all he needed from her. She gave dashing young Major Gurov, whose hair at that time was just beginning to be streaked with grey, what only a bored wife left alone for a whole week in summer can give. All that and more, he thought, remembering the keys to the cavernous No. 2 cold store at the regional meat processing plant where they kept the freshly cured meat.

"Alibek! I've just remembered. Get us some smoked meat as well, would you?"

3

Since Tsarist times disarming expeditions in the Caucasus had been known as "horse-shoeing". Russian troops would surround the fighters but not fully close the encirclement. Just one way out would be left. Bolting down this path the fighters would become extended into a straggling single file. Mounting an ambush to the right or left it was then possible, if not exactly straightforward, to pick them off one at a time, dragging them into the bushes (or leaping out and knocking one off the path into the ditch and disarming him there). The operation was, of course, carried out to the accompaniment of much firing in the air to encourage them to leave the encirclement.

They both managed to infiltrate the disarming squad, but Vovka was spotted and chucked out: Lieutenant Savkin only trusted men he knew. His eyes flickered over the solid physique of Rubakhin without snagging, and no rasping order to take "Two paces forward!" ensued, most likely because Savkin simply hadn't noticed he was an outsider. Rubakhin was standing among a group of the most powerfully built soldiers. He fitted in well.

The minute they started shooting Rubakhin moved fast into position in an ambush. He had a quick smoke in the bushes with a corporal called Gesha. They were both old timers and reminisced about others who had already been demobbed. They didn't envy them. Why the fuck should they? Who was to say who was better off anyway?

"Nifty movers, this lot," Gesha said, not bothering to raise his eyes to the shadows flitting past in the bushes.

At first the fighters ran by in twos and threes, crashing noisily through scrub that had sprouted up on the little used path, but now one or two stragglers were being caught. A shriek, a scuffle... and silence. ("They took him?" Gesha's look asked, and Rubakhin answered with a nod, "Yup".) The sound of someone again crashing towards them through the scrub was growing louder. The fighters could still just about shoot (and, of course, kill), but charging through scrub clutching a rifle and with an ammunition belt round your neck while under fire is not good for morale. Scared shitless and running into sporadic fire from the ambushes, the fighters needed no urging to keep to a path which seemed to be getting narrower, leading to the mountains and out of trouble.

"This one'll be mine then, okay?" Rubakhin said, half rising and moving fast towards the light.

"Go get him!" said Gesha, hastily finishing his cigarette.

"This one" turned out to be two running together, but having leaped out of the bushes Rubakhin could not change his mind. "Halt! Halt!" he yelled terrifyingly as he ran after them. He had not got off to much of a start. He was a muscleman not a sprinter, but once he built up speed neither the trampled bushes nor the loose scree underfoot could slow him. He flew like a bird.

He was pounding along six yards or so behind the second fighter. The first one was nippier than Rubakhin and pulling away. The second he was not too worried about (he was very close to him now). He could see the tommy gun round his neck, but either he was out of ammunition, or perhaps he just didn't know how to fire it on the run. The first was more dangerous. He did not have a gun, so he must have a pistol.

Rubakhin turned on the heat. He could hear running feet behind him. Gesha. Great! Two against two...

Catching up, he made no attempt to grab or tackle the fighter. By the time you had wrestled him to the ground, the other would be miles away. With a murderous left hook he sent him spinning off the path into the brittle bushes, shouting to Gesha, "One in the ditch! Get him!..." and raced after the first one with the long hair.

Rubakhin was running flat out, but his opponent was a good runner too. Whenever Rubakhin started gaining on him he speeded up, keeping a steady eight to ten yards between them. Half turning, Rubakhin's quarry raised his pistol and shot at him. Rubakhin saw he was very young. He took another shot at him (and lost ground. If he had not tried shooting he would have got away).

He was shooting over his left shoulder and the bullets were going very wide. Rubakhin did not even bother crouching when he saw him raising his hand. The fighter had enough sense, however, not to use up all his cartridges. He started pulling away again. Rubakhin saw his chance and without more ado flung his tommy gun at the fighter's legs.

The fugitive cried out in pain, jerked and started to fall. With a single leap Rubakhin was on top of him, immobilizing the hand that held the pistol with his own right hand, except that the pistol had vanished. He must have flung it aside as he fell, a fighter to the last! Rubakhin twisted his arms behind his back, wrenching his shoulder painfully, of course. "Ouch!" his prisoner cried, and stopped resisting. Rubakhin, still on a high, pulled a thong out of his pocket, tied the prisoner's hands, and sat him down by a tree, pushing his slight body against the trunk to tell him to sit still. Only then did he straighten up and walk back along the path, recovering his breath and scanning the grass, his attention already refocussed on the search for his own rifle and the discarded pistol.

Rubakhin again heard the approach of pounding feet. He leapt from the path back to the gnarled and stunted oak where his captive was sitting. "Not a squeak!" he commanded. The next instant several luckier fleet-footed fighters ran past, followed shortly afterwards by grunting and cursing Russian soldiers. Rubakhin left them to it. He had done what he came for.

He glanced at his captive's face, and was surprised. Firstly by how young he was, although it was not uncommon to find youngsters of sixteen or seventeen among the fighters. He had regular features and his skin was soft, but there was something else about the Caucasian's face. What? He had no time to think about it.

"Let's move," Rubakhin said, helping him to his feet (since his arms were tied behind his back).

As they marched back he warned him:

"Don't try to escape. Don't even think about it. I won't shoot you, but I'll hit you. Hard. Understand?"

His young prisoner was limping, his leg injured when Rubakhin threw the rifle at him. Or was he putting it on? Prisoners when caught often attempt to enlist their captor's sympathy by limping. Or heavy coughing.

4

A lot of fighters had been disarmed, twenty-two in all, which may have been why Rubakhin had little difficulty holding on to his prisoner. "This one is mine!" he repeated, resting his arm on the boy's shoulder among the general commotion and that final hubbub when attempts are being made to get the prisoners lined up to take them back to base. There was no falling off in the tension. The prisoners crowded together fearing that they were about to be split up. They held on to each other, shouting among themselves in their own language. Some did not even have their hands tied. "What do you mean, he's yours? Look how many we've caught. They belong to all of us!" Rubakhin shook his head, making it clear that while those might belong to all of us, this one belonged to him. Hot Shot Vovka appeared, as always, at just the right moment. He was miles better than Rubakhin at pulling the wool over someone's eyes while more or less telling the truth. "We've got to have him. Leave him be. We've got a note from Gurov... exchanging prisoners," he lied with his customary panache. "Well, you'll have to see the lieutenant about that." "We already have. He says that's okay!" Vovka effused, adding that the lieutenant colonel was presently at home drinking tea (which was true), and that the two of them had just come from there (also true), and that Gurov had signed this note for them personally and it was at the command post...

Vovka looked all in. Rubakhin glanced at him in puzzlement. He, Rubakhin, had just chased this long-haired lad through the scrub. He was the one who had caught and bound him. He had sweated blood, and here was Vovka looking knackered.

Having finally managed to line the prisoners up, the soldiers led them to the trucks. The weapons were carried well away from them, and somebody was counting: seventeen Kalashnikov rifles, seven pistols, a dozen grenades. Two of theirs had been killed during the hunt and two wounded. One of ours had been wounded, and Korotkov killed. The covered trucks were drawn up and, with an escorting armoured personnel carrier fore and aft, the column headed off, picking up speed, back to the unit. The soldiers in the trucks talked excitedly about the day's events and yelled at each other, and they were all ravenous.

The minute they arrived and climbed down from the trucks, Rubakhin and Hot Shot Vovka got themselves and their prisoner over to one side. Nobody argued. The prisoners were no great prize in themselves. The youngsters would be set free. More seasoned fighters would be imprisoned for two or three months in the guardhouse. If any of them attempted to escape they would be shot, not without some satisfaction. There was a war on. It could quite well have been these fighters who shot Boiarkov in his sleep (or just as he was opening his eyes). There wasn't a scratch on his face, just ants crawling over it. That first moment, Rubakhin and Vovka had started brushing them off. When they turned him over there was a gaping hole in his back. Boiarkov had been shot at point blank range, not sprayed with bullets. They had been pumped into his chest, shattering his ribs and blasting out his innards. On (and in) the ground was a mish-mash of ribs with his liver, kidneys, and loops of his guts on top of them, all in a great pool of coagulated blood. Several bullets had been stopped by his still steaming intestines. Boiarkov lay where they had turned him over with an enormous hole in his back, his guts and the bullets impacted in the ground.

Vovka turned to head for the canteen.

"He's a hostage. Lieutenant-Colonel Gurov has approved an exchange of prisoners," Vovka rattled out, pre-empting questions from the soldiers they met from Orlikov's squad.

The soldiers, full from their meal, shouted, "Say hello to the guys." They wanted to know who had been captured. Who was he being exchanged for?

"Exchange of prisoners," Hot Shot Vovka repeated uninformatively.

Vania Bravchenko laughed:

"Exchange of hard currency, you mean!"

Hook-nosed Sergeant Khodzhaev shouted,

"Well done, guys, he's quite a catch. They like ones like that. Their commander," he nodded in the direction of the hills, "likes ones like that very much." To make himself quite clear Khodzhaev laughed, showing his strong white soldier's teeth, and added: "You can get back two, three, five men for one like that. They love them like girls." Coming alongside Rubakhin, he winked suggestively.

Rubakhin grunted. He suddenly realized what it was that had been nagging him about the boy he had captured. He was very beautiful.

The prisoner did not speak Russian too well, but of course he understood everything. With squawking, guttural sounds, he shouted something back at Khodzhaev. His face and his cheekbones flushed, which only made it even more obvious how beautiful he was, with his dark, shoulder-length hair an oval frame for his face, with the set of his lips, and his straight, slender nose. Rubakhin's gaze was arrested by his large hazel eyes, wide set and with a slight oriental slant.

Vovka quickly talked the cook round. They needed a good meal to set them up for the return journey. Their fellow diners at the long plank table were a noisy, sweaty bunch, and it was very hot. They sat down at one end and Vovka immediately slipped the half-full bottle of wine out of his knapsack and furtively passed it under the table to Rubakhin who wedged it between his knees and finished it off unobserved by the others. "I left you exactly half, Rubakha. I trust you appreciate my bigheartedness."

He put a plate of food in front of the prisoner too.

"Not want," he responded curtly and turned away with a toss of his head.

Vovka pushed it nearer to him. "At least get stuck into the meat. It's a long march."

The prisoner said nothing. Vovka was afraid he was going to shoulder the plate away and the extra ration of stew and barley, which he had coaxed from the cook with such skill, would end up on the floor.

He quickly scraped the third portion on to his own and Rubakhin's plates. They finished it up, and it was time to go.

5

They drank at a stream, taking turns with a plastic cup. The prisoner must have been very thirsty. Advancing purposefully he fell to his knees, the pebbles grinding under him. He did not wait for them to untie his hands or give him a drink from their cup. Kneeling and bowing his face to the fast-flowing water, he drank at length. His hands tied behind his back were raised high in the air and were turning blue. He seemed to be praying in some bizarre manner.

Then he sat on the sand wet faced and pressed his cheek against his shoulder, trying his best to rid himself of the remaining drops of water on his face without the use of his hands. Rubakhin came over.

"We would've let you drink all you wanted, and untied your hands. What's the hurry?"

No reply. Rubakhin looked at him and wiped the water from his chin with his hand. His skin was so soft that the soldier's hand jerked back. He had not been expecting that. It was true. Just like a girl's, he thought.

Their eyes met, and Rubakhin immediately looked away, caught out by a sudden and none too moral impulse.

A sudden breeze blowing through the undergrowth put Rubakhin on the alert. Was someone there? His irresolution subsided (but it had only gone to ground: it was still there). Rubakhin was a simple soldier. He had no defence mechanisms to protect him against sheer human beauty, and now the same new and unfamiliar feeling seemed again to be coming over him. He remembered very well what Sergeant Khodhzaev had shouted, and the way he had winked. He really was going to have no option but come face to face with his captive in a moment. His prisoner could not cross the stream on his own. There were loose stones on the riverbed, the current was fierce, and he was bare-foot. His ankle had swollen so much that he had had to take off his excellent trainers just as they were setting out. (They were in Rubakhin's knapsack for the time being.) If he fell once or twice in crossing the stream he might be lamed completely. The current might drag him downstream. There was obviously no choice, and of course it would be for Rubakhin to carry him over. It was, after all, Rubakhin who had hurt his foot in the first place when he threw his gun at it in taking him prisoner.

A feeling of compassion came to Rubakhin's aid at just the right moment from somewhere up above, possibly heaven (although from the same quarter there again flooded over him the sense of irresolution, together with a renewed awareness of the boy's subversive beauty). Rubakhin was lost for only a moment. He caught the youth up in his arms and carried him over the stream. He resisted, but Rubakhin's muscular arms were strong.

"Now, now, stop kicking," he said, in much the same rough way as he would have spoken to a woman in a similar situation.

As he carried him he could feel the boy breathing. His prisoner had pointedly turned his face away, but his arms (untied while they crossed the stream) held on to Rubakhin tightly. He did not, after all, want to fall into the water or on to the rocks. Like anybody carrying someone in their arms, Rubakhin could not see where he was going and trod warily. Squinting sideways he could see only the water of the stream flowing in the distance, and against that background of leaping water, the profile of the boy, soft, pure, with his unexpectedly full lower lip pouting sulkily as if he were a girl.

They made their first halt on the other side. For safety they moved downstream from the path and sat in the undergrowth, Rubakhin's gun on his knees with the safety catch off. They were not hungry for the moment, but drank water several times. Vovka lay on his side fiddling with the dial on the little radio. It chattered barely audibly, gurgled and miaowed and exploded into alien speech. Vovka relied implicitly on Rubakhin's experience. He could hear a stone crunch under a stranger's foot a mile away.

"I'm going to have a kip, Rubakha. All right?" he warned and instantly fell into a soldier's light sleep.

When the eagle-eyed Lieutenant Savkin winnowed him out of the disarmament squad, Vovka, having nothing better to do, went back to the young woman's shack (next to the lieutenant-colonel's house but Vovka was suitably discreet). Not surprisingly she berated the lover who had so unceremoniously abandoned her at the shop, but a minute later they were again looking into each other's eyes, and a minute after that they were back in bed. Vovka was consequently now pleasantly fatigued. He was all right for marching, but whenever they halted he immediately fell asleep.

Rubakhin found it easier to talk when they were on the march.

"... when you think about it, how can we be enemies? We are all one family. For heaven's sake, we were friends only recently, weren't we?" he asked agitatedly, even insistently, hiding the feeling, which was so unsettling him behind hackneyed (Soviet) utterance. They were marching at a cracking pace.

Hot Shot Vovka snorted,

"Long live the indestructible friendship of the peoples of the Soviet Union..."

Rubakhin registered the sarcasm, but just said tersely,

"I wasn't talking to you."

Vovka dried up, but the boy too said nothing.

"I am just the same kind of human being as you, and you are the same as me. So why should we fight each other?" he persisted, but to no avail. He might as well have been mouthing his platitudes to the scrub and the path heading, since the stream, straight up into the mountains. Rubakhin wished the boy would at least disagree with him. He wanted to hear his voice, he wanted him to say something. (Rubakhin was feeling more and more disquieted.)

Hot Shot Vovka (without pausing) moved a finger and the radio in his knapsack twittered back to life. He tuned it some more and found a marching song, but Rubakhin went on talking. Eventually he tired and gave up.

Marching up a mountainside with a sore ankle and your hands tied behind your back is not easy. The captive was stumbling and finding it hard going. In one place where the ascent was steep he suddenly fell. He got himself up somehow and didn't complain, but Rubakhin saw his tears. He suddenly blurted out, "If you won't try to escape, I'll untie your hands. Promise me."

Hot Shot Vovka heard (through the music on the radio) and exclaimed,

"Rubakha, have you gone nuts?"

Vovka was marching ahead of them. He swore, registering his opinion of Rubakhin's soft-headedness. The radio was playing loudly.

"Vovka, turn it off. I need to be able to hear."

"Right."

The music was turned off.

Rubakhin untied the prisoner's hands. He wasn't going to get far from him, Rubakhin, with an ankle like that.

They were moving along at a fair pace, the prisoner in front, the semi-somnolent Vovka next to him and, slightly behind them, Rubakhin, wordless, his instincts ablaze.

You get a good feeling from freeing somebody, even if it is only their hands, and only for the duration of a march. There was a sweet taste in Rubakhin's mouth as he swallowed his saliva. It was a moment to remember. For all that his eye was as sharp as ever. The path became steeper. They skirted the mound where they had buried that piss-head Boiarkov. It was a lovely spot, bathed in the evening sunlight.

When they halted for the night Rubakhin gave the boy his woollen stockings to wear. He would wear his boots on bare feet. Everyone needed to get a night's sleep (they kept the campfire very small). Rubakhin confiscated Vovka's radio (not a sound at night). As always he kept the gun on his knees. He sat shoulder to shoulder with the captive and with his back to a tree in a huntsman's posture he had long favoured which allowed you to be ready for anything, but also to fall into a light slumber. It was night. He seemed to be asleep, but in parallel to sleep he was aware of the boy sitting by his side. He was so alert to him that he would have reacted instantly had his charge thought of making even the slightest unusual movement. But the captive was not thinking of escape. He was very down-hearted. (Rubakhin could sense what was going on in his heart.) Now the two of them fell into drowsiness (trusting each other), and Rubakhin could again feel the boy being overwhelmed by sadness. During the day he had tried to appear disdainful, but now he was plainly sick at heart. Why should he be so sad? Rubakhin had earlier hinted unambiguously that they were not taking him off to a military prison or for some other dark purpose, but purely in order to hand him back to his own people in return for safe passage for themselves. No more to it than that. They would hand him back to his own side. Sitting here next to Rubakhin he had nothing to fear. Even if he had not actually been told about the trucks and the blocked road, he must surely know, he must be able to feel, that he was in no danger. More than that, he must know that he, Rubakhin, liked him. Rubakhin was suddenly again overcome with confusion. He squinted sideways. The boy was looking miserable. Darkness had fallen now and in the firelight the captive's face was just as beautiful, but very sad. "There, there," Rubakhin said kindly, wanting to raise his spirits.

He slowly reached out. Afraid of disturbing that face half-turned towards him and the breath-taking beauty of that motionless gaze, Rubakhin barely touched the fine cheekbone with his fingers, as if brushing back a long braid of hair flowing over his cheek. The boy did not pull away. He said nothing. It even seemed, but perhaps it only seemed so, as if his cheek responded, oh, barely perceptibly, to Rubakhin's touch.

Hot Shot Vovka had only to close his eyes to relive those sweet elusive minutes that had flown so swiftly in that village shack, moment by moment, the throbbing, too fleeting joy of intimacy with a woman. He could sleep sitting up, on his feet, even on the march. It was no wonder that he fell soundly asleep at night (even though it was his turn to keep watch), and failed to register an animal charging past them, quite possibly a wild boar. That made them all sit up. The sound of it crashing off through the undergrowth died away very, very slowly. "Do you want all of us to get shot in our sleep too?" Rubakhin gently tweaked the soldier's ear. He stood up listening intently. All quiet.

Adding more wood to the fire, Rubakhin walked round in circles, stood for a time looking up the defile, and came back. He sat down next to the prisoner again. After their fright he was sitting there looking tense and hunched. His handsome face had been swallowed up by the night.

"Well now, how do you feel," Rubakhin asked almost too straightforwardly. Under such circumstances a question as to his welfare is asked primarily as a means of keeping the prisoner under surveillance. Was his drowsiness perhaps feigned? Had he found himself a knife? Was he contemplating escape under cover of darkness while his captors were asleep? (Only if he was mad. Rubakhin would have caught up with him in an instant.)

"Fine," he answered laconically.

Neither of them spoke for a while.

Having asked the question, Rubakhin stayed there sitting next to him. He couldn't be forever changing his position by the fire.

Rubakhin patted his shoulder.

"Don't let it get to you. I told you, when we get you back we'll hand you over to your lot straight away. All right?"

He nodded. Yes, all right. Rubakhin gave an awkward chuckle,

"You really are good-looking, though."

They sat in silence some more.

"How's your foot?"

"Fine."

"Right. Get some sleep. We're short of time. Let's get a bit more kip before it's morning."

And then, as if agreeing they needed to get a bit more kip, the young captive slowly inclined his head to the right and lowered it on to Rubakhin's shoulder. It didn't mean anything. It was just the way soldiers always make the best of their short sleep, huddled against each other. But now the warmth of his body, and with it a current of sensuality, in separate waves, began to reach Rubakhin, flowing through, wave after wave, from the boy's shoulder into his own. No, of course that wasn't it. The lad was asleep. He was simply sleeping, Rubakhin told himself, wrestling with temptation. He suddenly tensed as a great charge of warmth and unexpected tenderness passed through his shoulder and into his tremulous heart. Rubakhin froze, and the boy, feeling or guessing his alarm, also delicately froze. Another minute and the sensuality had gone from their contact. They were simply sitting side by side.

"Yes. Time to sleep," Rubakhin said to no one in particular, his eyes firmly fixed on the little red flames licking up from the fire.

The captive changed position, settling his head a little more comfortably on Rubakhin's shoulder, and almost immediately the flow of warmth, yielding and inviting, was there again. Rubakhin detected that the boy was trembling slightly. What could that mean, he wondered in turmoil, and again ran for cover, holding himself back, fearful of being given away by his own answering trembling. But that was not his real fear. He could cope with that. What terrified him was the thought that at any moment the boy would quietly turn his head. (All his movements were quiet and insidious, while at the same time seemingly without significance. Someone shifts while half asleep, what of it?) He would turn his face to him, almost touching him, and Rubakhin would inescapably feel his young life breathing in him and the closeness of his lips. That moment was very near. Rubakhin experienced a moment of weakness. His stomach was the first of his organs to protest at such an unwonted overloading of his senses and spasmed. Immediately the feel of the battle-scarred soldier's shoulder became as unyielding as a washboard. He was next convulsed by a fit of coughing, and the boy, as if taking fright, lifted his head from Rubakhin's shoulder.

Hot Shot Vovka woke up.

"You're booming like a cannon, you maniac. You can be heard half a mile away."

The carefree Vovka promptly fell asleep again and, as if in response, himself began snoring and wheezing sonorously.

Rubakhin laughed, as if to say, that's my fighting partner for you. Sleeps all day, sleeps all night.

The captive said slowly and with a smile,

"I think he had woman, yesterday."

Rubakhin feigned amazement: you reckon? Then, thinking back, he promptly conceded,

"You just might be right."

"I think yesterday in afternoon."

"You're right. Spot on!"

They laughed together, man to man.

But immediately afterwards, and very cautiously, Rubakhin's captive asked him,

"And you, you have woman long ago?"

Rubakhin shrugged.

"Long ago. A year ago, near enough."

"Not good-looking? A stupid cow? I think she was not good-looking. Soldiers have no good-looking women."

The pause that followed was long and awkward, and Rubakhin felt as if a great rock were pressing down, down on the back of his head...

Early in the morning the fire was completely out and Vovka, freezing cold, moved over to join them, pressing his face and shoulder against Rubakhin's back. The captive was snug by Rubakhin's side, and his sweet, warm body had beckoned him through all the hours of darkness. Thus the three of them, giving each other warmth, saw out the night.

They put a billycan full of water on the fire to boil.

"Tea-time everybody," Rubakhin said, a little guiltily after the unusual experiences of the night.

This guiltiness had come alive in him at first light, unsure of itself but now out in the open. Rubakhin had suddenly started courting the boy. (He was perplexed. This was the last thing he had expected of himself.) There was restlessness in his hands, like a sickness. He twice made him tea in the plastic cup, dropping in lumps of sugar, stirring them noisily with a teaspoon, and serving it to him. He let him keep the stockings, evidently for good. "Wear them. You needn't take them off. You can walk on in them today." That was how considerate he had suddenly become.

He had started fussing, and kept stoking up the campfire to keep the boy warm.

The captive drank the tea, sitting on his heels, his eyes following Rubakhin's hands.

"These warm socks. Fine," he praised them, shifting his gaze to his feet.

"My mother knitted them."

"Oh..."

"Don't take them off. I told you, they'll help you walk. I'll find something to wind on my own feet."

The boy took a comb out of his pocket and busied himself with his hair, combing it at great length, proudly shaking his head from time to time, and then again with a practised hand smoothing it down to his shoulders. Taking pleasure in his beauty was as natural for him as breathing the air.

In the strong, warm woollen stockings the boy walked noticeably more confidently. In fact all in all he had perked up considerably. The sadness had gone from his eyes. He undoubtedly knew that Rubakhin had been thrown into confusion by the way their relationship was taking shape. He might even have been pleased a little. He would glance sideways at Rubakhin, at his arms, and his gun, and smiled a fleeting smile to himself, as if having gained a playful victory over the huge, powerful yet hopelessly bashful soldier.

When they again came to a stream he did not take the stockings off, but stood waiting for Rubakhin to come and catch him up. The boy no longer only clung to Rubakhin's collar. His gentle arm unashamedly circled the soldier's neck as he forded the stream and sometimes, as they lurched forward, he slipped his hand under his shirt to be more comfortable.

Rubakhin again took the radio off Hot Shot Vovka, and signalled them to silence. He was in charge. Here where the much trodden path widened out he would trust nobody until they made it to the white cliff already in sight. This was a dangerous spot, redeemed precisely by the fact that two narrow paths went their separate ways there (or, depending on how you looked at it, came together).

The cliff was known to the soldiers simply as the Nose. A large white triangular promontory of stone, it now bore down, looming towards them like the prow of a ship.

They had already begun climbing up through the tangle of scrub at the very foot of the cliff. This mustn't be happening, flashed through the soldier's mind when he heard danger bearing down on them from up there (from the right and the left simultaneously). People were coming down both sides of the cliff at once. Their steps were sure-footed, rapid and irregular. The enemy. Shit! For two hostile detachments to coincide minute for minute, blocking both paths at once, just mustn't be happening! The cliff's one saving grace was that you could hear someone coming and pass them unseen up the other track.

Now, of course, they had no time to get through either way, or even to dart back from the cliff across the open ground and into the woods. There were three of them, one a prisoner. They would be spotted straightaway and all instantly shot down, or simply chased into a thicket and surrounded. This mustn't be happening, his reason cheeped piteously for a third and final time before deserting him. Now everything was down to instinct. He felt a prickling in his nostrils. He was aware not only of their steps but, in the almost total absence of a breeze, he could even sense the slow straightening up of the grass they had trodden.

"Shhh."

He pressed a finger to his lips. Vovka understood, and nodded in the direction of the prisoner. What about him?

Rubakhin glanced at the boy's face. He too had instantly taken in the situation (his side were coming). His cheeks and forehead slowly flushed (an indicator of unpredictable behaviour).

"Oh, to hell with it!" Rubakhin murmured to himself, quickly readying his gun for action. He felt his cartridge belt, but the idea of taking them on (like any other idea in a moment of danger) also moved aside (deserted him), shying away from responsibility. Instinct told him to listen, and wait. The prickling in his nostrils, the quiet, meaningful straightening of the grass, the steps coming nearer. No. There were a lot of them. Too many... Rubakhin glanced once more at his prisoner's face, trying to read from it how he would react, what he would do. Would he keep down and stay silent (which would be fine) for fear of being killed or would he rush out towards them with mindless joy in huge half-crazy eyes and (the killer!) with a yell?

Without taking his eyes off those coming down the left path (this detachment was already close and would be the first to pass them), Rubakhin moved his hand back and cautiously touched his captive's body. The boy trembled slightly, like a woman anticipating love. Rubakhin touched his neck and felt upwards to his face. Gently touching the beautiful lips, he put his hand over the mouth which must stay silent. The boy's lips were trembling.

Rubakhin slowly drew the boy closer to himself (never taking his eyes off the approaching rank of men on the left path). Vovka was following the progress of the right-hand detachment whose steps could already be heard. Pebbles were cascading down. One of the fighters had slung his gun over his shoulder and it kept rasping against the gun of the man behind.

The boy did not resist. Putting his arm round his shoulder, Rubakhin drew him round to face him. The boy (less tall) moved closer, pressing towards him, his lips crushed against the spot under Rubakhin's unshaven chin where an artery was throbbing. He was trembling, not understanding. "N-n," he breathed, like a woman whose "No" did not mean no, but only testified to her modesty, while Rubakhin watched him and waited for any sign of a shout. How his eyes widened in fear, trying to avoid Rubakhin's look and see, through the expanse of air and sky, his own people. He opened his mouth, but did not shout. Perhaps he only wanted to breathe deeply, but Rubakhin had lowered his gun to the ground, and with his other hand smothered the half-opened mouth and the beautiful lips and the quivering nose. "N-neh", the captured boy wanted to tell him something, but was given no chance. His body stiffened, his legs straining, but there was no longer anything for them to strain against. Rubakhin had lifted him clear of the ground. He held him tightly in his arms, not letting him kick against the telltale bushes or the stones which would have gone clattering down. Rubakhin hooked the arm with which he held him round the boy's neck and crushed him. His beauty could not save him. A few convulsions and it was over. Had Rubakhin been in too much of a hurry? Or not? Accursed hands. Rubakhin's mind, which had deserted him in his moment of peril, now came stumbling back with a phrase half-remembered from his schooldays.

Beneath the cliff where the paths joined up guttural cries of amity were soon to be heard as the enemy detachments discovered each other. The two Russian soldiers could hear salutations and questions. How come you are here?! Which way are you going? The fighters slapped each other's backs. They laughed. One of them, taking advantage of the halt, decided to relieve himself and ran over to the cliff where it was less public, not suspecting that he was in a Russian gun-sight. He was standing only a few yards from a clump of bushes behind which two live men and one dead boy lay stretched out. He urinated, hiccupped, did his trousers up, and hurried back.

When the detachments had passed and the sound of their voices and their feet marching down to the open ground had died away completely, two soldiers with tommy guns carried a dead body out of the bushes. They brought it to a sparse nearby wood along a path to the left where Rubakhin remembered a clearing, a dry patch of bare, soft, sandy earth. They dug a hole, dredging the sand out with flat stones. Hot Shot Vovka asked Rubakhin if he wanted to take his stockings back. Rubakhin shook his head. They said not a word about a human being to whose presence, in all truth, both of them had become accustomed. They sat half a minute in silence by his grave. What more could they do? There was a war on.

6

No change. As they approached Rubakhin could see the two trucks still stuck where they had been.

The road narrowed down to a tight corridor between two rockfaces, but the strait was guarded by hillmen. The trucks had been shot at in a desultory sort of way (but if they attempted to come any nearer they would be riddled with bullets). The trucks had been stranded here for three days already, waiting.

The fighters want weapons before they will let them through.

"We are not transporting guns! We haven't got any weapons," they shout from behind the trucks. A shot from the cliffs is their reply. Or a hail of bullets, a long burst of machine

45

gun fire, capped with laughter, gusts of joyful, jubilant, childish laughter echoing from the heights.

The escorting soldiers and the drivers (six men in all) have settled in by the roadside bushes, shielded by the bodies of the trucks. They are leading a simple nomadic life, cooking their food on a campfire and sleeping.

When Rubakhin and Hot Shot Vovka get nearer, Rubakhin notices a pale, daytime campfire, up on the cliff where the fighters lie in ambush. They are cooking their lunch too. It is a low-key war. Why not eat properly if you can, and enjoy a mug of hot tea?

Of course, those up on the cliff have also observed the approach of Rubakhin and Vovka. The fighters are keen-eyed. Even though they can see that the same two who left have returned (without visibly bringing anything back with them), they loose off a couple of rounds from the cliff just to be on the safe side.

Rubakhin and Hot Shot Vovka make it back nevertheless.

The sergeant-major sticks his belly out and asks Rubakhin, "Reinforcements on their way, then?"

"Like fuck."

Rubakhin does not elaborate.

"You didn't manage to get a prisoner?"

"Nah."

Rubakhin asked for water and drank long from the bucket, splashing it on to his tunic and his chest before blundering off and collapsing among the bushes to sleep. The grass was still flattened there. It was the same place where he had been lying two days before when someone prodded him in the side and he was sent for reinforcements (with Vovka as back-up). He sank face down with the crushed grass tickling his ears and deaf to the sergeant-major's grumbling. He was pissed off. He was tired.

Vovka sat down in the shade of a tree, stretched his legs in front of him and tilted a panama hat over his eyes. He started winding the drivers up: what had they managed to do while he was away? Hadn't they found an alternative route yet? Seriously? There was no alternative route, he was told earnestly. The slow-thinking drivers were lying in tall grass. One deftly rolled himself a cigarette from a piece of old newspaper.

Sergeant-Major Beregovoi, bugged by the unsuccessful outcome of the foray, attempted to re-open negotiations.

"Hey, listen, guys. Hey," he shouted in a voice calculated to instil immediate trust. "I swear, we haven't got anything in these trucks. No weapons, no food. We are empty. You can send someone down to check it out. We shall show him everything, and we won't shoot him. Hey, are you listening?"

His reply was a burst of shooting, and merry laughter.

"Fuck your mother's soul," he swore.

There was sporadic fire from the cliff which went on for so long and so pointlessly that the sergeant-major swore once more and called, "Vovka. Come over here a minute."

The two drivers lying in the grass came to life. "Vovka, Go on. Show those cloth-heads how to shoot."

Hot Shot Vovka yawned, lazily detaching his back from the tree. (He had found a really comfortable position.)

As soon as he took up his rifle, however, every trace of lethargy vanished. He settled himself comfortably in the grass and, raising his rifle, centred in the telescopic sight now one, now another of the figures prancing about on the cliff towering over the road from the left. They were all in full view. He could have picked them off even without the telescopic sight.

At just that moment one of the hillmen standing on the cliff edge started ululating mockingly.

"Vovka, do you feel like giving it 'im?" a driver asked.

"I don't give a fuck about him," Vovka snorted.

After a moment's silence he added, "I like aiming at them and squeezing the trigger. I don't need a bullet to know when I've scored."

The impossibility of it all didn't need putting into words. If he did kill a fighter the trucks would have no chance at all of getting through.

"That one who's kicking up all that din, consider him rubbed out." Vovka pressed the trigger of the unloaded rifle. He was enjoying himself. He aimed again, and again recklessly pulled the trigger. "That's another off the list. And this one, I could rip half his arse off. Not waste him, no, he's got cover from that tree, but half his arse, all yours on a platter!"

Sometimes, if his eye was caught by some possession of the hillmen glinting in the sun, a bottle of vodka, say, or (since it was morning) a prized Chinese thermos flask, Vovka would meticulously take aim and shoot the conspicuous item into tiny pieces. Just at the moment there was nothing tempting.

Rubakhin meanwhile was sleeping fitfully. The same guilty, disconcerting vision kept coming back to him (or was Rubakhin, burrowing there in the grass, conjuring it himself): the handsome face of the captive.

"Vovka. Let's have a smoke."

(What sort of fun was just aiming at them anyway?)

"Hang on a second." Vovka was well away by now, aiming at one after another, sweeping his cross-hair along the skyline of the cliff, down the edge of the rock, over the mountain scrub, along the trunk of a tree. Aha! His eye lighted on a scrawny fighter standing by the tree and snipping away at his greasy locks with a pair of scissors. Cutting your hair is a deeply personal matter. The mirror flashed, signalling to him, and Vovka instantly loaded the rifle and took aim. He pressed the trigger, and the silvery puddle fixed to the trunk of the elm tree shattered into a thousand pieces. The response was a volley of curses and the invariable random gunfire (as if a flock of cranes were calling beyond the cliff overhanging the road, giyaow, kiyaow, liyaow, kiyaow...). The tiny figures up on the cliff started running about, yelling, ulullating, but suddenly (evidently on a command) quietened down. For a time they did not show themselves so brazenly (and were generally better behaved). And, of course, they deluded themselves that they had taken cover, although Hot Shot Vovka could see not only their supposedly hidden heads, but the Adam's apples on their throats, their stomachs, even the buttons on their shirts, and he playfully moved his cross-hair from one button down to the next.

"Vovka. Pack it in," the sergeant-major restrained him.

"Sure," Vovka responded, lowering his rifle and heading back to the tall grass (with the soldier's eternal simple intention of having a sleep).

Meanwhile Rubakhin was losing something: he could no longer hold the boy's features in his mind's eye for long, the face broke up almost as soon as it appeared. It lost definition and left behind only a general sense of prettiness, blurred and uninteresting, just somebody's forgotten face. His presence was melting away. But then, as if in farewell (perhaps, too, in forgiveness) the boy's features again became clear. How his face now blazed, but not only his face, the boy himself stood there physically present before Rubakhin as if he were about to say something. He stepped even closer and suddenly threw his arms round Rubakhin's neck (as Rubakhin had done to him at the cliff), only his slight arms were as soft as a young woman's, impulsive but tender and Rubakhin (alert to the danger) had just time to register that man's weakness was about to come over him now in his sleep. He ground his teeth, forcibly driving the vision away, and immediately woke up, aware of an aching fullness in his groin.

"I need a smoke," he said hoarsely as he woke, and suddenly heard the shooting.

Perhaps it was the shooting that woke him. Tuk-tuk-tuk-tuk-tuk, a thin stream of rifle fire sent the stones flying and raised fountains of dust from the road beside the forlorn trucks. The trucks were going nowhere. (Rubakhin was not too bothered. At some point they would have to let them through.)

Hot Shot Vovka was asleep in the grass not far away, his rifle cradled in his arms. He had strong cigarettes for once (bought in the village shop at the same time as the wine), and they were conveniently sticking out of his breast pocket. Rubakhin selected one as Vovka snored quietly.

Rubakhin inhaled slowly. He lay on his back looking up at the sky, while to left and right (crowding in on his peripheral vision) the mountains of the Caucasus had him surrounded and would not set him free. Rubakhin had served out his time in the army, but whenever he decided to send it all to the devil and go back home for good (to the steppes beyond the Don), he would pack his belongings into his battered suitcase, and then stay. "What is it about this place anyway? The mountains?" he said out loud, with a vindictiveness directed solely at himself. What was so great about the monotony of life in the barracks, or the mountains themselves, for that matter, he wondered rattily. He was going to add, after all these years, but thought instead, after all these centuries... A slip of the tongue. The words had come up out of the darkness, and the startled soldier now mulled over this quiet thought which had been lying there somewhere in the depths of his mind. Grey, moss-covered gorges, the poor, grubby little huts of these mountain people, moulded like birds' nests. Was it the mountains? Their summits yellowed by the sun, crowded randomly together. The mountains. The mountains. The mountains. For how many years their majesty, their mute grandeur had given him no peace. What was it their beauty was trying to tell him. Why had it called to him?

Vladimir MAKANIN is among the best known Russian writers of the last 20 years. Born in 1937 in the Urals, he was trained as a mathematician and later a film-maker. But he made his name with his highly individual stories, which won him instant fame among the Russian intelligentsia in the 1960s. Many of his novels have been successful in translation in Germany, France, Spain, Eastern Europe and elsewhere. His better-known works are available in English: *Voices* (in *Dissonant Voices*, Harvill, 1991), *Antileader* (Abbeville, USA), *Blue and Red*, *The Laggard*, *Two Solitudes*. His latest novel *The Hero of Our Times* has also been translated into many languages.

His novel *Manhole* was short-listed for the Booker Russian Novel Prize in 1992 and published by Ardis (US), his *Baize-covered Table with Decanter* won the Booker in 1993 and was published in English by Readers International in 1995. See also Makanin's work in *Glas* 4 (*Klyucharev and Alimushkin*), *Glas* 7 (excerpt from *Baize-covered Table*), and *Glas* 8 (*The Safety-valve*).

Victor
PELEVIN

The Tambourine for the Upper World

Translated by James Escombe

Entering the railway carriage, the policeman cast a cursory glance at Tanya and Masha, looked over into the corner, and stared dumbfounded at the woman sitting there.

She did look pretty wild.

It was impossible to tell her age from her Mongol face, which resembled a stale pancake turned up at the edges. The more so, since her eyes were hidden behind dangling leather thongs and threads of beads. In spite of the warm weather, she was wearing a fur hat with three broad strips of hide attached to it. The first went round her forehead, and from it hung ribbons with small copper figurines on them, little bells and brasses. The other two strips of hide were joined across the crown of her head, and at the join was fastened a crudely fashioned metal bird with its twisted neck stretched upwards.

The woman was dressed in a hand-woven shift, adorned with strips of reindeer fur, embroidered with rawhide laces, and hung with shiny discs and any number of little bells, which made a pleasant tinkling sound with every lurch of the carriage. Apart from this, all sorts of small objects of no discernible purpose were fastened to her shift — serrated metal arrows, two Orders of Labour, bits of tinplate with mouthless faces etched on them, while from her right shoulder, on a crepe ribbon, hung two long rusty nails. In her hand she held an oval tambourine, also made out of hide and embellished with many little bells, while the edge of another tambourine protruded from the capacious tennis-bag on which she was sitting.

"Your papers, please," the policeman finally said.

The woman produced absolutely no reaction to his words.

"She's with me," interjected Tanya. "She doesn't have any papers. And she speaks no Russian."

Tanya spoke wearily, like someone who has to repeat the same thing several times a day.

"What do you mean, she hasn't any papers?"

"Why should an elderly woman carry her papers with her? All her papers are in Moscow, at the Ministry of Culture. She's here with a folklore group."

"Why does she look like that?" asked the policeman.

"It's her national costume," answered Tanya. "Her culture."

"Ah," said the policeman, "national culture, I see. We had a Chechen down at the station the other day, explaining why he had a sawn-off shotgun on him. He said it was part of his national costume: battle-green trousers, you know, leather jacket and an automatic rifle!"

"That was a bandit," Tanya said. "This is an honoured artist. She even has a medal, look, there, to the right of the bell. She's an Honoured Reindeer Breeder."

"So what? This is not the tundra. Here we'd call this a breach of the peace," said the policeman.

"What peace?" Tanya's voice rose. "The puddles of piss here on the platform? Or those thugs over there?"

She nodded in the direction of the connecting doors, from behind which drunken cries were clearly audible.

"Just riding on this train is dangerous, but rather than keeping some sort of order, you go about checking old ladies' papers."

The policeman looked doubtfully at the person Tanya referred to as an "old lady". She sat there silently in the corner of the carriage, rocking in time with the train's movement, and taking no notice whatsoever of the scene she was creating. Despite her bizarre appearance, her small figure radiated such peace and contentment that, after looking at her for a minute, the policeman softened, smiled to himself at some distant memory, and relaxed his clutch on the truncheon hanging from his belt.

"What's her name?" he asked.

"Tuimi," answered Tanya.

"OK," said the policeman, pushing open the heavy door to the next carriage. "Only, just watch it..."

The door closed behind him, and the shouts from the next carriage grew a little fainter. The train braked, the doors opened, and for a few damp seconds the girls glimpsed an uneven asphalt platform. Behind it stood some low buildings with numerous chimneys of different shapes and sizes; smoke curled weakly from a few of them.

"Crematovo Station," announced an impassive female voice over the loudspeaker, when the doors were already closed. "Next station, Nameless Heights."

"Is that ours?" asked Tanya.

Masha nodded and looked at Tuimi, who continued to sit in the corner, taking no part in the proceedings.

"Has she been with you long?" she asked.

"Three years," answered Tanya.

"Is she difficult?"

"No," said Tanya, "she's quiet enough. She sits all day long like that, in the kitchen watching television."

"Does she ever go out?"

"No," said Tanya. "She just sleeps on the balcony sometimes."

"But doesn't she find it hard? I mean, to live in a town?"

"Yes, she did at first," said Tanya, "but then she got used to it. She used to beat her tambourine all night, fighting with invisible ghosts. Now they seem to obey her. See those two nails hanging from her shoulder? She's defeated them. Now she only hides when there are fireworks, in the bathroom."

The station platform at "Nameless Heights" fully lived up to its name. Usually there are at least a few signs of human habitation alongside a railway station, but here there was nothing, except for the brick ticket office. Immediately beyond the fence enclosing the platform the forest began, and it stretched as far as the eye could see. God knows from whence the few shabby passengers on the platform could have come.

Masha, staggering under the weight of the tennis-bag, led the way. Tanya followed, with another bag on her shoulder, and Tuimi brought up the rear, her bells tinkling, lifting the hem of her shift as she stepped over the puddles. On her feet she wore blue Chinese sneakers, and her legs were clad to the knee in thick leather leggings, stitched with beads. Turning round to look, Masha saw the round face of an alarm clock on the left legging, and on the right, hanging from a length of toilet chain, was a hoof, reaching almost to the ground.

"Listen, Tanya," she asked quietly, "what's that hoof for?"

"It's for the underworld," said Tanya. "She says everything's covered in mud down there. The hoof's so she won't sink in."

Masha wanted to ask about the clock-dial, but thought better of it. Somehow, its purpose was clear enough.

A good paved road led into the forest, lined with two rows of old birch trees. But after three or four hundred yards any order in the way the trees had been planted was lost. The asphalt petered out, and wet mud squelched beneath their feet.

Masha thought that, sometime, some local Party functionary must have given the order to pave a road through the forest, but then it had become obvious that the road led nowhere, and so they had forgotten about it. The sight of it depressed Masha. Her own life, begun twenty-five years before by whose will she knew not, seemed to her like this road — first straight and even, lined with rows of simple truths, then forgotten by some unknown authority, before turning into a winding path that led she knew not whither.

"Must get away from here," she murmured, "must get away from here, never mind who with..."

"What's that?" asked Tanya.

"Nothing," answered Masha, "I'm just mumbling."

A length of white tape gleamed in front of them, tacked to a birch branch.

"Here we turn right into the forest," said Masha. "Another five hundred yards or so."

"It's so close," Tanya said doubtfully. "I can't believe it's still there."

"Nobody comes this way," said Masha. "There's nothing here, and half the wood's surrounded by sagging barbed wire."

Indeed, there soon appeared before them a low concrete post, from which barbed wire stretched in both directions. Several more posts then became visible. They were old, and all around them the undergrowth grew thickly, so that the barbed wire could only be seen when you got right up to it. The girls walked wordlessly along the wire fence, until Masha stopped beside yet another piece of white tape hanging from a bush.

"Here," she announced.

Several strands of the wire had been pulled together and twisted. Masha and Tanya climbed underneath without difficulty, but Tuimi crawled through backwards, getting her shift caught on the barbed wire, and her bells tinkled as she slowly negotiated her way through the narrow aperture.

On the other side of the wire the forest was just the same, without any sign of human presence. Masha walked confidently ahead, and after a few minutes stopped at the edge of a gully with a small stream gurgling at the bottom of it.

"We're here," she said. "Over there, in the bushes."

Tanya looked downwards.

"I can't see anything," she said.

"There's the tail sticking out," said Masha, "and there's the wing. Come on, there's a way down here."

Tuimi did not go down. She sat on Tanya's bag, leaned her back against a tree and froze into stillness. Masha and

Tanya, hanging on to the branches and slipping on the wet soil, went down into the gully.

"Listen, Tanya," said Masha in a low voice. "What's up with her? Doesn't she need to look? How's she going to do it?"

"Don't you worry," said Tanya, looking into the bushes. "She knows better than we do... Yes, there it is, it's still there."

Behind the bushes lay something a dirty dark brown in colour, and very old. At first sight it suggested the humped grave of some minor tribal chieftain who at the last moment had been hurried into conversion to some rare form of Christianity. From this long narrow hump there emerged askew a broad, cross-shaped construction of twisted metal, in which it was possible to discern the half-destroyed tail of an aeroplane, which had become detached from the fuselage at the time of the crash.

The fuselage was almost buried in the ground, but a few yards ahead, through some hazel trees and long grass, the outline of the wings could be seen, and on one of them a swastika gleamed blackly.

"I looked it up in a book," Masha broke the silence. "It's a Heinkel bomber. There were two modifications — one had a 30-millimetre cannon under the fuselage, the other had something else, I can't remember. Anyway, it doesn't matter."

"Did you open the cabin?" asked Tanya.

"No," said Masha, "I'd have been too scared on my own."

"Suppose there's nobody inside?"

"There is," said Masha. "The cabin's undamaged. Look."

She pushed aside the branches, and with her palm wiped away the layer of vegetable detritus built up over the years.

Tanya bent down and brought her face close to the glass. Behind it could be seen something dark and wet.

"How many of them were there?" she asked. "If it was a Heinkel, there ought to be a gunner as well, oughtn't there?"

"No idea," said Masha.

"All right," said Tanya. "Tuimi will find out. It's a pity the cabin's closed. If we could just have a lock of hair, or a bit of bone, how much easier it would be."

"You mean she can't do it without?"

"Oh yes, she can," said Tanya, "only it takes longer. It's getting dark. Come on, let's gather some branches for a fire."

"No, but, doesn't that hurt the quality?"

"What do you mean, quality?" asked Tanya. "What sort of quality are you expecting?"

The fire was burning well, and gave out more light than the evening sky, which was obscured by low clouds. Masha noticed her shadow dancing impatiently across the grass, and she felt odd — the shadow obviously felt so much surer of itself than she did. She felt stupid in her city dress, while Tuimi's costume, which people had been staring at all day, seemed in the flickering light of the fire the most fitting and natural dress for a human being.

"Now what?" asked Masha in a whisper, after a few moments of silence.

"Wait," replied Tanya in an equally low voice. "She'll start all on her own. We mustn't say anything to her now."

Masha sat on the ground beside her friend.

"I'm scared," she said, and rubbed the place on her windcheater, which covered her heart. "How long do we have to wait?"

"I don't know. It's different every time. Last year, a couple of times..."

Masha started. The snap of the tambourine, alternating with the tinkling of many bells, sounded across the clearing. Tuimi was on her feet, bending forward, and looking into the bushes on the edge of the gully. Striking her tambourine one more time, she twice ran counter-clockwise round the clearing. Then, with amazing agility, she leapt over the wall of bushes and disappeared into the gully. From below came her plaintive cry, full of pain, and Masha thought she must have broken her leg, but Tanya reassured her by closing her eyes.

From the gully rose frequent slaps on the tambourine and a rapid chattering. Then everything became still and Tuimi reappeared from the bushes. Now she moved slowly, ceremonially. Reaching the middle of the clearing, she halted and began rhythmically to tap the tambourine.

Masha closed her eyes, just in case.

A new sound was added to the tambourine. Masha was not aware of the precise moment when it started, and at first did not understand what it was. It seemed to her as though someone were playing on a stringed instrument, but then she realized that it was Tuimi's voice producing this piercing and sombre note.

It was as though the voice were emerging from some totally foreign space, which the voice itself was producing, and through which it moved, colliding on the way with numerous objects whose nature was unclear, and each forcing Tuimi to utter disjointed, guttural cries. To Masha it suggested the image of a net being dragged across the bottom of a dark pool, gathering everything that fell into its path. Suddenly Tuimi's voice snagged on something. Masha felt she was trying to free herself from it but couldn't. Then her voice fell silent, and Masha opened her eyes.

Tuimi was standing not far from the campfire, and was trying to withdraw her hand from this space, this void. She pulled with all her strength, but the void would not let her go.

"Nilti doglong," cried Tuimi in a menacing voice. "Nilti dzhamai!"

Masha was quite convinced that the void before Tuimi was saying something in reply.

Tuimi laughed and shook her tambourine.

"Nein, Herr General," she said, "das hat mit Ihnen gar nichts zu tun. Ich bin hier wegen ganz anderer Angelegenheit." The void asked some question, and Tuimi shook her head in emphatic refusal.

"What's she doing, is she talking German?" asked Masha.

"When she's in a trance she can speak any language."

Tuimi tried to extricate her hand again.

"Heute ist schon zu spaet, Herr General. Verzeihung, ich hab' es sehr eilig," she said, angrily.

This time Masha felt a threat emerging from the void.

"Wozu?" cried Tuimi scornfully, and she tore from her shoulder the crepe ribbon with the two rusty nails, and swung it above her head. "Nilti dzhamai! Bla budulan!"

The void released her hand so quickly that Tuimi fell back on to the grass. As she fell, she laughed, turned to Tanya and Masha, and emphatically shook her head.

"What's the matter?" asked Masha.

"It doesn't look good," said Tanya. "There's no sign of your client in the underworld."

"Maybe she didn't look far enough?" asked Masha.

"What do you mean, far enough? There's no far or near down there. No beginning and no end either, for that matter."

"So what do we do now?"

"We can still try the upper world," said Tanya, "only the chances aren't good. We've never managed it so far, but of course, we can always try."

She turned towards Tuimi, who was sitting on the grass as before, and raised her finger. Tuimi nodded, went over to the tennis-bag lying by the tree, and took from it the other tambourine.

The tambourine for the upper world sounded different, softer and somehow thoughtful. Tuimi's voice, on a long-drawn, plaintive note, was also changed, and instead of terror it aroused in Masha feelings of peace and a gentle melancholy. She repeated the same ritual as a few minutes earlier, only on this occasion the procedure was not sinister, it was exalted and yet unfitting. Why it was unfitting even Masha could understand. It was quite inappropriate to disturb those parts of the world to which Tuimi was now appealing, as she lifted her face to the dark sky between the branches, lightly tapping her tambourine.

Masha remembered an old cartoon film about the adventures of a little grey wolf in dense, dark, gloomy woods near Moscow. Every now and then in the cartoon all this would disappear and be magically replaced by a new scene of a road flooded in noonday sunlight, so overexposed as to be almost transparent, and along a washed out watercolour road a barely sketched wanderer was making his way.

Masha shook her head to bring herself back to her senses, and looked round. The objects surrounding her, the undergrowth, the trees, the grass and the dark clouds which had until now merged together into one mass, seemed to be separating in response to the sounds from the tambourine, and in the gaps between them a strange, luminous, and unknown world momentarily opened out.

Tuimi's voice stumbled against some object, tried to go forward and then lingered on one insistent note, as though it had hit a concrete wall.

Tanya tugged Masha's hand.

"He's there," she said. "We've found him. Now she'll catch him."

Tuimi raised her arms, gave a piercing cry, and fell back on to the grass.

The distant drone of an aeroplane reached Masha's ears. It was impossible to tell from where it was coming and the sound continued for a long time, but when it ceased there came a whole series of noises from the gully. The crash of breaking glass, the rending of rusty metal, and the soft but clearly recognizable sound of a man's cough.

Tanya stood up, walked a few paces towards the gully, and then Masha saw a dark figure at the edge of the clearing.

"Sprechen sie Deutsch?" Tanya asked hoarsely.

The figure moved silently towards the fire.

"Sprechen sie Deutsch?" cried Tanya, backing away. "Are you deaf or something?"

The reddish light of the fire fell on a strongly built man of about forty, dressed in a leather jacket and flying-helmet. Coming up to them, he sat down in front of the giggling Tuimi, crossed his legs and looked up at Tanya.

"Sprechen sie Deutsch?" Tanya repeated her question.

"Oh, do give over," the man said quietly in Russian.

Tanya whistled in amazement.

"Who on earth are you?" she asked, sitting down.

"Me? I'm Major Zvyagintsev. Nikolay Ivanovich Zvyagintsev. And who might you be?"

Masha and Tanya looked at each other.

"I don't understand," said Tanya. "How can you be Major Zvyagintsev if that plane is German?"

"The plane was captured," said the major. "I was flying it to another airfield, and then..."

Major Zvyagintsev's face twisted in a grimace. Evidently he had remembered an extremely unpleasant experience.

"So you're what?" asked Tanya. "Soviet?"

"You could say that," replied Major Zvyagintsev. "I was Soviet, but now I don't know. It's all a bit different where we come from."

He looked up at Masha. For some reason, she blushed and turned her face away.

"And what are you girls after here?" he asked. "After all, the ways of the living and the dead are not the same. Isn't that so?"

"Oh," said Tanya, "please forgive us. We're not out to disturb Russians. It's all because of the plane. We thought there was a German inside."

"Whatever do you want a German for?"

Masha raised her eyes and looked intently at the major. He had a broad, placid face, with a slightly turned-up nose, and several days' stubble on his cheeks. Masha liked such faces — though it was true that the major's looks were rather spoiled by the bullet-hole in his left cheekbone. But Masha had already come to the conclusion that perfection doesn't exist in this world and she didn't seek it in people, least of all in their outward appearance.

"Well, you see," began Tanya. "Times are so hard today, everybody has to manage as best they can. So she and I..."

She nodded in the direction of the unconcerned Tuimi.

"In short, we're in a sort of business. You see, everybody's getting the hell out of Russia. To marry a foreigner costs four hundred bucks. We usually charge five hundred ourselves, on average."

"What, for corpses?" asked the major incredulously.

"Just think. The nationality's still there. We bring them back to life on the condition they get married. It's usually Germans. For a dead German we charge about the same as for a live Zimbabwean, or a Russian Jew without an exit visa. Best of all, of course, is a Spaniard from the Blue Division, but they come dear. And they're rare. Then, we get Italians, and Finns. But Romanians and Hungarians we don't touch."

"Well, well, well," said the major. "And do they live long afterwards?"

"About three years," replied Tanya.

"That's not long," said the major. "Aren't you sorry for them?"

Tanya thought for a moment, and her pretty face grew serious. A deep furrow formed between her brows. There was silence, broken only by the crackling of the logs on the fire and the quiet whispering of the leaves.

"That's a hard question," she said finally. "Are you serious?"

"Absolutely."

Tanya thought a moment longer.

"Well, the way I heard," she began, "is there's this one rule for earth and another one for heaven. Get the power of heaven going on earth and you set all creation astir and the invisible becomes visible. It has no substance of its own, being by nature but a fleeting condensation of darkness. That's why it doesn't stay long in the vortex of transformations. In fact it's just a lot of emptiness, which is why I don't really feel sorry for them."

"That's just how it is," the major said. "You hit the nail on the head."

The furrow between Tanya's brows was smoothed away.

"Honestly, there's so much work you don't have time to think. We usually move about ten a month, fewer in winter. Tuimi's got a two-year waiting list in Moscow."

"These people you bring back to life, do they all agree?"

"Practically all of them," Tanya replied. "It's desperately sad where they are. Dark, overcrowded, no grace. You grit your teeth and bear it there. Mind you, I don't know what it's like with you — we haven't had a client from the upper world before. Still, dead folk are all different in the underworld too. It was like that near Kharkov last year — terrifying. We got hold of this tank driver from the Death's Head Battalion. We dressed him, washed him, shaved him, explained everything to him. He agreed — I mean, we had a really good bride for him, Marina, from the Faculty of Journalism. We fixed her up later with a Japanese sailor... Lord, you should see them float up to the surface... I remember... What was I saying?"

"The tank driver," said the major.

"Oh yes. Well, to cut a long story short, we gave him some money to make him feel he'd got a life, and of course he started to drink; they all do at the beginning. Then at some private bar or other they wouldn't sell him a drop. They wanted roubles, and all he had was German occupation marks. So the first thing he did, he smashed their windows with his revolver, and that night he rolled up on his Tiger tank and flattened every last bar around the station. Ever since that day they often see his tank at night driving around Kharkov, flattening all the private shops, but come daylight it disappears. Nobody knows where it goes."

"The world's a funny old place," the major said.

"Since then we've only worked with the Wehrmacht. We won't touch the SS. Their brains are all scrambled. Before you know it they'll seize a village council, or start singing in chorus. And anyway, they don't want to get married — it's against their regulations."

A blast of cold air swept across the clearing. Masha lifted her fascinated gaze from Major Zvyagintsev and saw three indistinct, ghostly figures emerging from behind three tree trunks at the edge of the clearing. Tuimi gave a squeal and hid behind Tanya.

"There," gulped Tanya, "it's beginning. Don't be afraid, you silly old thing, they won't touch you."

She rose and went to meet the ghostly figures, making calming gestures as she approached them, like a car driver stopped by the traffic police. Tuimi rolled herself into a ball, put her head between her knees, and began trembling quietly. Masha, just in case, moved closer to the fire, then suddenly felt with her whole body the full force of Major Zvyagintsev's eyes upon her. She looked up. The major smiled sadly.

"You're so beautiful, Masha," he said quietly. "You know, I was working in the garden when your Tuimi began calling me. She went on and on. It really got on my nerves. I wanted to chase you all off. I looked out and saw you there, Masha. There is no telling how much I liked you. There was a girl at school like you. Varya, her name was. She was so like you, the same freckled nose, but she wore her hair longer than you do. I was in love with her. Would I really have come if it hadn't been for you?"

"Have you got a garden there then?" Masha asked, blushing a little in embarrassment.

"Yes," replied the major.

"What's it called, this place where you live?"

"We don't have any names there," said the major. "That's why we live in peace and happiness."

"What's it like there, though?" Masha asked.

"It's all right," the major said, and his lips again parted in a smile.

"Do you have things, you know, possessions, like people here do?" asked Masha.

"How can I put it, Masha? On the one hand, we sort of do, but on the other, we sort of don't. Everything's a bit approximate, a bit blurred. But only when you think about it."

"Where do you live?" Masha asked.

"I've got a kind of cottage, and a bit of ground," said the major. "It's so quiet there, nice."

"Have you got a car?" Masha asked, and instantly drew back. It suddenly seemed such a stupid question.

"If you want one, you can have one," said the major. "Why not?"

"What sort?"

"It all depends," said the major. "You can have a microwave too, and, what's it called, a washing machine. Only there's nothing to wash. And a colour television — mind you, there's only the one channel, but we get all your channels on it."

"Does it all depend, what kind of television you have?"

"Well," said the major, "sometimes it's a Panasonic, sometimes a Shiwaki. But when you try to remember, it's not there any more, it's gone. There's just a shimmering cloud there. I told you, it's all the same as here, except that nothing has a name there. Everything is nameless. And the closer you get to heaven, the more nameless everything becomes."

Masha could not think what else to ask him, so she fell silent, pondering the major's last words. Meanwhile, Tanya was making some very emphatic point to the three ghostly figures.

"How many times do I have to tell you, she uses thunder for her magic," her indignant voice could be heard saying. "It's all perfectly above board. She was struck by lightning as a child, and the spirit of the thunder gave her a piece of tin, to make herself a peak for her hat... Why should I produce it for you? She's under no obligation to carry it around with her. We've never had any problems of that sort... You should be ashamed of yourselves being so suspicious of an old woman. You'd be better employed going after the faith-healers in Moscow. It's positively scary living there now, and all you can do is pick on a poor old woman. I'll lodge a complaint and all..."

Masha felt the major's hand on her elbow.

"Masha," he said. "I'm going now. There's something I'd like to give you to remember me by."

Masha noticed a note of intimacy in his voice. She was pleased by it.

"What's this," she asked.

"It's a reed pipe," said the major. "When you get tired of this life, come to my plane. Play on it and I'll come to you."

"Could I come and visit you?" Masha asked.

"Certainly," the major replied. "Just wait till you taste my strawberries!"

He rose to his feet.

"You'll come then?" he asked. "I'll be waiting."

Masha gave an almost imperceptible nod.

"But what about you... Aren't you alive again now?" she asked.

The major shrugged, took a rusty TT revolver from the pocket of his leather flying-jacket, and put it to his ear.

A shot rang out.

Tanya turned and stared at the major in alarm. He staggered but kept his feet. Tuimi looked up and giggled. The cold wind came again, and Masha saw there were no longer any ghostly figures at the edge of the clearing.

"I'll be waiting," Major Zvyagintsev repeated, walking unsteadily towards the gully, over which a barely visible opalescence was hovering. A few steps more and his figure dissolved in the darkness, like a lump of sugar in a glass of hot tea.

Masha was looking out of the train window at the passing cottages with their vegetable gardens. She was weeping quietly.

"Don't, Masha. Don't be so upset," said Tanya, looking at her friend's weeping face. "Never mind, it just happens that way sometimes. Would you like to come to Arkhangelsk with the girls? There's an American B-29 Flying Fortress lying in a bog there. Eleven bodies. Enough for everybody. Why don't you come?"

"When are you thinking of going?" Masha asked.

"After the fifteenth. By the way, come and see us on the

fifteenth, it's the Festival of the Pure Hearth. Tuimi's going to cook some wild mushrooms. We'll play on the tambourine for the upper world for you, as you like that so much. Hey, Tuimi, wouldn't it be good if Masha came to see us?"

Tuimi looked up and answered with a broad smile, displaying the brown stumps of her teeth sticking out of her gums at odd angles. It was an unnerving smile because Tuimi's eyes were hidden behind the thongs of hide that hung down from her hat, which made it seem as if only her mouth were smiling, while her unseen gaze remained cold and attentive.

"Don't be frightened," said Tanya. "She's a good person."

Masha, however, was already looking out of the window, clasping in her pocket the reed pipe Major Zvyagintsev had given her, and thinking intently about something.

Victor PELEVIN (b. 1962) is one of the most acclaimed writers of his generation. Few people are capable of creating wonderful new worlds. Pelevin's are fantastic worlds of dreams, talking sheds, philosophising chickens, computer games, Soviet werewolves, drug addicts. He possesses enormous erudition which includes knowledge of Chinese philosophy, information science, mysticism, metaphysics, and much else. As a true artist Pelevin reflects the dominant moods of the times.

His better known books include *The Blue Lantern*, *Omon Ra*, *The Life of Insects*, *Yellow Arrow*, *Chapayev and Pustota (Buddha's Little Finger)*, *Generation P*, *Numbers, The Werewolves' Sacred Book*.

Vassily AKSYONOV

Palmer's First Flight

Palmer's Second Flight

Translated by Alla Zbinovsky

Palmer's First Flight

The artist Modest Orlovich sat in his studio, located behind the old wall of Moscow's Kitai-gorod with windows looking out on the Bolshoi Theater. Outside, in December of 1991, Soviet communism was in its death throes. Meanwhile, in Orlovich's studio, something violet with crimson bruises was taking shape and a stormy blue with a lead underbelly was materializing — the new waves of an acrylic revolution.

In the dismal studio, the television was expressing itself with colorful flashes. That frightening fiend of a rock-star Kierkegorenko wailed predictably: "Red swine, get out of the Kremlin! Out of the Kremlin, the ground is groaning!" The smell of roasting turkey was wafting through the whole studio: Orlovich's girl friends Muse Borisovna and Hamayun Bird were preparing to receive guests on the occasion of the end of violet and the onset of blue.

The zinc-coated door began to shake: it was clearly being kicked. In former times, Orlovich would definitely have thought: "The vipers are here," although he hadn't given the "vipers" much reason for coming, except for his famous leap into the trowel of the "Belarus" bulldozer, sent to plow down an unofficial outdoor art exhibition in the fall of 1974. His yellow-green scarf then flew over the dispersed modernist paintings, until it was thrown into a ditch along with everything else.

Now then, after all the events at the barricades during the August coup, the "comrades" won't be coming again, thought

Orlovich. However, the door continued to shake as if being kicked by proletarian boots. With the help of his long levers, Orlovich climbed out of the crushed couch to open the door. Instead of a boot a bare foot pushed its way into the studio. The proletarian turned out to be his déclassé neighbor, Misha Chuvakin. "What are you locking yourself in for? What's happening, are you pigging out on sausage?" He made his way inside, spreading the disgusting smell of potato salad, akin to vomit.

Orlovich saw himself together with Chuvakin in the crookedly hung nineteenth-century mirror. "We deserve each other," he thought. "What vile slovenliness in our faces, our hair and clothing. But you know, I've got two good suits, razors and eau-de-Cologne, to somehow set myself apart from Chuvakin."

"Does anything need fixing?" asked the neighbor, for some reason looking behind the mirror. Everyone in the apartment building knew that for all his appearance of a "Russian handyman", he could never fix anything and never intended to, and that his main business was — to meddle in people's affairs so that he could get things from them, which was why he always appeared with proposals to fix something.

"Misha, what is it you need right now?" asked Orlovich.

"Some German woman is here, Modest. Maybe you could chat with her awhile," said Chuvakin.

"This is something new. Perhaps she's even an English-woman?" said the surprised artist.

Misha Chuvakin told this short story. In principle, he was sleeping already, having eaten some noodles in chicken broth. When this rock festival began, he shut himself off and even turned out the slutty Smaragda. "Modest, if you think I'm wiped out because of a hangover, then you're dead wrong! I'm just tired, working till dawn in the brigade dismantling the Kalinin

75

monument, the All-Union elder. Why so many details, Modest? What is there for people to talk about, if not the details?"

Casually pouring himself a glass of wheat vodka from an open bottle, and gulping it down as if it were beside the point, as if this were not the real reason he had come, Chuvakin continued. He had heard some sort of knocking through his dreams, somehow it seemed like an alien kind of knock, well you know, not the way the local police inspector knocks. The slutty Smaragda went to open the door and returned with a German woman. A young woman, not at all a slut. A slightly lame Englishwoman, as if a flower, well, a German. Trembling and holding out a baby in blue ribbons.

Here is a Dickensian story for you, with a Kitai-gorod twist to it, thought Orlovich. Christmas is coming, a lame German-Dutch woman with a blue-ribboned baby. Moscow, anarchy. "Chuvakin, aren't you twisting things just a bit, indulging in mythological thinking?"

Chuvakin was suddenly very offended. He addressed his neighbor in a friendly way, called him by his first name, Modest, and that one condescended by calling him by his surname Chuvakin.

"You're fucking around with me, Modest, you're not treating me like one of your own, as if I'm not your neighbor. I come to you for help, to translate what this single mother is saying, and you keep me at arm's length, as if I were a drunk." After splashing down another half-glass with the same casualness, as if he didn't attach the slightest importance to the main liquid in his life, the déclassé Chuvakin stomped to the door.

"What ribbons, you ask, what baby? See for yourself!"

Orlovich now saw with his own eyes an Englishwoman in the stairwell, or maybe a German or a Swede, in a black down coat and thick ear-muffs perched on the sides of her elongated head. She was wearing enormous down-filled gloves, with which she pressed a substantial package tied with blue string to her chest.

This was one Kimberly Palmer from the town of Strasburg, state of Virginia, USA (we beg you not to confuse it with the Strasbourger Torte found in the center of Western Europe). She was 29 years old. For some unknown reason, any mention of Russia, even as a small child, caused her throat muscles to spasm, and her tear ducts to well up. This strange emotional reaction brought her to the Russian program at Vanderbilt University, located in Nashville, Tennessee. She spent a whole semester in a state of agitation while taking courses in Russian geography and history; well, and in her Dostoyevsky class she lost all control. One night all her suite mates came running into her room, alarmed by the sobbing: Palmer was reading Dostoyevsky's "Netochka Nezvanova" in Andrew MacAndrew's translation. She would have made an excellent Slavist if she hadn't been forced to cut her education short. It so happened that her father, Mr Palmer, went mad from the endless life in the scenic Shenandoah Valley and cut his capers, completely in keeping with the spirit of Dostoyevsky's heroes. Without a word to his family, he re-mortgaged their house, took all the cash and went somewhere to the devil, maybe even to Las Vegas, for good. The mother, Mrs Palmer, collapsed under the weight of the monthly payments, the younger brothers went wild, and Kimberly, almost repeating the heroic act of Sonechka Marmeladova, sold herself to a bank called Perpetual. And so, she got stuck there for some years in the car loan department behind an all-glass window with old-fashioned calligraphic lettering and a view of a Strasburg intersection: a traffic light, a competitor bank First Virginia, Max's pharmacy and a shop called Helen's Pottery.

She did well at the bank, that is to say, by the time she hit twenty-seven, she had been made department head and was making $32,000 a year, which meant that even after making the monthly payments, she could afford a more or less up-to-date lifestyle. This whole time, she never stopped considering herself a student at a prestigious institution of higher learning and never forgot to renew the university sticker on her Chevrolet; over ice cream at Max's she often told Helen: "You know, at my university, Vanderbilt..." Twice a week she drove to Woodstock for an aerobics class. Naturally, all pocket editions of the Russian classics were on her shelves, and at night they roamed all over her pillow. In the mornings, she ran three miles around sleepy Strasburg, and sometimes in the evenings she ran three miles, and sometimes in the middle of the night she ran three miles, and sometimes she didn't feel like stopping at all, if it meant not having to return to the car loan department. Naturally, while running, a tape of Russian phrases or a Russian symphony played on her Walkman. "This Palmer returned from Tennessee a very different person," the locals said. Men did not dare ask her out on a date, and rightly so: none of them reminded her of Lermontov's Pechorin, nor of Chekhov's Gurov. By the way, in her literary celibacy she had begun to dry up a bit already, in spite of her vivid imagination.

It was Helen Hoggensoller who understood her best. She was the owner of the popular local shop that sold various types of pottery: pots and vases for your flowers, flamingos and marmots for your lawn, cherubs for your graves and, in general, objects of good taste, my dear. Three-hundred-pound Helen, in counterbalance to her obesity, had a light disposition, inquisitiveness, and even a degree of erudition. She managed to wear her oversized things with extravagance, including the ceramic necklaces that were constantly rattling on her breast, reflecting the centuries-old culture of a Shenandoah Indian tribe who called themselves "Moon Meditators". Our heroine could talk only with Helen about passion, about a faraway country which could not be understood with any computer, could not be measured with any calculator, in which you could only believe, believe... During Palmer's intense spasms, chest pressure and dampening eye sockets, Hoggensoller would press her hand and tell her that Sergeant Isaac Isaacson, a deputy sheriff from Front Royal, had again asked about her and sighed, just like, my honey, your Pushkin.

It was at Helen's Pottery that the Strasburg women's club began to meet, about twelve of the better representatives of this settlement, founded back in the eighteenth century, with the overall number of souls exceeding a thousand. They gathered on Fridays among the ceramics and velvet poinsettias and demonstrated their capabilities, each in their own way: brownies or danish, or homemade raisin cookies, or a small bucket of pasta salad, and even celery and carrot sticks accompanied by a thick sauce which, in accordance with local tradition, was for dipping vegetables, thereby producing a pleasant moistening effect during the chewing process. If the conversation turned out to be good, they would wave away the high calories, and each chipped in two dollars for a cheesecake from Max's across the street. The conversations often turned out to be interesting, and the instigator almost always turned out to be Kimberly Palmer. The ladies sighed, listening to her stories about the suffering in Russia, and enjoyed repeating interesting words after her: "gorbachev", "kremlin", "kaygeebee", "perestroika". They especially liked the word "glasnose": to them it sounded superior, in transparent opposition to the expression "hard-nose", that is, dark dogmatism and blunt-nosedness.

So it was there, at Helen's Pottery that the idea arose of contributing to the world's humanitarian aid effort to the all-suffering Russians. For Christmas, let's send them food packages: each of us will contribute our mite. We'll set an example for other Christians, other Americans, other women!

They began to collect money, that is, began fund-raising. The "Blue Ridge" newspaper reported on the initiative to the public at large. With increasing frequency, cars began to stop in front of the shop window filled with vases and pots. Some gave a dollar, some gave two. Deputy Sheriff Isaac Isaacson donated thirty bucks, that is, enough for the purchase of six six-packs.

Palmer got so carried away with this wonderful work that she now always ran out of her home with none other than a dazzling smile on her lips. Then suddenly, an unpleasant event transpired: her daddy returned, her sinful papa, in the flesh. He now looked like half the splendid man he had once been: second in the county in bowling and a salesman in the town's main enterprise, the "Antique Emporium". Apologizing to his family for causing so much trouble, this man of indeterminate age and a strange lightness clarified that the goal of his return was not the resumption of family life, but the restoration of his right of access to a state hospital, where he could die for free, or almost for free. Keep calm, boys and girls, don't panic! As a matter of fact, he had already registered in the hospital, he had only stopped by the old house to pick up his collection of baseball cards, so he could sort through them while dying.

Kimberly was stunned by the remarkable qualities of her almost unrecognizable daddy and attached herself to him for the remainder of his life, that is to say, for fifteen or so days. Papa suffered, but he never ceased smiling in expectation of painkillers. Pharmacology submerged him into a state of almost total bliss. He took the hand of his eldest daughter and continued smiling, either from recollecting something not all that bad, or perhaps he was already traveling in some sort of extraterrestrial sphere. He died in a superior mood, even while sort of whistling something from the big-band era.

The stunned Kimberly now began running not three miles at a time, but all of six at once. Tchaikovsky's Fifth Symphony hovered over the sleeping Strasburg as it trailed after the runner. It seemed the night skies reflected the happy smile of her cast-off father. Isaac Isaacson frequently escorted her in his patrol car. While holding back tears, he told her about group therapy for the treatment of sexual sublimation, about family planning, about balancing budgets.

Once, just before dawn, the friendly hand of Helen Hoggensoller intercepted our runner. It turned out the Pottery Club at its latest meeting had decided to assign one of their members to accompany the humanitarian aid packages to Moscow. This representative, of course, was to be Palmer. After this, how can we still call our era the manifestation of mercantilism?

As a matter of fact, take a look at the arena of world events and you'll find all sorts of things there: gangsterism, sadomasochism, romantic cruelty, hypocrisy and compassion, a great deal of exalted idiocy, rather cheerful but also excruciatingly mean swindling, but you'll never find any displays of common sense associated with mercantilism. Million-strong crowds of people commit reckless acts, both individuals and governments live beyond their means; they are capable in three days of destroying socialism or throwing three ten dollar bills to the wind. It's only China that is systematically increasing its economic potential with no regrets for the students killed on the way to achieving this goal. However, that which applies to China does not apply to the rest of mankind.

And so, here was this 29-year-old girl called Palmer with the humanitarian aid package, mistaken for a baby bundle by the déclassé worker in Moscow. She had thirty such packages in her luggage. Not quite enough to save a large country, but the most important thing was the initiative! If thirty packages

81

came from every thousand Western Christians, then that would make seven and a half million from the USA alone! It goes without saying that our Russophile flew to Moscow in a state of exultation.

In the initial minutes of acquaintance, the longed-for city shocked Palmer by its smell. Possessing the keen nostrils of one who grew up among the relatively not-so-nasty smells of the Shenandoah Valley, Palmer immediately caught the essence: a mixture of urine and disinfectant. This basic smell, by the way, was constantly enriched depending on the presence of certain elements such as concentrated sweat, universal rottenness, chemical alcohol, exhaust fumes; in a word, the whole bouquet of communism's death agony. She caught herself with a strange sensation: it seemed to her in the presence of such a smell it was somehow awkward to conduct regular human activities. One should just stand and wait until the smell evaporated.

She had a room reserved for her in a huge hotel near the Kremlin. Masses of people constantly walked down the endless corridors. Out of her window, Palmer saw a narrow river with blackened ice and a monstrous building with six hellish smokestacks and mighty letters displayed on the facade. She had barely read the word "Lenin", when two fat women entered her room and began counting the towels, pillow-cases and quilt covers. Taking refuge in a corner of the room, Palmer looked at the flabby embodiments of "Russianness" in the coarse and wretched features of these two specimens.

"Where is your second towel?" asked one of them, but upon seeing the wide-eyed look of the new arrival, they brushed her aside: "Ay, this dummy doesn't know a word of Russian!" They looked at her more closely and added: "As far as money goes, I dare say the ugly dog doesn't have any. She's traveling on a shoestring!"

Palmer paced past the Kremlin with the first trial package of humanitarian aid. It was far better here — the smell was gone. The frost stung at her cheeks and nose. Seeing her reflection in the shop-window of GUM, she was astonished by her own beauty. A tall American woman with a humanitarian aid package. She was startled at the density of the throngs. People walked quickly, not paying any attention to the fairy tale architecture surrounding them. An adolescent girl stood on a corner with a sign, written in English: "We were deprived of all basic rights — please help my family to survive." Palmer extended 25 rubles to her. The girl motioned to a tin can with her chin and turned away contemptuously.

Endless lines of people stretched around the corner along the sidewalk. Palmer, shocked by the vast quantities of fur hats, attesting to the massive abuse of small animals, decided to begin a campaign against fur hats in the future! She tried to listen carefully to the Russian spoken around her. She frequently heard a Russian obscenity that sounded like Chinese, an unfamiliar hoarse exhalation on "khu". In general, the people standing in line were not talkative, it seemed they had exhausted all topics of conversation. One man had a small wooden board hanging on his chest with hard currency signs. She heard the word "kaufen" and dashed away to the side.

Suddenly, she found herself on the front steps of a building that looked as if it had been smashed by an earthquake. A baby stroller was being carried out of the door with a creaking sound. An apartment building. Palmer went inside. A cave-like entryway permeated by the smell of cat freedom. Boards lay on top of a high stack of beat-up Dutch tiles. It was as if a Pennsylvania mine shaft gaped into the entrance of a long hallway. Of course, there are needy people living in these slums. The first Christmas present from Strasburg will be delivered right here, to the door labeled 7-a.

"Don't open it, don't you dare open it, you parasite!" someone howled from inside. The door opened. It seemed to Palmer that she had ended up in a New York ghetto, known to her only through the movies. This was all because the déclassé Chuvakin, from his many years of drinking plonk, had turned substantially blue-grey, if not completely dark. His wife, Smaragda, was either Chuvash or one of those Lithuanian Karaites, so she could pass for a Puerto Rican. Palmer wanted to greet them in the normal Russian way, but from nervousness she said something totally senseless: "Zdravevichi" instead of the greeting "Zdrastvuite". Frightened, she began to poke at her package, as if entreating them not to suspect her of evil intentions. Then she noticed that the husband and wife were barefoot, and something was wrong with their oral cavities. She almost began to sob: these poor people, poor people!

"Take it!" she muttered. "Enjoy! Merry Christmas!"

"What a stupid cow," yawned Smaragda. "Whoa, look at her! She wants to abandon her goddamn baby!"

"You don't understand a fucking thing, you slutty Smaragda," said Chuvakin, scratching himself all over, from his ears to his toes. "She's a Swede, they are really frightening. I'll take her to the artist, he can speak their language. I've heard him myself."

"You're going to get smashed at the artist's again!" howled the wife. "Don't you dare come home, you bastard! I wish all you pricks would get smothered by a giant cunt!"

Chuvakin, with a diplomatic twist of his body, showed the way upstairs. They climbed up staircases. This house was once opulent, thought Palmer: in places you could make out marble, ornamental cast-iron and mosaic fragments. She recalled a lecture on "The World of Art" given by Kostanovich, a Vanderbilt professor. They climbed all the way to the top, just under the roof. This should be where the neediest roost. This self-sacrificing barefoot man didn't think of himself, but of others. Such depth to these characters. Some nice smells suddenly reached them from behind the zinc-coated door on the top landing. Smelled like home-cooking on Thanksgiving.

When the "Englishwoman" was led inside, Muse Borisovna and Hamayun Bird had already begun setting the table in the far corner of the cavernous studio. The Hungarian turkey legs stuck up to the cathedral ceiling like two mortars. The first fragrance of fish pie came from the oven. A soft mountain of caviar rose over the edges of a crystal bowl. This last substance was known to Palmer only from literature, and in its actual embodiment it remained unidentified by her until the very end of the story.

It was with great pleasure that the ladies continued their creative work around the table. By the way, both of them were Moscow celebrities, Ostankino mirages, as well as the "darlings" of the commercial and corrupted plebs. They didn't have any problem "using their faces", walking through any crowd into the office of a store manager and acquiring any hard-to-get item they pleased. And look — Modest has all the luck! Both prominent celebrities of different generations for some reason took it upon themselves to present the artist's studio as a "horn of plenty". Of course, this horn was constantly and obscenely being emptied by the crowd of motley bohemians, gathering at night in the loft, from where you could see the coachman's head and the back of the monument to Marxism's founder, and also, if you were to peer through the drunken gloom, the chariot on top of the Bolshoi Theater.

Modest Orlovich knew one solid English interrogatory sentence, "Ver are you fram?" and in addition, a fairly good number of individual words, mostly nouns. This supply of nouns helped him to speak with foreigners in the mode of "telegraphic speech" created by the Italian futurist Marinetti, that is, without verbs. He usually presented himself as "paintor", patting himself on the chest with his hand. "Great paintor. My houz," followed by a circular gesture around the studio. "Guest goot. Frost, ah? Russia. Vinter. Ver are you fram?"

Meanwhile, Palmer looked with delight at the tall and gaunt painter — well, simply an incarnation of Prince Myshkin! Exclaiming in her own Virginian, occasionally adding sticky Russian words that sounded like caramelized popcorn. This is approximately what came out. "I'm from Strasburg, Virginia. We also have winterovs. No, no, I'm not afraid of Russian frostniks. I'm so gladski, many thanks! So you're a house painter, sir, and this is your friend, the barefoot gentleman, a plumber, right? That's just marvelous! Thanks for your gospitality!"

Orlovich replied quickly and boldly: "Good. Food. Vodka. Beer. Fuck. Table. Chair. Glass. Plate. Painting. Great. Voilà!"

Chuvakin even dropped his jaw in admiration. An almost understandable conversation took place before him in a foreign language.

"Ask about the baby, Modest!"

Orlovich asked about the blue bundle with his two palms and chin.

"Chaild? Child? Mazer? Fazer?"

Palmer didn't get a chance to answer. The zinc-coated door flew open, never to close again that night. A drunken crowd with rosy cheeks burst into the studio. Agitated, distorted faces and elegant clothing. Designer coats with capes fell into a heap, colorful scarves were unwrapped. A whole team of leggy tarts. Some fat Sicilian. A fine, large Russian fellow, a bare chest with a cross under a shaggy vest. Everyone talked at once, nobody listened to anyone.

"Where shall I put this humanitarian aid package?" asked Palmer, suddenly becoming timid. Nobody answered her. A rhapsody of kisses. The men sucked in parts of each other's badly-shaved cheeks. The women ground their groins into the host instead of shaking his hand. It was obvious they were all quite drunk already, and the table now held even more bottles, like pins in a bowling alley. "So you're all ripped already, my gang!" yelled Modest happily. "You need to catch up with us, our genius genie!" The Russian hunk grabbed the host by the beard and shoved a bottle of champagne into his mouth. Foam sprayed all around them. One heavy drop hit Palmer right in the forehead. Her head spun and made a wild circle around the vaults of the enormous loft. It was only now that Palmer realized that the walls glowed with paintings and glimmered with the deep gold of icons. Hamayun lightly shook Palmer out of her down coat and hugged her around the waist. "Put the child right here, under the icons, and have a seat at the table, here!" A red mouth illustrated an invitation to the internationally intelligible "yum-yum." "Why, little mother, you've turned blue!" Muse Borisovna placed a bowl of hot broth before Palmer. "You need to boullionize yourself, my dear!" An amber slick of cholesterol covered the surface. The only thing that was still needed for total suicide was a glass of vodka, and here it was.

"Let's drink to Bruderschaft, my country schoolteacher!" the Russian stud Arkashka Grubiyanov yelled into Palmer's ear. He sat on the arm of her chair, and when, after the vodka, he leaned over to kiss her according to Russian custom, he fell with his thick thigh between the Samaritan's two shapely extremities, accidentally pushing the palm of his hand into her crotch.

Her thin lips quivered under Arkashka's wet sausage lips. It's not his fault, this is tradition, such sincere national character, Russianness, this man is not to blame, one shouldn't pick on him. What passion, what freshness of feeling, even though he does reek of something sickening.

Grubiyanov shoved a tablespoon of caviar into her mouth.

"You must have it, eat our treasure, the last caviar of a dying Russia! You can't swallow it? Hey everyone, she takes it in her mouth, and then she can't swallow it!" Muse Borisovna cut off Grubiyanov's boorishness with a dramatic gesture. "Stop your swinish antics, Arkashka!" Then someone at the table began playing Eine Kleine Nacht Musik on the violin. A group of European and Russian menfolk dressed in fancy suits got up at the far end of the table, drinking some sort of separate toast to a joint venture. Arkashka had already forgotten about Palmer, and was grabbing a big-headed critic by the chest. "You just don't get the Russian idea, you jerk! You still don't comprehend Rozanov!" One more big-headed man crawled up to Palmer from her other side. "Je vous voudrais de ride on a Russian troika!" The leggy girls wouldn't sit at the table, they kept getting up, as if trying to slip out of their tiny dresses, and then they would pull them down with rather enigmatic smiles. Suddenly, the whole company, no less than thirty mouths, all sang at once: "Let's take each others' hands, our friends, so we don't perish one by one."

The candles were already burning. Palmer, dumbfounded, looked at all the faces lit up with inspiration. The slightest puffiness in the cheeks or under the eyes appeared exaggerated, any sunken spaces sunk in twofold. A living sculpture of a suffering people. Pouring herself some vodka from the octagonal carafe, the girl Palmer rose with a toast.

"Gospodin i gospodan!" she said, meaning to say "Ladies and gentlemen". And she went on in Virginian: "I have the distinctski privilege of sending you heart-felt and warm regardovs from the peopleniks of the Shenandoah valley, particularly from Mrs. Hoggensoller's Pottery Clubchik. Let me emphasize that this humble donation reflects just a small part of a great sympathy for a large people at a very, very important crossroads in historich!"

The women looked at her with great surprise, as if they had just noticed her. The men leaned out of their chairs, trying to check out her backside. Even those sexually satisfied or with poor appetites considered it necessary to demonstrate their libidos were not asleep. Only Arkashka Grubiyanov for some reason right at this moment became gloomy. Somehow it was during the toast made by this goggle-eyed sort-of Swede he thought of his KGB basement, which because of the disintegration of the USSR, might suddenly be opened only to expose a stunning stench.

Palmer pointed out the blue bundle under the glimmering icon to everyone. The déclassé Chuvakin sat next to the bundle, his feet no longer bare, but sporting Muse Borisovna's large steel-spiked Italian boots. He took the bundle and passed it to the host, Modest Orlovich, who took it in his arms somewhat tenderly. "What's his name?" he asked the guest in Russian. "Nom? Navn? Name?" Rocking the bundle, himself swaying over the table, a perfect papa. Warm feelings streamed out of the artist's childish, if not donkey eyes. The menfolk laughed, not very maliciously. "Fess up, Modest, you knocked up the Swede! Now take the baby for upbringing."

Palmer quickly de-diapered the bundle right on the table next to the octagonal decanter of Czarist vodka, the crystal Slavic bowl, still heaped with Caspian caviar, the half-gnawed turkey leg from the Hungarian plains, a scattering of cigarettes of the more prestigious brands at that troubled time in the Russian winter, that is Marlboro and Dunhill, and also items of Western preserved delights, which had already struck an irreparable blow to Soviet Marxism, well, so as to not bumble around this disgraceful phrase any longer, next to some cans of beer. The assortment, so painstakingly collected by the Pottery Club ladies, now appeared before the gathering: two boxes of Uncle Ben's quick-cooking enriched rice, a packet of thick mushroom sauce, a big box of oatmeal cereal called Common Sense (which as we can see, is still available in the context of today's civilization) — a goldmine of beneficial fiber with good vitamin combinations, including riboflavin, magnesium, zinc and even an optimal quantity of copper, moreover, with the full absence of saturated fat and cholesterol, two packages of Town House spaghetti, and two necessary ingredients to go with it — a tube of ketchup and bottles of powdered Parmesan, three boxes with an ideal supply of protein, that is, tuna fish in spring water, so that every mouth, if just for a while, could feel like a sponger, Wiler bouillon cubes, the obligatory three cans of Andy Warhol's Campbell Soup, well, a package of Lipton Tea, (drink 100 strong cups, or 200 moderate cups, or 300 sensible cups), and a jar of Maxwell House instant coffee, whose last drop was appreciated even by Mayakovsky, while refusing to remove his cap from his head, well, a packet of pseudo-cream to go with the coffee, so that the hungry people would still not gain weight, hot cocoa mix, a mixture of McCormick spices consisting of ground parsley, celery and sweet basil (note the indubitable good taste of Helen Hoggensoller), well, Head and Shoulders shampoo, Crest toothpaste, a selection of miniature Proxa Brushes, to purge the Russian inter-dental spaces of the remains of American food, a jar of Geritol vitamins, Bayer aspirin and Preparation-H suppositories for the successful outcome of everything listed above, well, and finally, some delicacies for children — crunchy chocolates, Danish cookies, gummy jellybeans, and also, in conclusion, something for the soul, an American Father Frost — a Santa Claus figurine.

"That's all of it!" exclaimed Palmer, her voice ringing with joy. "Alas, not a lot, but from the very bottom of our heartniks!"

"Foreign grub!" howled Chuvakin, throwing himself on the

unwrapped package and fishing out the life-giving contents. As Grubiyanov pulled the package toward himself, it all spilled out on him. Everything whirled around in a cheerful greedy mess. Her lavender eyes blazing, Hamayun Bird flew by with some Chicken of the Sea cans. The other girls were powdering themselves all over with the Parmesan cheese. Even the joint venture businessmen did not refuse the gifts, although they had the same goodies, in the Italian version, stored away in the event of a many months street battle in the Russian capital. Even the Slavophile critics, a very proud bunch, didn't mind helping themselves to a packet of mushroom sauce each. In the midst of all this bedlam, only the violinist didn't allow himself to be distracted. Biting a small tube of macaroni, he tediously forced out the melody "Yesterday". And Muse Borisovna, unexpectedly smitten with wet nostalgia, cried without any sadness, while holding up her still-lovely breasts. Between them lay a set of McCormick spices, giving a special meaning to the fleeting moment.

It seemed that the host, the future Sotheby's exhibitor, Modest Poligamenovich Orlovich, was the only one left without a souvenir, which was soon found for him. Looking over the ripped package at the illegitimate baby's narrow-shouldered mama, he suddenly decided that this was exactly what was left for him: a symbol of motherhood, a model for a new acrylic "World of Art" in blue. "Mazer! Chaild! Painting! Je vous aime! Lav! Seance!" He seized Palmer by her trembling wrists, her pulse beating like large grasshoppers, and brought her through the labyrinth of partitions, into the holy of holies, where the stretched canvas stood, where Russian history dimly shone through the window: a granite statue with a coachman's mane, very high spotlights which knew the better days of socialism, and the imperial yellow yolk of the Malyi Theater was mixed with the sinister tar of the rows of empty shops, and the classicism of the Bolshoi Theater, out of place in 1991, with its completely other-worldly chariot.

The half-raped Palmer was placed on the window ledge to pose in her ripped-apart form. "He didn't even notice he popped my cherry," she thought with some tenderness, gazing, as it was said, "into the murk of this goddamned Byzantium", and only slightly trembled in her stupor. The artist was in the middle of a burst of inspiration, or as they said in a circle of jazz musicians, he "grooved" at his canvas. From time to time, through his wiry beard littered with caviar, chocolate and lipstick, nouns would break through: "Solitude. Alienation. Engagement. Weltgeist!" From behind the partition, the noise of the party's intensifying wildness reached them.

Two hours passed like this, after which two small explosions reached them from the square still carrying the name of that humble Bolshevik, Yakov Sverdlov. The lights went out everywhere. The dreary gloom was filled with smoke.

The session lasted still another whole hour. Palmer's silhouette was now reflected in the enamel basin stuck to the wall. "Thanks to jogging," she thought, "I managed until age 29 to preserve myself in the form of the Dream Princess." A whole series of loud sounds reached them from the refectory. From various directions, no less than a dozen mugs flooded with wild happiness thrust themselves into the creative corner. "Ride, ride! Let's go riding on horses!" Modest threw away his brushes. "Ay da, Kimberlylulochka!" Carnival masks were raving around them. "The horses are shaking their manes out there!" Palmer quickly but carefully packed up her small breasts.

"Troika?!" she said, suddenly recalling the word. "Troika russki?!" Grubiyanov grabbed her, intent on hoisting all of her one hundred and ten little pounds on his shoulders. A crowd of guests poured down from the top floor like a giant wave. They leapt out to freedom, which was still called 25th October Street, although right on the verge of throwing up all of its Communist past.

The carriage was already waiting. Ordered through the armed company "Alex". Safety fully guaranteed. The troika turned out to be super-luxurious, not even a troika, but a chariot, cast according to the finest traditions of the imperial designer Baron Klodt. The stomping hooves struck many sparks and crumbled the old asphalt. The stability of Russia's fundamental core was guaranteed by the enormous, broad peasant back of the coachman. Palmer pressed her cheek to this roughly chiseled Russian monolith. An inorganic cosmos, isn't it? Could it be a flight to bumpy celestial roads?

Palmer's Second Flight

Kimberly Palmer spent almost all of 1992 in Russia, but by autumn she returned to her hometown of Strasburg, in the state of Virginia. "Palmer came back from Russia a very different person," said the pharmacist Ernest Max VIII, at the forefront of the current generation of Strasburg milkshake beaters, who although they didn't get monstrously rich from this popular food-stuff, had never once gone bust since the last quarter of the 19th century, preserving their enterprise as the leading attraction on Main Street and introducing the best life had to offer into the lives of eight generations of local German cherubs; oo-oops, someone dropped a glass with a pink shake while staring at the "adventuress Palmer" crossing Main Street. "Never mind," exclaimed Ernest, "did you notice that she even has a different walk now!"

"She obviously lost her innocence over there," some well-wisher whispered to Sergeant Isaac Isaacson, almost deserving a bullet in the forehead, which he would have gotten, if the sergeant's sense of duty hadn't prevailed over his personal emotions. Meanwhile, Palmer, wrapped in a multipurpose Slava Zaitsev cape, crossed the street heading toward Helen Hoggensoller's Pottery Club, where ladies were already hopping around outside waiting to envelop her in their embraces.

"It feels weird to see you all, dear friends," said Palmer at an extended meeting of the club, where canaries twittered among the refined ceramic objects, and Helen shone proudly in her oversized Russian double-headed eagle T-shirt as she brought in miniature cups of coffee — ! — espresso! "Oh, how strange it is, my friends, to return to my homeland, to this quiet town, after ten months in that incredible country!" Then she was silent, and her eyes opened wide as if she had completely forgotten about what was around her at that given moment. And the awestruck ladies also widened their eyes.

Now, in the quiet of the Shenandoah Valley, this ten-month "Russian film" turned itself on in Palmer's mind like virtual reality, in absurdly scrambled pieces, sometimes at night on her pillow, sometimes at the wheel of her Toyota, then in the supermarket, at times while jogging, then while watching television, sometimes while smoking — this harmful habit, acquired in Russia, somehow seemed like an infectious disease among the enlightened inhabitants of Virginia — and the "film" even surpassed the blazing Indian summer, fleetingly glimpsed squirrels, the marching of the school orchestra, the usual TV series, which one should say she really had missed while in Russia, while they were still in her mind.

She would suddenly have visions of the giant commercial strife of Moscow, dirty slush underfoot, and overhead, crows crazed from all the wild capitalism, women's blouses hanging next to bunches of dried fish, stalls of tinned goods lying in a mess next to doorknobs, bottles of vodka, lipstick, books by Sigmund Freud and Elena Blavatskaya. In her deepest sleep she saw glimpses of Russia, containing something more than feelings or thoughts, imprinting themselves into the darkness, like images of her own agony. The Mesozoic plate under the Russian continent stirred like a sluggish toad, a meter every millennium.

Shaking herself awake, she smoked in the bedroom — only Marlboros, which for some reason were considered to be the hippest brand in Moscow — and again watched her fragmented "film": Vietnamese merchants fighting on the train from Saratov to Volgograd, tiny and ferocious in their denim "Army USA" shirts, spraying each other in the face with poisonous atomizers and dragging about some sort of bales; distribution of humanitarian aid to the children at the orphanage near Elista, where she had traveled during a joint effort of the British Red Cross and a German group called "Redemption"; hanging out in Moscow's bohemian attics and basements, and the men, a plenitude of them, not always strong, but always insolent, smelling of sweat no perfume could eradicate, cursing coarsely or soaring to the heavens; dragging her into a corner, shoving vodka at her, and immediately letting down their flies, as if feminist ideas had never spent the night in this country.

Sometimes she cried out in horror: could it be that she subconsciously anticipated such SOBs when she thought about Russia? No, no, there was also something else which matched her youthful ecstasy: violin concerts, poetry readings, and spontaneous rushes of mass inspiration — a crowd suddenly waltzing to the flute, tuba and accordion in the spit-filled passageway under Pushkin's statue — "The Blue Danube!" After the waltz, however, everyone ran off like a herd of jackals, with the accordionist howling after them: "Sons of bitches! Motherfuckers! And who's going to pay, Pushkin?!" Left alone in the void, he closed his eyes and played "Yesterday".

There was so much of everything, and still, Kimberly Palmer, admit it, your main discovery in Russia turned out to be men. At first she met with them as if prompted by some sort of tearfulness, a motherly atavism, and then, the truth is, something exclusively physiological appeared, a kind of bitch in heat, ma'am. It was likely that in the Kitai-gorod art studio there wasn't one regular who didn't get to know the "Englishwoman" intimately, or, as she was called after that memorable night in December 1991, when the humanitarian aid package was mistaken for a baby, "single mother". It got to the point that something that she didn't quite understand was said about her: "the broad's out of control".

The most horrific memories were connected with the Sokolniki abortion clinic, where Orlovich brought her to a doctor he knew. In sterile, clean Virginia one couldn't even begin to imagine comparable medical care, orderlies and nurses, not to mention the patients. Palmer was sure she wouldn't get out of there alive, and it was even more amazing that everything turned out well, leaving nothing but pride like the kind that remains with hostages after an ordeal in Beirut.

The stunned Sergeant Isaac Isaacson, who got from her on the first night of her return what he had wished for during many years of Tantalus torments, muttered with a touch of tragic sarcasm: "I can see you must have gone through group therapy for overcoming sexual sublimation, am I right?" "I wonder if it wasn't group surgery," smirked Palmer.

Sergeant Isaacson, in the course of duty, often came across displays of madness; however, until recently, he hadn't really understood where it came from in human nature. Now, when he himself had to sometimes suppress his own outbursts of madness, his views on human nature broadened significantly. And even somewhat deepened. Yes, exactly, sometimes he said to himself while off-duty, sitting in front of a grunting television with a six-pack, now I somehow look at all those swine in a deeper way.

He proposed marriage to Palmer, and she unexpectedly consented, which again shook his conceptions about human nature; in which direction, he couldn't quite tell yet. Now they appeared together in public, sometimes at the Ascot bowling alley, as an engaged couple.

Life settled into routine. Of course, another Kimberly Palmer sat in the car loan department of the Perpetual Bank, if that could be said about a sloppy broad from West Virginia perpetually chewing on something. However, the competitor bank quickly hired the local celebrity who had fulfilled her Christian duty in a very faraway and dangerous country, thereby attracting new clients to their financial sources. On the streets of Strasburg, enormous maples, poplars and chestnut trees accepted the prodigal runner under their boughs with tranquilizing rustles. Nobody in Moscow responded to Palmer's letters, and Russia again began to fade into an academic abstraction from a university curriculum. At best, it was still associated with Tchaikovsky's "Sixth Symphony", which Palmer listened to during her five-mile run; violins and brass, piercing flights of the small pipes... and this is Russia? The object of inspiration and the product of inspiration existed in different planes that never merged. The music was in frightening contrast to matters olfactory.

"Even if you really love all that rubbish, that doesn't mean you have to go there. Go back to the university and learn about 'em all," the reasonable Isaac would say. He began applying for a vacancy in the law-enforcement agencies near Vanderbilt University in Nashville, Tennessee. He had some savings from his temperate bachelorhood that would allow him to hold out for two to three years until our girl received her MA.

Things flowed along for almost a year in this undemanding way, until the end of September 1993, when an extracurricular phone call resounded in Palmer's home at three o'clock in the morning. It was Arkashka Grubiyanov. Well, to put it in the old-fashioned way, he was "on the line". In the reality of the night, the frightened Palmer thought she heard a cosmic echo in this fateful call from the eternal Moscow playboy, "user" and "boozer." "Hi, old girl," he said according to the rules of Moscow jargon, which not all that long ago elated the humanitarian aid pioneer, but now evoked only a feeling of slight nausea. "I hope you haven't forgotten those fiery nights yet? I'm calling you from your capital. No, not from ours, but from yours, from your-not-our Washington-not-Russianton, you get it? Insomnia, old lady, Homer, tight sails, a list of ships, well, I read it halfway through and thought: why not call good ol' Palmer, it's great to have a chick across the ocean, isn't it? No, I didn't emigrate, why should I emigrate when things are fine at home too. Business, of course, not private, but state. You can't measure us with ordinary yardsticks, mama, I'm here on an official state visit."

From the reckless Grubiyanov's faraway chatter, some-times lazy and sort of slurping, then tongue-twisting and sort of choking, Palmer understood, that he had recently become a member of the government, namely the Minister of Cultural Communication — not to be confused with the Minister of Culture — of the Russian Federation, and now here he was in Washington, heading a delegation. "We're having negotiations, old girl, five, fifteen negotiations a day, five thousand negotiations in all! Ten thousand agreements are being signed! Couriers are flying here and there, thirty thousand couriers! Faxes, modems, things are really cooking! I'm already getting hot as well, that's why I'm calling you! Come on over to the Ritz-Carlton, and ask for Minister Grubiyanov!"

Palmer could only assume this nocturnal outburst was none other than a ridiculous joke by a Moscow buffoon in the role of a "hero-lover." He was even now almost totally plastered while talking rubbish with his mighty, but not very obedient tongue about a government fitness center, where he swam daily with Rubleskauskas himself and jumped off the diving board into the water after Pelmeshko himself, prone, on his belly, a fountain coming out of his ass, and where he was offered, among splashes of champagne, a ministerial seat. Palmer didn't really understand the specifics of the revolutionary situation and that was why it was difficult for her to imagine how some mostly-mad actor could become a minister, and in addition, that a ministry could be created for him right at the edge of a swimming pool. "I'll send a car for you, if you want! With a bodyguard! Five bodyguards! Ten!"

"Listen, Ark, I'm in no position to go see you at three o'clock in the morning," Palmer finally formulated. "Now then, you're talking in Finnish again," sighed the minister distressingly, and then he completely stunned her by saying that in that case Mohammed would come to the mountain himself, that the next evening he would be ten miles away from her in "what's-its-name-Strasburg," namely at Korbut Place, well yes, at those same Korbuts, who are throwing a dinner in his honor, and he was inviting her in his capacity as minister. "Come on over, no fucking excuses! You know that Stanley Korbut — he's a normal guy, one of us, a great guy, hung up on Russian Art, Hamayun has turned him into a horny beast!" Korbut Place! Even if this estate was located ten miles from Strasburg, the local inhabitants could see its rooftops only from a scenic stop high up in the Blue Ridge, thirty miles away. All the approaches

99

to this wooded territory, the size of which did not concede to the dwarf kingdoms of Europe, such as Andorra or Liechtenstein, were closed off by roadblocks. For a local girl, an invitation to the castle of the kings of the meat-milk business was equivalent to some Oprah-Ivanna-Vannaesque fulfillment of her dreams. Palmer was already not quite a local, but she went anyway. For some unknown reason, she wanted to see Grubiyanov's full red lips again. And about feeling timid in front of the meat-milk aristocracy, Palmer, after hanging out with the bohemian crowd for almost a year, or as they said then, the "free-buffet gang", had learned one cardinal directive: "go fuck yourself" or, in indirect translation, "no problem!"

Without saying anything to her sergeant, she took off in her Toyota. Maybe, Arkashka had made it all up, but why not take a chance? At the first barrier, some large men from the Korbut Guard were on duty. Upon learning that she was there on the invitation of Minister Grubiyanov, they respectfully showed her the way with their beefy hands. Right after the checkpoint, the forest turned into a park. Beyond the avenue of tall trees, you could see hills rolled smooth with an ideal cut, antique sculptures, terraced Versailles-style gardens descending into a pond with a fountain. The chateau windows reflected the Shenandoah sunset in all its grandeur, and even surpassed this phenomenon of nature by adding an architectural symmetry to it. "My whole life I've lost my senses in these sunsets," thought Palmer, entering the castle. Only after crossing the threshold did she realize that a footman in tights and gloves had opened the door for her.

The guests, no less than two dozen in number, sat in an oak-carved dining room, which had enough oak-carved sidings for a frigate squadron. It was as if the naked shoulders of the women widened the scale of the lavish spread. Palmer removed her antique Russian scarf: her shoulders were not the worst parts of her equipment. "I slept with these shoulders, I lived with them," recalled Minister Grubiyanov. He was the embodiment of etiquette. Instead of his usual ragged sweater with rolled up sleeves, he had on a complete black tie outfit, rented through the service bureau of the hotel. With a gracious smile he showed Palmer to a free seat, a few places to the right of him. An even more ceremonial peculiarity appeared to be Madam Vetushitikova, a maiden with lilac peacock rings around the eyes, known in certain circles of the Russian Federation as Hamayun Bird, currently the head of a youth exchange division. From afar, she blew a kiss to Palmer barely moving her lips. I can just imagine what will happen when they all get drunk, thought the kiss's addressee.

A lively conversation was taking place at the table, naturally, it was about Russia. Leonid Brezhnev was a real leader, gentlemen, and then there was his daughter — the picture of femininity. I'm in complete agreement, I knew both of them. Leonid was tough, but his daughter Brezhnev turned out to be utterly charming! An old woman with bluish-grey curls was gradually taking over the floor, a certain wealthy, well-known half-mad enthusiast type, who came up with a new pet project every year: either giving Winnie Mandela an award for "moral heroism", or flying some overfed poets to Portugal on her personal jet, or setting up a visit to Disneyland for hoods, to distract them from guns and crack. Currently, the old lady was engaging herself with dollar infusions into the Ministry of Cultural Communications, MCCRF, and this is why everyone listened to her with great attention. Naturally, this woman was called "Jane", and she explained:

"Colossal impressions, folks, indelible! We visited the house of a great Russian poet near Moscow, whose name starts with the letter 'P', I'll think of it in a moment, oh yes, Potemkin's house!"

The minister and the members of the delegation respectfully nodded their heads. Nobody interpreted for them, and they of course didn't understand a thing. Upon the word "Potemkin" someone laughed inappropriately. "The poet Potemkin?" asked Palmer, to make sure she had heard correctly. From her early studies at Vanderbilt University, this name was connected with something not quite poetic, but something from 19th-century secret wars, the assault on Turkey: a scepter with a diamond bulb on top, a glass eye, the Onassis yacht, no, that's already from a different story altogether.

"Not just a poet, but a great poet," Jane said, frowning sternly, looking as if she herself was from the Potemkin epoch with her bluish wavy hairdo. "He lived in the town of Peredelkino," unexpectedly pronouncing the name almost in Russian.

"Pasternak!" Palmer then exclaimed, and Grubiyanov roared with laughter, almost splitting at the seams. "Where?" asked the billionairess, quickly looking around, and then it dawned on her. "Well, of course, I mixed it up a little, it's Doctor Pasternak!"

Palmer trembled as she began to cut up something that resembled a pacific atoll served on a porcelain plate. "The son of the great Doctor Pasternak showed us the house," continued Jane. "Poor, poor man, how he lived! Listen, I said to the son, please, would you mind if I took a picture of you at your father's desk? Oh, boy, the son became so indignant! He yelled and waved his arms, rejecting my modest proposal! I never imagined that the father and son had such a tense relationship!" "Oh, boy!" exclaimed the Cinderella of the evening, who nobody knew, except for a few Russians. "Don't you see, dear Mrs. Caterpillar, that your proposal was sacrilege to this man?"

"Sacrilege?!" the lavish old lady proudly placed her arms akimbo against a background of carved oak, just like Admiral Nelson. Then Grubiyanov burst out laughing, despite his ministerial title. It appeared that someone had translated a part of the women's dialogue, and he bellowed across the philanthropic Russian cultural communication table: "Why Jane, old girl! Don't you see that your proposal was like asking to try on the shroud of Christ in the Cathedral at Turin! Don't you see that Pasternak is a saint for us, and his house a shrine! Hey, someone please translate for her!"

Nobody of course translated anything, but everyone began to laugh, looking at the Russian minister who it seemed would at any moment burst out of his tight tuxedo with an abundance of emotion. The first one to get drunk, however, was not the minister, but the host, Stanley Korbut, the slender business veteran, constantly occupied with golf, sex and champagne. This last thing, it appeared, didn't completely disappear into the depths of his body, but partially settled into the turkey bags under his chin, which made him a walking symbol of negligent and don't-give-a-damn capitalism, the kind that had already lost all interest in profit. "Dancing!" he howled. "Let's waltz!" He grabbed Madam Vetushitikova by the arm and twirled her around in the direction of his bedroom.

Then again, we didn't have to wait long for the guest of honor to follow suit. With no less spontaneity, he shoved a pair of cigars from the cigar table into his breast pocket and a bottle of "Glenmorangie" from the cocktail table into the deep wings of his trousers, after which he decisively led his girlfriend Palmer to the exit. The reciprocity principle in action. Russians don't surrender, they just become allies! All our prophetic birds, Alkonost, Siren, Hamayun, real, not tarts, soar in space, but the all-important Phoenix rises from the red ashes, matures with both heads, and demands a double ration! We're still to see the sky in diamonds! A man is not a flea! The Russian Federation is vast, but there is nowhere to retreat!

When he calmed down and fell asleep on the sofa bed, Palmer went out under the plentiful moon and sat on a heavy cast-iron chair, the best item from her grandmother's inheritance. A human shadow crossed the meadow, moving out into a forward position. It was Sergeant Isaacson with his full hip collection: a club, pistol, walkie-talkie, handcuffs. "I guess this here is one of your Russians?" he said with sufficient inflection. Palmer nodded thoughtfully. "You know, these Russians today aren't really quite Russian. That one, sleeping over there now, a minister, is less Russian than I am British, or you are Swedish. Alas, the age of literature is no longer." "I'll still shoot him before sunrise," surmised the sergeant.

"No, you won't," she resonated, not in the sense of echoing, but because she put forth a reason to restrain him from using force. "Why? At least because you respect me and look upon me as more than just a vagina!" Steel objects shook on the sergeant's hips. To be honest, he wasn't capable even of imagining a comparable reason, and so now he shuddered. As she rose the moon enveloped her with its light, around the body of a future Boston marathon champion. "Well then, let's go to the garage, Isaac."

In the morning, over breakfast, Minister Grubiyanov, still in his rented tuxedo, gave Palmer's nephew Fritz Germenstadt a Tissot watch on a bracelet, and to the boy's mama, Rosalyn, he gave two bills, from a stack of hundreds rumpled inside his bosom. Having eaten a fairly substantial mountain of Virginia buckwheat pancakes with maple syrup, he asked if he could switch on CNN. It appeared that in Moscow a "Second October Revolution" was developing in full force, to use the expression of the new president, Sasha Rutskoi.

From that moment on, the whole weekend went by under Atlanta's eye, if one could say it that way for the sake of beauty, having in mind the CNN cameras, swooping over the assembly of Moscow buildings, including Grubiyanov's own ministerial mansion. In the end, the tuxedo ripped at the seams. The unshaven minister smoked a stolen cigar in a deep chair in front of the telly and guzzled Glenmorangie malt whiskey. Meanwhile, newly maddened Bolsheviks swept by the screen in waves. Bonfires made of rubber tires burned along the Garden Ring Road. A mob with pounding hammers, swishing sickles and rolled swastika chariots settled scores with the police. Along with the big, raging fellows with Lenin and Stalin profiles in their hands, the Komsomol girls from the forties and fifties flew with the mob as old valkyries. Shock-workers tightened nooses made of bicycle chains on the cops' necks, old women completed the affair with banner poles.

Grubiyanov punched his hand with his fist, laughing a bit, wildly turning to Palmer as if looking for confirmation of his unspoken thoughts. Everyone around him walked on tiptoes, pressing their fingers to their lips. It seemed to the members of the household that a typhoid-ridden man or alcoholic had moved into their living room.

The hours went by like this, the minister's stubble grew, in Moscow the Reds were winning. The siege was broken! Sub-machine gunners in camouflage came out in a line formation from the enormous building, as if fittingly constructed in the style of a socialist apotheosis. On a roll, they hacked their way through the neighboring skyscraper with heavy trucks, threw out tri-color rags, raised the triumphant red calico. The glass walls of capitalism were coming down. "Oh, now they've done it! Oh, good job! Go on, Sasha, go ahead!" yelled Grubiyanov, all carried away. From the huge balcony, the head of the Moscow uprising, no less swollen than the Virginia viewer, proclaimed victory and sent the proletariat to the TV tower at Ostankino and to the Kremlin!

Not long afterwards, close-ups of the carnage appeared at the television station: American television covered the demise of Russian television. A general with a hyena's face and a beret pulled down over his ears directed the assault. "When comrade Stalin sends us into battle and Makashov heads our fight," wailed the masters of tomorrow's executions. A rocket grenade flew past the central entrance with a roar. Glass flew and concrete collapsed. "Oh wow! Oh wow!" laughed the minister of the overthrown government into the Virginia night.

"My God, what's with him," whispered Palmer. "It's all intertwined here, Stavrogin and Svidrigailov mixed in with all this modern filth! Who is he if not a fiend from Russian literature?" She dozed off a bit in the corner of the century-old Palmer sitting room and woke up when the television began to rattle at higher speeds and when something in Moscow toppled over with a thundering crash, prompting a new burst of laughter from Grubiyanov. History was turning backwards, and the fiend was laughing!

However, history, while turning back, really only stomped around in place, and then spun around and drove the red-bellies back, under the protection of the Soviet constitution. Minister Grubiyanov continued to enjoy the spectacle. Kantemirov tanks began to flog the headquarters of the "Second October Revolution," and he laughed with the same delight: "Oh, they're giving it to them! That was great! Forward, Pasha!" The leaders went to surrender, and then he laughed until he began to hiccup: "Far-out!"

When the next day began over the innocent Virginia, and evening began in the putrid Moscow under falling ashes, the minister fell with a crash to his knees, embracing Palmer's legs as if embracing all of mankind, and began to wail rapidly in a theatrical manner, sometimes plunging his nose into the edge of her female grove, a bit prickly even through the jogging bottoms: "Take me, my cursed Kimberlylulochka, single-mother, I am your only humanitarian aid package! Nobody, nobody knows what I'm really like, and if anyone ever finds out, they won't believe it! Take me away, away from myself with all of my dollars all stuck together! I still dream of a good life, beyond the meanest horizons! In Trinidad, or Tobago, let me find myself in the tropic of feelings, cleanse myself in a waterfall of confession! Don't leave me, Maiden, in the apotheosis of my desire for worldwide democracy! Lady of kindness, only in your bosom do I see universal grace, trust my fucking words, angel of humanity!"

Palmer lifted her head up to the ceiling and waited for the outpouring to cease. The question of kindness was a tortuous one for her. In her early youth, when she looked in the mirror at her face and caught an expression of kindliness in it, she would think masochistically: "With my looks, kindness is the only thing I can rely on." These thoughts tortured her. "What people and particularly men perceive as kindness is really a self-inflicted mask, but it's possible that deep down I'm sly and evil." The trip to Russia intensified this contradiction. The mask, it seemed, had fastened itself too tightly to her lips and to the creases between her nose and lips. Everyone around her drank to her kindness. "I'm insincere," she tortured herself, "I'm doing tricks with my kindness, and all because of these cursed men."

"Elevez-toi, Arkashka, s'il tu plait!" she said neither in English, because of her confusion over the next twist of fate, nor in Russian. The French language program from school suddenly splashed out from her depths, yet another springy fountain of mercy.

A hundred-mile-long tourist highway called Skyline Drive weaves south along the very crest of the Blue Ridge over the Shenandoah Valley. Stunning sunsets' unfold from the right, beneficial sunrises from the left. Depending on the time of day or night, of course, though if you're in flight in the heat of a humanitarian action, it might seem to you that the sky is blazing from both sides simultaneously.

Palmer instinctively chose this road, and only later understood that she was trying to get away from the law enforcement authorities. She drove her car, trying to rid herself of any hints of kindness in her face. The body of the minister, his tux split open at the seams, settled into a heap next to her. Not seeing any manifestations in the skies, he snored unconsciously, still jerking occasionally and clearly answering some unheard questions: "Never joined! Wasn't there! Didn't sign! Didn't inform! Didn't take it!" Once his body suddenly distended, and he muttered: "Lord have mercy, Lord have mercy, Lord have mercy, forgive and protect me!" — and again he crashed.

After half an hour, Palmer glanced in the mirror and saw a Chevrolet with a red crossbeam on top following her steadily. The Viking mask behind the windshield was missing just two horns on the sides of the head. Well now, Sergeant Isaacson, now your true character will be put to the test!

Vassily AKSYONOV was born in 1932 in Kazan (Tatarstan) and trained as a doctor in which capacity he worked for many years while writing stories which won him a reputation as one of the most original talents in Russian literature. He has an ear for the slangy racy Russian of students, bohemians, and ordinary people, and an eye for urban landscape and street scenes. His heroes are in constant search of their identity and refuse to settle down spiritually or physically. Aksyonov was forced to emigrate from Russia in 1980 and settled in the USA where he taught Russian literature at George Mason University in Virginia. Aksyonov has been widely published in the West. All his major novels are available in English translation: *Generations of Winter*, *In Search of Melancholy Baby*, *The Island of Crimea*, *The Burn*, to name a few. His latest novel, *The Male and Female Fans of Voltaire* won him the Russian Booker Prize in 2004.

Alexander
TEREKHOV

The Rat-killer

summary and excerpt from the novel

Translated by Andrew Bromfield

Summary

[The town of Svetloyar is bidding to be included in the list of historical towns making up Russia's famous "Golden Ring" around Moscow, which is a major tourist route. The town is due to be visited by the President of Russia and the Secretary-General of the United Nations. Apart from the relatively minor difficulty that the town has no historical past, having been entirely constructed during the Stalinist period (there are, after all, ways of adjusting history), it has one serious problem: rats. They have infested the place, and they have to be removed, if only temporarily, if Svetloyar is to avoid disgrace and acquire the coveted and profitable "Golden Ring" status.

Two exterminators, or "rat-killers", are summoned from Moscow to deal with the most sensitive site, the town's central hotel, where the rats simply drop from the ceiling in the banqueting hall.

Svetloyar's historical (and geographical) credentials are created by burying exhibits from museums in the region, together with ill-assorted bones, to create a fake archaeological site (when the army workers accidentally uncover the genuine site of an ancient graveyard, it is rapidly reburied to avoid unnecessary complications):

"What's this you've dug up for me, you bastard? Where did you get this garbage from?..."

"Right, lads, bury the fucking tombs again. Cover them with clay and smooth it all over... Smash the bones to pieces and scatter them in the fields..."

"For history?" Sviridov twisted his face into a grimace. "You shut up about history. I know what kind of history we need around here."

Pipes have been laid from the Don to establish a "source" for the great river on the territory of the town, and a connection has been invented with the hero of old Russian folklore, Ilya Muromets (he must have passed through here at some point on his travels!).

In order to greet the President and the UN Secretary-General in fitting style, the real inhabitants of the town are evacuated and a motley collection of soldiers, actors, blind women and female prison-camp internees is put into training by the local army command as a "welcoming crowd" stage-managed with immaculate, if ludicrous, care.

Meanwhile a power struggle develops, involving factions in the army and the security forces. The outcome, inevitably, is the emergence of a provincial military dictator. Pretence becomes reality as different military factions become embroiled in bloody combat. Eventually Svetloyar (now populated entirely by the military) is threatened by a new wave of rats, turned against the town by the competition rat-killers who were brought in to help exterminate the rodents.

The narrative is told in the person of the younger of the two rat-killers (he refers to his boss simply as "the Old Man"). A biologist by education, he is supporting himself as a rat-killer while he struggles to complete his dissertation on flies.

When he and the Old Man have successfully rid the hotel of rats, they are about to leave, but instead are arrested because they protest against the army's plans to set captured rats on fire in order to destroy their burrows. The young rat-killer becomes ill, and as his condition worsens the narrative assumes more of the characteristics of a delirium or nightmare.

The resemblances between human and rodent behaviour become greater when his own constant attentions to women (including the bride of the military dictator Gubin) are strangely mirrored in his pursuit of a particularly cunning female rat that takes refuge in the local savings bank. Only at the end of the book do we realise that the rat-killer is in fact mortally afraid of rats. And in metaphorical terms, of all that they stand for. Throughout the book he has been engaged in far more than a simple struggle with destructive rodents].

"Still dribbling into your pillow?" I asked the Old Man when I phoned and woke him up. "You can get the money tomorrow and pay for the basement, before they turf me out of it." Then I dropped and slept, right there in the basement. We'd rented a basement for our office because we were struggling to make ends meet on small orders.

For millions of years the common and black rats known as sinanthropes after their home country of China remained dammed into the rice-swamps, locked into that foul place by the Himalayas, the desert, the jungles and the ice. When people moved in there looking for gold, they melted the glaciers and cleared the passes, and in a flash rat hordes broke out. Skirting round the Himalayas, up to the North! — to Korea and Manchuria. To the fleshpots of India — South! The East submitted without even raising its head to protest. The first to congratulate Buddha on the New Era was a rat, the symbol of joy and prosperity.

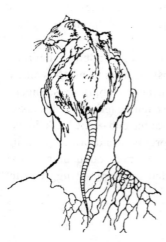

From the twelfth century Europe complained and would not accept its fate — for it was believed there were no rats in Golden Hellas! — not knowing that black rats in ships and attics pressed ancient Egypt so hard that even the accidental killing of a cat was punished by death. Greece and Rome had only one refuge: they kept mum, or they mumbled "mice". And we used to be proud of their cleanliness, what fools we were! Excavations have made it quite

Drawings by V. Losev

clear just what kind of creatures it was that Aristotle described: born of the filth in the ships, conceived by licking salt. Who did Diogenes reproach with lust? Who was it Cicero reproached for his gnawed sandals? The god of "mice" is Apollo. Their history began when the Gods overthrew the Titans and the earth shook and split open. And 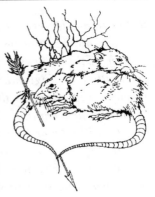 *the mice came pouring and tumbling out of the black cracks.*

And they put the people under siege.

There were no windows in the basement. The night was coming to an end when the Old Man switched on the light. He stuck the key into the lock and picked up the piece of paper that had unstuck from the door: "RAT Cooperative".

I went to bed late. The Old Man was a real swine, he could have shown up later just as well.

Streaming after their black brothers came the common rats, the victors! With the Arabs they crossed the Persian Gulf and the Red Sea, the Crusaders carried them further on from Palestine, Venetian mariners delivered the plague-carrying rats to Europe together with pearls and spices. In the fifteenth century the Church cursed them. It was too late. The bones of a common rat were dug up in the palace of Shirvan-shah in Baku.

The common rats made their way across medieval Rus. Convicts in the stocks at the Solovki Monastery paid with their noses and ears for the commercial liberty enjoyed by the towns of Pskov and Novgorod. The rats moved into St. Petersburg with Peter the Great. In 1727 the earthquake in the Kuma Desert drove a huge army of common rats to Astrakhan. The pincers were closed.

In 1732 a vessel from the East Indies delivered retribution to England. Thirty years later Paris fell, and twenty years after that the beggars ate rats during the siege of the French capital.

In 1775 America capitulated.

In 1780 it was Germany's turn.

When the Russians reached the Aleutian Islands, they were swarming with rats, and so that was what they called them, the Rat Islands.

In 1809 Switzerland fell to the horde.

The Old Man walks about, sneezing, the pig, stands a carton of milk right under my nose, puts a bread-bun beside it, rummages in his bag. He's the boss, he gets the table, and I get the camp-bed. I have to sleep with my legs bent up.

They carried on. At the end of the nineteenth century they celebrated the capture of Tyumen, Tobolsk, the Crimea. The Russo-Japanese War bequeathed rats to Omsk and Tomsk, and by 1912 the common rats had occupied the Siberian Railway.

The First World War gave the black and the common rats more fodder than they could eat, and not a single place was left in Europe without them. During the Siege of Leningrad the rats warmed themselves in the children's beds and occupied the front lines of defence (where the corpses had more meat on them). The evacuation carried them off in all directions.

"Get up out of that bed," said the Old Man. "Enough sleeping. I've paid for the basement."

I ripped open the carton of milk and took a bite from the bun. A thickset, grey-haired man came in, scratching his neck. He produced an advertising supplement out of his pocket:

"Here," he said.

The advertisement I had put in read as follows: "An opportunity not to be missed. Rats and mice exterminated anywhere in the world. Prices well below international rates. We saved the Vandome Islands from rats. We saved Thuringia and the public toilets in Geneva (three hundred seats). The 'RAT' Cooperative, winner of a special award from the Swedish Academy! Reach us via metro station Medvedkovo and bus No. 661 to the stop for the State Polytechnical College. Walk along the concrete wall on the opposite side of the street to the break, then through the car park. Ask for the All-Union Society of the Blind. We are in the basement at the first entrance, sixth door on the left. Telephone such-and-such, from 22.00 to 24.00, Vladimir and Larissa."

"Yes, that's us," said the Old Man. "Have a seat."

"I'm glad I found you," said the man. "I have a way for you to earn some good money."

* * *

We had the meeting in the school gym.

On the floor lay a huge sketch map of the town. An army colonel, dressed in field uniform, was pushing a string of toy trucks across it, as if it were the president's cavalcade.

"Mokrousov Street, transit time sixteen seconds. Welcoming crowd," the ginger-haired Baranov read from a piece of paper, "one hundred and seventy-six. Twenty-four on balconies. Sixteen at windows. Nine posters, forty-six flags. Dress from the civil defence reserves."

"Okay," agreed the Governor, and climbed down from the volleyball umpire's tower.

Take a gutful in the evening and next day you'll suffer for it. I sat by the mineral water, close up beside a bald old man in glasses. He didn't even turn his shrivelled skull of a head, he was too busy watching the governor.

Shestakov towered up in front of the flags of Russia and the United Nations, leaning with his fists on the oak table that was crowded with telephones and winking army walkie-talkies, waiting for me to finish opening a bottle of mineral water with my teeth.

"Time. We're losing time," Shestakov hissed, as soon as I'd drunk my fill and wiped my mouth. "The job is a big one, but we don't have enough people. We're expecting three companies of police from the district centre. The reserve has been called up. Just in case there's any nonsense the district command has provided another three battalions. They're training in Kriukovo Forest. For a day like this there should be a division, with tanks. Our garrison is keen for action, isn't it, Comrade Gontar?"

"Very keen," agreed the army colonel.

"On the fourth we start operation 'Clear Field'." Shestakov glanced down at the telephones, and his cheeks quivered. "Expulsion from Svetloyar of all outsiders. On the sixth, operation 'Clear Sky', removal to village schools of residents from the town centre and the visitors' entry and exit routes. Responsible officer, Baranov of the police. I am in overall control. We'll have no nonsense. No attempts to contact the President. Or any questions. Please don't make any notes."

Everyone glanced around cautiously. Especially at the Old Man. And at the door, which was guarded by two men in civilian dress with automatics sticking out from under their jackets.

"From our side Colonel Klinsky's people will be the closest to the visitors." The governor pointed to a puny bureaucrat with slick, wet-looking black hair. He was the only one without a tie and he had ear-phones glued to his head.

"The town is almost in ruins. That's what the mayor's office has done for it. The evacuated residents will have to be paid for two days off work and given hot meals. We'll have to guard them. To be on the safe side. Do not explain anything to them! If you do, it will all be turned against us. Two areas are causing me concern. First, we have to have people who look right to play the part of the residents along the route of the procession and at the festivities by the monument to the 'Source of the Don'. The organisers figure we need about ten thousand. Men are no problem. We can dress up soldiers and cadets. The theatre will help out with hair styles. There aren't many children, but we do have some. Two nursery schools have been assigned. Our people in the front rows."

Shestakov sighed loudly. "The women are a problem. Where can we get so many women? The blind workers' cooperative will give us fifty units, they can be paired off with soldiers as guides and kept at a distance. Maybe the ballet dancers will have time to get changed after their concert. But we've had to request most of the women from the corrective labour camp. Special train here and then back again. Five hundred women with shattered lives. How do we explain the march from the station and back again under guard? Maybe we could say it's a cross-country march of soldiers' mothers? We'll have to arrange them on the square with officers, three to one. It's hard to keep an eye on people in a crowd. We were thinking perhaps we should take their shoes off. Or perhaps handcuff them together at the elbow. We'll come up with something. We'll put together a task force out of actors and police veterans, about a hundred men. They'll be following the visitors in two vans, just in case..." Shestakov put his palms against his cheeks and continued in a hollow voice, "in case the visitors want to speak with the people. An extreme situation, as you appreciate. Personally, I don't believe it will happen.

But everyone has to be able to smile and say hello. The reception and the dinner will last one hour forty minutes, but the escort will arrive earlier, so the festivities will drag out for about six hours. I understand, believe me, it's all really far too much for us. But as they say, we have to go for bust. The life of our town depends on it, from now on forever, comrades. If we do a good job, then the government will include Svetloyar in the "Golden Ring" of Russian towns and the list of national historical monuments. And that means hard currency, comrades."

His audience came to life and began applauding.

"The second thing worrying me," Shestakov cast a significant glance towards our corner, "is the rats, comrades. Repulsive creatures. They gnaw everything, that's why they're called rodents, it means they gnaw. They've been building up here for decades, and in the last few years the mayor's office has fallen down badly on the job. They bite the dogs. People are afraid for their children. On my initiative we've set up a rat control corporation, 'King Rat'. They'll use a traditional folk method to rid the festivities area of rodents. In a single night, just before the visitors arrive. Free of charge."

Now even the guards were applauding. Skull-face beside me was lashing away so hard, his spectacles slipped down his nose. The Old Man stared gloomily at the map.

"But the banqueting hall in the hotel 'Don'... You know yourselves what it's like. Some of you... had first-hand experience. We had to go to the capital for help. The governor employed them, but we'll have to pay, and it's a lot of money." I was watching the governor as he spoke. He had turned pale. "It can't be allowed to happen, it just can't be, not even for a moment. Not even for a fraction of a moment. Imagine. During the celebrations... One drops on to the table. Or the floor. Or on someone's head. Even just droppings. It's absolutely out of the question! So let me warn our highly paid businessmen here and now, in front of you all. Just so they have things clear."

The gathering turned to face us. I smiled. The Old Man fidgetted.

"Colonel Gontar will announce the orders of the day."

"Right. Let me inform you that from six o'clock the H.Q. will be under barracks regime. Sleeping quarters have been laid out in the staff room and the head teacher's office. The mess is in the library. The latrines remain where they were. Military rank must be respected. On the ground floor two classes will begin the normal school year. The external guard will be in the queue for kvas and in the school lunch van. Passes to be shown to the sentry with the pram. Duty officers will inform you of the colour of the pram. Dismissed!"

Everyone got up, kicking aside the basketballs skittering about the floor. I winked at my neighbour. Well?

"So you're the ones who are robbing us blind."

"And who are you?"

"Here? Captain Larionov."

"Well, captain, all this reminds me of a mad house."

The old captain grimaced:

"I'm no doctor. I'm the town's architect."

He said goodbye and left. The Old Man sat on his chair. It had been a long time since I'd sat in a schoolroom until blue twilight filled the windows. Just like being at a dance, not a single girl in sight. I said:

"Tell me, Old Man, what did we come here for?"

* * *

On the square a cordon in full-dress uniform was dying of boredom as they taught Alsatians to lie and stand, lie and stand.

In the centre, an officer in a peaked cap stood on a wooden crate, blowing down a megaphone to test it, with a herd of bodies pressing around him. Plodding piously over to join them came a portly priest with a big round medallion hanging on a chain round his neck. Mincing behind him at a respectable distance came several rosy-cheeked lay-brothers in gold surplices, carrying an icon, a censer, a cross and a gonfalon.

"Stage one!" roared the megaphone. "Put out that cigarette! Who's that there spitting on the ground? Sviridov, the visitors, who are the visitors?"

"Comrade lieutenant, com..." A rotund warrant officer with sweaty eyebrows who had the look of a light-weight wrestler came shooting across to me. "Comrade lieutenant, seven seconds. This way please." He dragged me over, clutching my wrist in his moist palm. "Here's your visitor, comrade colonel. He's the right size."

Garrison commander Gontar looked me over from up on top of his crate: "He'll do."

A captain clambered up on the crate and held the megaphone to the colonel's mouth with both hands.

"Stage zero. Comrades, general rehearsal. Remember, total security, responsibility. The goal: determine who follows who. Finalise the general picture. Right then, to your starting positions. One run-through, and we're done. Sviridov, who's visitor number two?"

The crowd stirred and formed up into ranks.

"This way, please." The warrant officer prodded me toward the crate. "You're still in the car. Now who else... Comrade colonel, I can be guest number two myself!" He sniffed and wiped the drops of sweats from his eyebrows.

"Ten-shun! Listen. 'September twelfth. Twelve hundred hours. The sun has gilded...' Right, I'm not reading all of that. Right then, the President and the Secretary-General of the United Nations... they're out of the car, they've arrived!"

The warrant officer led me forward two steps and stopped. We were on the spot.

"Ours is on the left, the other's on the right. Who's that not looking? Remember who's where. Just to help you, theirs is an Arab. That's a kind of Gypsy. Orchestra!" Colonel Gontar waved his cap and over on the boulevard someone thumped a drum. "The blessing, the blessing, what are we waiting for?"

The warrant-officer moved aside and twisted his face into a pious grimace. The priest advanced, wrapped in something that looked like a water-proof army cape: cloth of gold embroidered with pearls, stuck all over with blue and scarlet flowers with six petals. Sharp reflections from the jewelry glittered on the faces of the meek-and-mild servitors; the priest waved incense over the crowd, crossing himself with broad, sweeping gestures. I stood up straighter and lowered my head with the rest. The warrant officer put his hands on his hips in a haughty gesture.

"Now comes the blessing. Kiss his hand," Gontar hissed.

The priest handed his censer to a lay-brother, then took my hand and kissed it respectfully.

"Kravchuk! What the..." the colonel swore in his exasperation. "Get that goat's beard of yours out of there! Who's the bishop? You're the bishop! You do the blessing, and he does the kissing! He holds his palms out, and you stick your mitt on top! He kisses it, and you make the sign of the cross over the back of his head! Stop tugging at your beard! Too hot? Sviridov, we can do without the beard today."

"What if he won't kiss it?" inquired the "bishop".

"He will. It's a clean perfumed hand... He'll be told what to do too. If he hesitates, then cross his fat face and move on. What d'you mean, where to? What about guest number two? You've got to bless the Gypsy! Girl, bring up the bread and salt!"

Suddenly there was music from horns and a psaltery, and a fine buxom girl with a face as red as a traffic cop's came bouncing over happily, holding an empty chased-metal tray.

"Girl: 'Pray taste of our bread and salt.' Hold it out, and don't straighten up, let him get a good look down the front of your dress! Don't look down. 'Smiles.' Give him a wink. Once. With your right eye. He takes a bite and chews it. Passes the bread to the nigger. 'Without straightening up the girl takes a present out of her bosom. Speaks:

"Beloved, I have sat up through the night waiting for you and embroidering the shorts'". Sho-orts? Is that right? Sviridov!"

"That's right, comrade colonel. That's what it says in the book."

"In the book! Sviridov, you'll end up in the guardhouse! He reads books now! Anybody here from the museum?"

"Yes, comrade colonel," someone shouted from the crowd. "It should be 'the shirt'."

"Alright then. Come on, girl."

"My beloved, I have sat up through the night waiting for you and embroidering this shirt." The girl ran her tongue over her moist lips and thrust a hand into her crowded bosom.

The colonel rapped out his approval:

"Good girl, good girl... God grant everybody will do as well. 'The girl runs off, the hem of her skirt rises so her underwear can be seen...' It doesn't say what colour, but it should. Sviridov, check that later. Cossacks, let's have the Cossacks!"

Two policemen on light-brown horses rode over from the boulevard and around the crowd, whooping as they went.

"'Out runs a girl.' Where's the girl?"

"Here!" A female gymnast in white sports shoes stepped forward. She was about twelve years old, with sharp pointed elbows and totally flat-chested.

Gontar thrust the megaphone away from his lips and hissed.

"Listen, Sviridov, haven't we got any healthier-looking specimens?"

"She's the district champion." The warrant officer shrugged and spread his hands, stung by the comment.

"Alright, alright, what does it say here? 'Out runs a girl feeding pigeons!' Alright then, she feeds them, turns a somersault, does a cartwheel. Then a thousand pigeons, the age of the city, go flying up in the air. 'The cover falls from the monument "The Source of the Don" and a stream of water raises up Ilya Muromets over the square, with the flags of Russia and the United Nations. Orchestra. Exultant citizens press the guards against visitor number one' (don't get him confused with the black!) 'and a woman with a blind child break through.' Right, quick march!"

The crowd pushed forward, and a woman with a face wasted from exhaustion lifted a boy in a blue T-shirt up above the swaying shoulders of the bodyguards, keening mournfully:

"Lay your hands on him, saviour."

The child stared upwards in torment, as though an invisible palm were pressed across the bridge of his nose, and he kicked his legs so hard his sandals flew off.

"That way they'll crush the woman," Sviridov hissed.

I tapped my hand stupidly against the child's scarlet forehead. His head trembled on his neck and he bawled out:

"I can see. Mama, I can see! The sun and the grass and our beloved city. Who is this good man?"

"He is your saviour," said the mother with a sob, pressing the child to her and caressing it. "I can hardly believe it myself but we shall pray for him..."

"'She is pushed aside'," Gontar read slowly. "Hold him good and close so he doesn't get photographed. 'The city's chief

125

medical officer certifies it as a case of healing. An ambulance takes him away.' On the corner of Sadovaya Street and City Father Mokrousov Street the midget gets out and the child gets in, and you go to the flat. 'An old woman tumbles out of the crowd.' Alright, Larissa Yurievna, let's see you tumble, please."

A woman with her face caked in powder, wearing a velvet jacket and silvery silk trousers, crept under the cordon of bodyguards. She spread out a newspaper at my feet and then knelt down heavily on it, supporting herself on the servilely extended elbow of the stooping Sviridov. She thrust a fat hand covered in rings and bracelets into my face.

"'The visitor attempts to raise her to her feet'."

"Oh, let me be, I am older than you are, and you must hear what I have to say." The woman gave a feeble smile and adjusted an imaginary head-scarf. "I never thought to see the face of an angel, but now I have I can die in peace. When I tell them in the village they won't believe me, they'll say I'm making it up. Hear now the one thing I must say. You are our hope, make our land beautiful, pay no heed to our transgressions, curb the power of despotism, dry the tears from the people's eyes. Do not forget you are Russian. Remember where you come from. If you ignore the earth it will not forgive. Do not give way to vain pride, do not be ashamed to repent, do not seek harm to others. We have waited for you so long." The woman sniffed and her tall bouffon hair-do swayed to and fro in its net. She held out an ordinary post-office envelope containing a sprinkling of sand. "A gift to guard you, earth I gathered from the burial mounds of our own Kriukovo Forest, it will save you in the dark hour of night."

"The old woman is carried away," Gontar prompted. "The visitor breathes in the smell of the earth. Song: 'O Russian land, beyond the hills afar...' Is that right? Isn't it 'so fair', not 'afar'?"

"A fart, maybe?" suggested the captain holding the megaphone.

"Five days' close arrest in the guardhouse! Sniff that earth! What kind of way is that to sniff? They're not offering you shit on a shovel! Watch this, I'll show you how to sniff your own native earth!" The colonel jumped down off the crate, took the envelope from me and stuck his nose into it. He took a deep breath, screwing up his eyes in ecstasy, then he suddenly grunted and barked out: "Sviridov, where did you get this?"

"I did as you ordered... I got sand," Sviridov said in a startled voice. "I got it from the sandbox, in the yard... Let me have a sniff."

"At the double. Take down all the dog owners' names, sieve all that sand, find out which animal shat in it and take it to the veterinary station. Put the mangy cur down! And do it now! Now for everybody: in three days' time full dress-rehearsal. Know your lines. First company, right turn! Second company, left turn! At the double. On the command 'at the double' elbows bent at ninety degrees, trunk inclined forward with the weight balanced on the right foot. Quick march!"

Warrant officer Sviridov slouched off about his business at top speed, holding the envelope up to his nose and then holding it away from himself at arm's length. I finally recovered my wits. Everything had been so well-ordered I didn't have any time to laugh or even think...

Alexander TEREKHOV (b.1966) graduated from Moscow University's Department of Journalism and originally won acclaim as a writer of short stories. His novel *A Winter Day Starting a New Life* was published in France. *The Rat-killer* was published by Beck Verlag in Germany. English translations of his work can be found in *Glas* 2 (*Buddy* and *Charon*) and in *Glas* 4 (*Black Void*).

Terekhov's literary early themes were largely drawn from his formative experiences during service in the Soviet Army (the Army High Command described his works as "slander"). He spent his childhood in a small industrial town in Central Russia, which still preserved "the spirit of the early builders of communism". This background and his own subsequent disillusionment underlie the complex structure of his novel *The Rat-killer*, in which the main action is set in a similar town named Svetloyar.

Overwhelmed by the dark embodiment of the narrator's nightmare the novel draws a clear parallel between the rats and human beings. As the political intrigue of phantasmagoric post-communist reality develops into nightmare the greed, cunning and malice of the humans more and more resemble the behaviour of the large communities of destructive rodents, while the rats acquire more and more human features.

Terekhov introduces descriptions and explanations of the complex social organisation of rat society, with its dominant and subordinate males, and of the means used to fight rats, up to and including other rats specially trained to kill and disrupt communities.

Terekhov's language is packed with forceful imagery and the slang of modern Russian. If we wish to identify precedents for his work we might look to Saltykov-Schedrin from the 19th century for his satire of provincial life, and Platonov in the early Soviet period for his range of imagery and individuality of language.

Terekhov, however, is a young and vital writer drawing very much on his own resources and experience, with a distinctive and individual intonation. In *The Rat-Killer* he has produced a racy read which is at the same time an extended metaphor and a satirical novel very much in the Russian tradition.

Vyacheslav
Rybakov

Hassle

Translated by Robert Greenall

Catastrophe

I felt the burning sensation under my shoulder-blades as I queued for tea. The crush and the heat were terrible, and I thought at first it was just the usual streams of sweat running down my spine and irritating my skin with unusual acridity. It was a while before I got scared. Things had gone well that morning and I was in a triumphant mood. It was my "ibrary day" and so I wasn't due in college, officially registered as working at the Public Library in the ancient manuscript room. I'd managed to sign on in my place in the queue for cottage cheese in the dawn cold. Cringing in the cool wind, yawning and sleepily screwing up its eyes, the long queue had formed outside the shop an hour before it opened, everyone afraid of losing their places. Fifteen or so lucky ones, who hoped to make their purchases today, nattered away good-humouredly close by the doors. "Have they said what's come in?" "She stuck her head out, yelled something and they locked the door again..." "You should have asked her again!" "How can you, when she slams the door in your face?" "They're selling children's curd pancakes for thirteen eighty. I saw the van being unloaded..." Some old prig trying to look younger than his age stood beside me without a bag, his hands in his pockets, surveying the subdued pushing and shoving, and grumbling aloud:

"Bloody perestroika! They've brought the country to its knees!" No one replied — they had other things on their mind. "Number eight hundred and three hasn't turned up — I remember him, with that moustache of his, and that white cap!"

"Have a look in the window, would you please, see if there's any butter on the shelf. Please, love, have a look for us! I can't squeeze through..."

I got away before eight thirty. The queue had moved forward seventeen places — not an awful lot but it suited me fine: at that pace I could hope to get in at the end of summer before my wife and Kirill moved back home from the country cottage. Anyway it was Kirill who needed the curds.

I had to queue for tea inside the stuffy shop. The cash till kept on breaking its ribbon so the queue moved slowly and kept on growing longer and longer. A lot of people had transistor radios pressed up against their ears. Yet another congress was being broadcast almost without a break. Chernichenko's ardour had not diminished in the slightest, he hammered away furiously:

"... And what happens? The bakers end up queueing at the chemist's, the chemists are queueing at the baker's, the engineers are queueing at both places, and there's nothing to buy because no-one's working, they're all in the queues! And if there's nothing to buy then the queues don't move!"

It was true. People listened with bated breath; an old woman in front of me cried quietly, wiping away her tears with the wad of ration coupons clenched in her fist. In the distance the cash till began rattling and pounding — everyone pressed their radios closer to their ears, looking daggers at the source of the noise, then sighed with relief when it screeched and spluttered to a halt again. The cashier, in a lather of sweat and flustered to a deep shade of purple, threw up her hands, jumped to her feet and darted out of her glass kennel as if the mafia hitmen were on her heels.

I stuck my hand behind my back to have a scratch, where my shirt was soaking wet, and felt quite clearly that it wasn't my skin that was itching, but something underneath it. Something deep inside me.

It was then I went cold all over.

I can't remember how I managed to stay on my feet. I

threw the June packet of tea into my bag with a trembling hand. Even the fact that it was Indian wasn't enough to cheer me up or even interest me. The words echoed in my head: "It can't be! It can't be!" I couldn't really believe it that quickly, but I was already overwhelmed by despair. By force of habit I pushed my way through on legs of jelly to the confectionery department where pretty tins of Italian baby food were piled high on several rows of shelves, but I didn't feel even a tremor of hope. For my own peace of mind I asked, with my usual embarrassment at the stupidity of the question:

"Are they for sale?"

The salesgirl yawned in slow motion, blinked and said:

"Ownly on prescripshun."

I thought so. We should have had a prescription, but for the third month in a row they hadn't delivered any forms to the polyclinic, and they'd run out of pink ones ages ago. The annoying thing was there were still heaps of pensioners' forms — the different types were issued in equal numbers, though if you thought about it, it should be obvious that pensioners have fewer young children than working people. But the local health authority, or whoever it was there, had got it into their thick heads that they were going to institute social justice. When our pediatrician's working day was over, I waited half an hour for her behind the parched, almost budless bushes opposite the clinic, shot out after her, caught up with her round the corner, so that her colleagues wouldn't see us from the windows, and tried to persuade her to write out a prescription on a pensioner's form. She just pursed her lips and shook her head: any inspection would spot it, and she'd lose her bonus. And when, driven to despair — Kirill just wouldn't eat what my wife and I could offer him, and at less than three years of age he was losing weight, not putting it on — for the first time in my life, stuttering and stammering, I offered a bribe, she looked at me contemptuously and hissed slowly: "And you a Doctor of Sciences!" I don't know what exactly she meant by it. When I reported back to my wife, she assumed that I had begrudged spending money on the child and not offered enough.

I staggered out into the street. It was getting on for midday, the sun was baking hot and the bright, scorching light sliced into my eyes. The itch under my shoulder-blades was growing stronger and becoming painful; from time to time I reached behind me and ran my hand over my back, my protruding shoulder-blades and the pronounced peaks of my vertebrae — everything was okay, no characteristic swelling or hard lump. That didn't prove anything though, it was too early. The pain spoke for itself. There was no point in doubting any more. But still I couldn't believe it; I just couldn't get it into my head that it had happened to me.

I stood in the middle of the pavement and people shoved me from the right and the left. Everyone was rushing somewhere. But I didn't feel like going anywhere any more, I didn't need to go anywhere. In the morning I'd been planning to go and pick up the washing from the laundry after I'd got the tea, — I'd heard it was open again; then go round the photo shops looking for some fixing solution — my wife was upset that I hadn't taken any snaps of Kirill for so long; then sign on in the queue for mutton — my turn ought to come up by the end of the month... and in the evening have a quick bite on the corner of Sadovaya Street — I'd noticed in passing that the "Medea" restaurant had set up its stall there again. Clearly, investigation had disproved the rumour that the pies were being filled with the meat of sick crows that were too weak to fly. Then after my snack, I was going to rush over to the library and work there till it shut, if only for an hour. No one had released me from my job, I was still getting paid. But now I couldn't, I just couldn't. I stood there and watched indifferently, as an excited crowd dragged a couple of perfectly decent-looking young men out of the "Golden Hive" cafe, shouting:

"Where you come from we can't get bread without residence permits, and you come down here to scoff our waffles!"

"Zere's only four million off us in our republic, but here zere's five million off you here in von city!" one of the young men tried to explain with a strong accent. "Ve von't eat all your food!"

"You could stuff yourselves with all the rice in China and still look for more!"

An old man walking past took in the whole situation at once. He was carrying a big bag, and the star of a Hero of the Soviet Union gleamed bright yellow on the breast of his shabby filthy jacket. Intent as he was on a spot of emergency bulk buying, he still proved capable of taking the viewpoint of the state. He shouted, straining his falsetto voice in obvious sympathy:

"Steady on! Take it easy, they might secede from the Union!" But that just fanned the flames.

"We'll bloody well secede before they do!"

"We're pissed off with greasing up to spongers!"

"Let them bugger off out of it!"

It didn't come to blows, however. The poor guys were simply shoved further away from the doors of the shop and people lost interest in them. They shook themselves down.

"Russian scum," said one under his breath as he straightened his tie and then checked his wallet.

"The rotten empire," said the second gloomily, checking his wallet and then straightening his tie.

"I still managed to grab one packet," the first one

announced, changing to the gentle, dancing rhythms of his native tongue. His friend slapped him on the shoulder and slowly, with dignity, they disappeared into the crowd.

I reached behind my back again — and felt it.

Below my left shoulder-blade the barely palpable swelling shifted beneath my fingers. A small hard spot.

A wing-embryo.

The fact that it was only under the left shoulder didn't mean a thing. In half an hour a knot would appear under the right one too. The pain would increase. Then, when the embryos took root, tearing apart the tight-packed layers of tissue, it would subside, a thin stalk of connective tissue would extend between the two rapidly swelling shoulder-blade nodes and across my spine, and then, with the embryonic growths nourishing each other, the process would proceed even more intensively...

How much more intensive could it be? It had only taken two hours to produce a node. I had a week left to live, at most.

If I didn't get to my family in that time, I'd never see them again.

They probably wouldn't even find out what happened to me. They'd wait, they'd cry... Kirill would ask his mum twenty times a day when I was coming and she wouldn't be able to tell him. Autumn would come; during the autumn, and maybe during the winter, my wife would still start at the sound of footsteps at night on the still, black street and run to the window to see who it was; or start if she heard a bell ring and rush to the phone or door... The police would tell her: he hasn't been located, but we're looking, don't worry...

Autumn?

I've got their coupon for the train tickets for September!

If I don't get to them, how are they going to get back to town when my wife's leave is over?

Labours

I trudged home, absolutely drained by pain and despair. I got thoroughly crushed in the bus, and this time the customary crush was unbearable — the embryos were incredibly sensitive, and the slightest pressure on them caused a shooting pain which pierced my lungs and my heart, setting it fluttering and pounding from the shock of the pain; I shuddered as I stifled a cry and bit my lip at every judder, every heavy jolt of the worn-out old bus over every pothole, when the packed crowd of people, glued together by sweat, shook in a single gelatinous mass, like a lump of frogspawn...

I tried phoning for a taxi, but the line was busy. Then, with a newspaper full of the verbatim texts of yesterday's speeches, I swatted the cockroaches from my desk and started writing a letter. All the time I wanted to pull my shirt off and look at my back in the mirror, it took all my strength to resist — what was the point of looking? The pain had eased. There was only the numb sensation of pins and needles, scuttling like cockroaches across on my skin as it stretched tautly under the pressure from within. "My dearest!" I wrote slowly, crossed it out and wrote: "Darling! I have done nothing wrong and I never wanted this to happen. You know that. But when something happens to your body — without you wanting it to happen, without any warning, of its own accord, as if it were somewhere far away, not there inside you — there's nothing you can do. It's like an earthquake. If I find I won't have time to see you I'll send this letter and enclose the coupon. But please believe me, I tried..." No, it didn't work. I dialled 312-00-22 again, and couldn't get through this time either. I got up, reached behind me and involuntarily felt my back. The fleshy membrane had already formed between the two subcutaneous swellings, round and firm like tree fungi. I could have howled like a baby, no one would have seen me. My eyes were burning, as though they were filled with acid, my throat tightened and shuddered. Why me? This was my house, I grew up here, I'd lived here thirty-six years, worked here — sometimes well, sometimes badly; I'd made love, played ice-hockey and soldiers with my son, read him books. I was going to carry on reading him that fairy-tale collection I'd managed to buy last week — such lovely pictures! And I had to leave all this behind! Outside the window the layered and humped roofs of the motley collection of surrounding buildings stretched away into the distance. Just as they had when I used to play soldiers with my dad — they hadn't changed, but I was changing ineluctably, and there was nothing that could be done about it, nothing at all. What state would I be in a week from now? Where would I be? I didn't want it to happen, I wanted to stay here! The distant glittering dome of St. Isaac's hung above the waves of the roofs, from this distance it appeared weightless, it floated in the air, giving off gleams as subtle as red-hot threads, from the sides of it not visible from here — but it was real and solid and it would remain. I again phoned for a taxi. There was no dial tone for ages. Sobbing and still stroking my back — the way your tongue keeps poking at a new filling or the hole where a tooth has been pulled out, and there's no way you can stop it — I waited and waited, quite sure I hadn't got through, the signal had faded away somewhere in the maze of wires and I'd have to redial. But then there was a click in the receiver and a melodious female voice began in mid-word: "...ply, you are on hold. Please wait for a reply, you are on hold. Please wait for a reply, you are on hold." Holding the receiver in place with my shoulder, I felt my back with my hand. I moved my piece of paper closer and picked up my pen. "Love and kisses to little Kirill" — "Please wait for a reply, you are on hold." — "I don't know where I got it from. But then no one knows what causes it. I was carrying on my life as usual, only feeling a bit more tired, but that can't be the reason, that's just me feeling my age, that and life becoming more of a strain." — "Please wait for a reply, you are on hold." — "I'll keep signing on in the queues as long I can. I'm in line for cottage cheese, mutton, grapes for September, I've signed on for a pressure-cooker... I'll try to explain to everyone that you'll be picking the stuff up. I'll sign over my numbers to you, but don't get them mixed up. The coupon for the tickets is valid from the first to the fifth of September, you go to the station at Roshchino, to the window on the far left, any day in that period, pay thirty-seven forty and they'll give you tickets for the same day. Only try to have the right money ready, they never have change there, the clerk gets really annoyed and might not give you a ticket." — "Please wait for a reply, you are on hold." — "I bought a book from someone for Kirill, I'll leave it on the table where you can see it. I think it's good — the illustrations are very well done — stars, cypress trees, the sea... Like the Crimea, remember? That moon shining in through the window as it hung over the mountain, and the cicadas... Fairy-tales for five-year-olds." — "Please wait for a reply, you are on hold." — "Kirill's probably not quite ready for it yet, but it will keep, and he can look at the pictures for now. All those people in loose Turkish pants, and minarets everywhere..." — "Please wait for a reply, you are on hold." I dragged the telephone after me — the long cord rustled as it trailed across the floor, I went over to the window, unable to write any more. "Please wait for a reply, you are on hold." On the square in front of the District Party Committee building there was a modest crowd carrying placards. The crowd was orderly and at one corner of it a long pole jutted up like the standard of a Roman legion, bearing an inscription in large letters on it — "Authorised demonstration." "Please wait for a reply, you are on hold." I couldn't make out all the slogans from that distance, but there were some I could read clearly. "Yes to perestroika! No to anarchy!" "We won't allow a wedge to be driven between the people and the Party, which has heroically taken upon itself the responsibility for the results of its actions and set in motion the processes of renewal!" "Criticise a soldier and you criticise the entire army! Criticise the entire army and you insult the memory of the fallen!" "Please wait for a reply, you are on hold." No one was looking at the demonstrators. People lathered in sweat rushed back and forth past them. It was the end of the working day, the streets were packed, everyone was in a hurry. No one seemed to notice the people standing in the blazing sun. But when a few hefty-looking lads filed out of the Committee building — the doorman held the huge door open for them — with trays laden with food from the private Party dining room, and began handing it out to the demonstrators so they could keep up their strength, the people hurrying by began to stop and many of them held spyglasses and binoculars up to their eyes to see what food it was these people were getting.

"Please wait for a reply, you are on hold. Please wait for a reply, you are on hold. Please wait for a reply, you are on hold."

I couldn't bear it any longer. My back ached as if the flesh were quietly crunching and cracking under the pressure of the hard-swelling neoplasm. I put the polite, blandly muttering receiver down on the table, on top of the unfinished letter, fished some change out of my jacket pocket and left the flat. I had to hold myself up very straight — for the first time in many years I paid attention to my posture. I'll tie a plank to your back to stop you hunching your shoulders, my mum used to say... I only had to stoop over a little in my usual manner and the red-hot wire of the connecting membrane would dig deep into the crack between my vertebrae, as if it were about to slice through my spine. For a few seconds at a time I had the feeling it was easier to walk, but it soon passed. A trick of the nerves, of course. I'd start to lose weight in two or three days. The course of the illness had been described in detail. I'd read everything about it, gasping in detached astonishment as I went. I knew it all, but it had never even occurred to me that I might be affected. It was impossible, impossible. Quite impossible... The disembodied telephone voice carried on murmuring in my ear. On the stairs stinking of rotten rubbish, I carefully felt my back with an already habitual movement, trying not to disturb the swellings. No, there was still nothing anyone else could notice. But just the same I pulled away my shirt, which was clinging to my sweaty skin, so that it could hang more freely, thus disguising the outline of my body! And just the same, out on the street among the tired people hurrying about their own business, I imagined everyone was looking at me and their eyes were boring into my back.

When the phone was free, I squeezed into the baking, smoky booth flooded with fierce late afternoon sunlight; I put in a coin and dialled the home number of my Institute's Director. There was a rapidly diminishing chance left — the Director had a country cottage at Gorkovskaya. In exchange for fruit and vegetables from their gardens, cottage-owners were issued with weekly passes on suburban transport to the districts where they had cottages. Although it was formally forbidden to let other people use these passes, it was practically impossible to detect a switch, only an inspector who happened to remember the face of the real owner could stop you — as yet the pass carried neither a photo nor a passport number. The Director was home. I felt as pleased as if we'd already agreed on it.

"Good afternoon, sir," I said. "Poimanov here."

"Afternoon, afternoon," he answered pleasantly, which pleased me even more. "And what can I do for you?"

"Er... I just wanted to know..." — the words stuck in my throat. I realised I didn't know how to ask him. I'd have to explain. "Are you... thinking of going to the cottage in the next few days?"

"Hm-m-m," said the Director in surprise, but then he immediately rose to the challenge. "You know, I think not. The weather's nice, but I'll have to stay in town. You know yourself how busy things are at the moment. And then our French colleagues are arriving on Tuesday, remember? By the way, that old friend of yours Professor Janvier's coming with them. I'm pleased to tell you, he specially asked whether he'd be able to see you, and he was most enthusiastic about your last article. Although, tell me now... didn't I tell you in Council?"

"Yes, yes, I remember," I lied. That is, not entirely — that morning I really had remembered and, as I queued outside the milk shop, I was even looking forward to the meeting because, for all their comfortable conditions, all the computers in their libraries and the air-conditioning in their studies, I'd managed once again to get the better of this nice guy from Bordeaux. I'd long since grown used to substituting intuition for information, and so far it had paid off pretty well. But in the intervening hours that followed all of this had evaporated from the convolutions of my brain and ceased to have any real existence. "I'm calling about something else. You see, my family's in the cottage at Roshchino at the moment. I have to get to them, it's urgent... not for long, I'll be at the Institute on Tuesday, of course," I lied again to reassure him. "It's entirely unexpected, and I've got no idea what to do. You know yourself, people have been signing on for the suburban trains since February..."

"Hm-m-m," said the Director, dropping his friendly tone. My heart sank; I hunched over and immediately straightened up again with a jerk from the razor-sharp pain. It is impossible to convey the horror of the sensation — like being cut open alive, like a sabre slash, not across your skin but deep inside you, across your bones, because the sabre is in the very heart of you.

There was nothing else for it. I asked desperately:

"Could you lend me your pass? Just for a day?"

"Hm-m-m," said the Director. "But you see, my friend, just at the moment I only have passes for the second half of June and later. We've already used up the old ones, we planted what we could in May... and the new harvest isn't ready yet, so there's nothing to trade in. I really don't see how I can help you."

"I see," I said blankly. Something in my voice must have worried the Director.

"What exactly is it that's come up?" he blurted out.

"Oh, nothing special," I replied, "family problems."

"Listen, my friend... After all, passes aren't the be-all and end-all. Maybe we can work something out..."

"Maybe, we can."

"Anyway, it's the fifth of June now. In ten days my document will be good. Is that any help to you, about eleven days from now?"

"Thanks, but no," I said tiredly. And suddenly added, without really knowing why: "I'll be flying away soon."

There was a long pause — just the rustling in the receiver, and some very faint music playing somewhere in the bottomless depths of the telephone network. I wanted to say goodbye, but then the Director asked:

"What?"

"I'll be flying away," I said.

"Do you realise what you're saying?" he inquired icily.

"Yes I do."

"The deadline for your project expires next year. I hope you haven't forgotten?"

"No. Now I can be perfectly honest with you — I probably wouldn't have got it finished in time anyway. I just can't get to grips with it somehow."

"You got five years' pay for that monograph!"

"You can try deducting it from... my widow's salary."

Another pause. Then he asked warily:

"Are you sure?"

"Absolutely."

"I'll try to think of something," he said hesitantly.

"On Monday our colleagues in the next laboratory are sending a truck to Vyborg for liquid nitrogen... The Finnish delegation is leaving by bus tomorrow... I'll try. Give me a call in two or three hours."

"Thank you, sir," I said almost without hope, and he put the phone down straight away.

Please wait for a reply.

I left the phone booth.

The city was adrift in a haze of heat. Some windows flashed in the glare, others were dark. The dense heat eddied to and fro. There was a smell of asphalt and petrol, unbroken walls of cars, unbroken walls of people, walls hemming in cars and people. Knowing that for me all of this would soon be gone forever, I wanted to howl out loud. I went home, holding myself ridiculously erect, almost leaning over backwards, and a single thought pulsed in my head and my throat: this is the last time. The last time. The last time for what? For everything.

A taxi.

"Taxi! Hey taxi!" I waved my arms so hard they almost dropped off.

A screech of brakes. "Can you take me to Roshchino?" — "Are you soft in the head or something, gov'nor?"

There was something in the letterbox — I opened it

mechanically. It was a postcard from the central children's shop notifying us that the queue for prams had moved on fifty places and requesting us to confirm our order. We'd signed on a year and a half before Kirill came along, but every month the queue got slower and slower, and now my wife and I sometimes joked that the pram would come at just the right time for Kirill's children. We had to improvise and make do: I glued up boxes made of paper, using my rough drafts, notes and the beginnings of articles which I hadn't been able to finish, because of a chronic lack of time, and which I already knew would never have time to finish; instead of wheels I used reels from an old tape recorder — this saved the day, but such contraptions proved short-lived — the paper would get wet and come apart. Kirill only had to wet himself while out for a walk and the thing would have to be glued back together again. A good thing I used to write so much — nowadays you just wouldn't be able to get that amount of paper anywhere. Tomorrow I'd have to run down to the children's shop and drop in the latest postcard. Tomorrow. Christ, tomorrow. But I had to leave town! I still ought to get down there. I couldn't lose my place. The telephone receiver twittered as it lay there on the letter. It was obviously just the phone twittering, but I held it up to my ear anyway with a hand clammy with sweat... "Please wait for a reply, you are on hold. Please wait for a reply, you are on hold." Two hours. Or three. That meant between seven and eight. Maybe he can do something? After all he's got influence... Half an hour had gone by already. What could I do? From the far corner of the table a half-read dissertation stared mockingly up at me. I had to oppose its presentation on Wednesday. Wednesday, huh! Trampling the cockroaches underfoot without mercy I went into the toilet and got a floor cloth out of the cupboard behind the pipes. Taking a masochistic pleasure in feeling my backbone being sawn in two, I began painstakingly washing the floor, every now and then pausing stock-still to listen to the voice on the telephone through the loud gurgling of my heart. "Please wait for a reply, you are on hold." Everything was going dark because of the pain. Take that, I muttered. Take that. I'm sick, but I can still do it. The corridor, the kitchen. The other rooms. The sleeves of my shirt were soaked to the elbows, but I didn't dare roll them up — the shirt would dry out, but what if the numbers written all the way from my wrists to my shoulders faded so you couldn't read them... So much for Zamyatin with his numbers instead of names! So much for the concentration camps where you got five or six neat little digits tattooed on! No one had abolished names, but then no one was interested in them; we write these numbers on ourselves: six hundred and eight in the bread queue, five thousand three hundred in the candied fruit jelly queue, and God help you if you get them mixed up! Finished. The floors gleamed damply, and the warm, slightly stuffy smell of wet parquet pervaded the flat. I froze listening. "Please wait for a reply, you are on hold." It had only taken me an hour to wash the floors. How long the daily chores take if you want to get on with something really interesting — and how quickly you can do them if you have time to kill! I washed the WC. Then I scrubbed the gas stove in the kitchen. Take that. I went back to the living room, collapsed into an armchair absolutely exhausted, then threw myself back forward with a groan, — it felt as though two red-hot iron bars had been thrust into my back. I couldn't even lean back comfortably now.

There was a click from the receiver, and a new voice came on. From that distance I couldn't make out the words but I could tell they were different. Throwing off my slippers, I sprinted for the phone. My heart stood still in disbelief: had I really got through? And then: I wonder what time I'll get a car? And then: better ring Arkhipov to say I don't need his help. And then: it's an hour to Roshchino by car, I'll be there before dark! They'll be pleased! Get the book, the book for Kirill! And the coupon... Christ, how am I going to tell her?! I grabbed the phone and managed to catch the end of the sentence: "...will be disconnected. Thank you for your attention."

"Hallo!" I cried. " I need a car as quick..." The voice paid no attention to me and began again, and my request died on my lips.

"This is the electronic accounts section of the IBM-Promin joint venture. Dear comrade! Your telephone conversation has exceeded the time limit allowed. You are overloading the public network and impeding the flow of normal communication between citizens. Your telephone is therefore being disconnected for a period of one week. Tomorrow at the latest you must pay a fine of seven hundred and forty-six roubles fifty kopecks at the following address: Urgent Payments Department, 14 Sinopskaya Embankment. If you fail to do so your telephone will be disconnected. Thank you for your attention."

I stood there for a second, saying nothing, wanting nothing, then replaced the lifeless receiver with a lifeless hand. It was silent — no distant music, no crackling. That was it. Please don't wait for a reply.

It was a quarter to eight. I felt my back carefully. I'd have to wear a jacket if I went outside. My shirt was stretched taut across two protruding humps that felt like moulded rubber.

The cameramen finished shooting the demonstrators, who began to disperse, rolling up their slogans and gobbling the remaining sturgeon sandwiches. The heat came in waves, interspersed with occasional gusts of stale cool air from connecting courtyards. The day was slipping away, the first of the six or seven I had left. I went into the phone box. During the last three hours a new piece of graffiti had appeared in it: "Keep the cockroaches away, kill a junkie every day!" Hardly anyone wrote rude words any more — new social interests had been aroused. Carved deeply and clearly right above the phone were the words: "Love your country!" And to the left, in wiry ballpoint: "Honest bucks aren't scared of AIDS. But sleep with anything on two legs and you'll snuff it like Stalin without the last rites!" I surveyed all of this as I held the hot receiver against my cheek, but the long ringing tones evaporated rhythmically into the air of the Director's flat and no-one heard them. Ten, eleven, twelve... I cut the phone off with my finger and dialled again. "Keep the cockroaches away, kill a junkie every day!" "We crushed the fascists, but we haven't crushed the corrupt bureaucrats yet." That's what it said. Fifteen... seventeen...

"Yes?" said a sleepy and extremely annoyed female voice.

"Good evening. Could I speak to Arkady Ivanovich please?"

"No, you can't speak to Arkady Ivanovich. Arkady Ivanovich has gone to Moscow."

The phone almost fell out of my hand.

"What do you mean? Gone where?"

"Don't you understand plain Russian? Moscow I said. On a business trip. An hour ago. Tomorrow is the sixtieth birthday of the academician in charge of the Department which Daddy's institute comes under." The voice said the words "Daddy's institute" so carelessly, and the word "academician" with such a flashy familiarity for titles, that the conversation's pointlessness was immediately obvious. But I asked anyway, amazed at my own calm indifference:

"This is Gleb Poimanov. We spoke three hours ago about some important business. Did he leave a message for me?"

"No," replied the voice, almost indignantly. "He was in such a rush..."

"Thank you. Goodbye," I said and hung up.

I went on standing in the phone box. Who else could I call? I couldn't think of anything. All kinds of wild ideas swirled around in my head: like dashing over to the Finland Station and bribing the dispatcher... if I could find him... Dodging the platform inspectors and going without a ticket, hoping that I didn't run into an inspector along the line... Walking out of town along the Primorsk Road and thumbing a lift, someone would take me if I offered them enough... I got out my wallet and counted my money. It wasn't exactly bulging. And when you thought that the following day I had to pay the fine down at Sinopskaya Street... Then I thought of Tonya.

She worked as a laundress in a nursery, and her brother was a mechanic in some factory garage. Their mother lived in the country, and they often went out to see her. They'd take off in a truck or minibus from the garage for a couple of days — getting the train or the bus was too much of a struggle, and anyway no one noticed the vehicle was missing — none of them were ever in the garage. I first met Tonya a year before, purely by chance. I was on my way back from some conference, looking exceptionally smart and feeling unusually buoyant and inspired, and that always makes you stand out in our hassled, nervous crowds, — and suddenly for no obvious reason a pretty girl decided to chat me up in the metro. I'd never been able to do that, I'd never even tried, but she managed it very simply: how do you get to so-and-so? Oh, I'll probably get it all wrong... Do you think you could show me, please? We sat for four hours in some little park, smoked a packet of Salems (a present to me — even though I was a non-smoker — from an exchange student of mine, Reggie Walker) into the July night. Tonya puffed on one cigarette after another, and she talked the same way — a chain of one tedious link after another, whose only purpose was to avoid parting by keeping up a pretence of conversation; then she somehow relaxed, became more natural and started talking about herself. I listened and soon began to sympathize with her, the way I always did: she told me how her hands were always raw from doing the laundry; how she loved looking after children and would have had a baby herself long ago, but she couldn't afford to support one; how a truck-driver had tipped her out of his dumper onto the road when she was still a school-girl — that evening she'd asked him to take her from Solnechnoye to Ushkov, but refused to give him what he wanted, and he pretended to agree, but just raised the dumper while the truck was moving — she hitched up her skirt without the slightest embarrassment and showed me a long scar on her hip — a tortured, lumpy blue zigzag, which disappeared beneath her clean cherry-patterned knickers... When the Salems ran out, she said: "I've never smoked so much, I feel quite sick..." "Why did you do it then?" "So as not to have to go." "You have to sooner or later." She took my words as a hint that it was time to say goodbye, her lips trembled, she stood up quickly and swayed — I jumped up to support her. "I must be going crazy," she said timidly. She gave me a sideways glance, well aware that the phrase was one more cliche, like one more cigarette. Afraid I wouldn't realise, she asked: "Will you take me home?" I took her home. We were scarcely inside the glass-panelled door of her flat, on the threshold of the depths of a huge communal labyrinth stinking of filthy living, when faces appeared and loud voices began exchanging opinions on us as we circumnavigated the knickers and slips strung out to dry across the corridor, the nappies, the sheets so worn the light shone through them, the garlands of socks darned and re-darned, grafted tightly onto each other, as we made our way past the piles of clinking empty bottles ranged along the wall, with the shaky painted floorboards bending beneath our feet: "Look, look, Tonya's brought another one home!" "Give her a break, Nikola, no-one's been round for, let's see, three months or so, the girl must be desperate by now!" "He's getting on a bit..." "They don't wear ties like that nowadays." "He's got a briefcase, like some major-general." We went in, she slammed the door, turned sharply to face me, and her eyes grew big and dark. "I've never talked like that to anyone before," she confessed and began to kiss me, and afterwards it was my turn to talk quite openly, though not too freely, about myself, and then we exchanged our numbers at work: there was no phone in that twilight pigsty, and I had a wife at home; I left, knowing for sure I'd never call her but feeling ashamed to throw away that scrap of paper with its hurriedly scribbled digits of invitation. But she phoned herself; summer, autumn, even at the start of spring she phoned me at work. She'd ask for me formally in a trembling voice, invite me round, promise to fry me some potatoes from her allotment, treat me to some mushrooms she'd gathered and pickled. It broke my heart the way she dreamed of having me round. "Tonya, love, don't waste your time on me..." "Who else is there to waste it on?" "What do you want from me?" "Everything."

I never did go to see her, but now, in my despair, I remembered her.

I recognised her voice straight away.

"Tonya? Hello, Tonya."

She recognised me too.

"Gleb. What a surprise! Hello. Is something wrong?"

I immediately felt more relaxed and hardly even ashamed. There was just my jacket stretched tightly and uncomfortably across my back.

There was a distant rumbling of washing machines in the phone.

"Yes, Tonya, there is something. Can you talk?"

"Of course!"

"Listen. Are you thinking of going to see your mum in the next few days?"

"You need a break? I've invited you often enough ..."

"No, Tonya... Tonya. I need... My family's in Roshchino at the moment, at the cottage, and I need to get to them as soon as I can. Sorry for asking you... But I'm in an absolutely desperate situation, and I've no-one to turn to except you."

She said nothing for a moment, and then:

"I'll phone Tolya, love. We weren't planning to go just now, but I'll find out," her voice had faded slightly, but it was still just as gentle. "Maybe he can help."

"How will I know?"

She paused again.

"I finish work in half an hour, I might even get away earlier, as it's such a... Come round to my place, I'll be there in an hour and a half and I'll know by then. You remember the way? You will be there?"

Now it was my turn to pause.

"Yes."

"By then I'll know everything," she repeated.

The Candle

"Actually, you know, Gleb, I haven't been able to reach him yet. He's not at home, his wife said he'd be back by eleven. But don't worry dear, I'll try again, I'll nip out and phone. Let's just stay here a while. You're not in a hurry, are you?"

"No."

"Sit here. Here, here's a chair for you, like last time. Have you had your tea?"

"No."

"I thought you wouldn't have. I fried some potatoes."

"Oh Tonya, you shouldn't..."

"Go on, go on! You'll be bored just sitting there. And look what else I've got!"

"Oh Tonya, why did you?"

"Just a little bit, one glass. It's been so long. We have to celebrate!"

"Thanks... Stop! That's enough..."

"Of course, and the same for me. Oh Gleb, my love, this is going to be such a treat! Hang on... The sun's in my eyes so I can't see you. Shall we draw the curtains? See, I've got new curtains! They're so thick you can't see anything through them. Last time that man was spying on us from that window over there. But now it's nice and cosy. Shall we light a candle? Or have a little drink first? Eat up, your food's getting cold! Look, isn't that a lovely candle! Sorry, I'm making too much fuss... I really thought I'd never see you again. But you phoned after all! Let's have a little drink..."

"Cheers, Tonya."

"Cheers to you, and your family. And look at this... only promise you'll take it. You promise? Well?"

"Promise..."

"Go-od. I bought this for your little boy today. Sweet, isn't it? Clever little thing! Chuff-chuff-chuff!"

"Tonya... No, I can't take it. It's too expensive."

"Can't I give you a little present once a year? You promised, you promised! It's yours! Well? Just a drop? Isn't that candle pretty when it burns? Go on, just a little sip."

"Tonya, where did you get the vodka? When a friend and

I wanted to have a drink we couldn't find anything but Azerbaijani cognac at a hundred and seventy-three roubles a bottle."

"You should've called me in. Remember Gosha? ... Well, never mind... he works at a bottling plant. He can always get vodka, and he doesn't add too much on to the price... I hopped round there after work!"

"How could you find the time?"

"Well, you see, after you phoned I began to move ten times as fast. I didn't feel miserable or tired..."

"Why not?"

"Because I was glad there was something you needed from me."

"Why were you glad?"

"Because you're not a bastard."

"What's that supposed to mean?"

"Oh, come on now, don't be silly. Why aren't you eating? Don't you like it?"

"I do, it's just that I've got no appetite."

"Have a drink then. And I'll join you."

"I feel dizzy enough already."

"Dizzy, my foot... You're just feeling relaxed, that's all, and your eyes don't look nearly so strained... You looked so shattered when you got here, it made my heart bleed for you."

"Everyone's shattered."

"No, they're not. A lot of people like things the way they are. Shouting, rushing around, grabbing — no need to actually do anything. But all you'd like to do is just work and work, I know that..."

"How do you know that?"

"I just do. Ooh, now I'm getting tipsy. It's lovely! Now you pour, it's man's job. That's enough. And for you, too! Let's drink to us. Hot, isn't it? I'm so happy for your family, out in the fresh air in weather like this. Your boy's probably got a tan, and his nose is peeling... It's stifling in here. Do you mind if I just slip into something more comfortable? Turn round for a moment. Now look at the nice little bathing suit I made. Like it?"

"Tonya, your scar's faded."

"Oh, don't, Gleb dear. You're just trying to be nice. It's still there, I don't care, I'm used to it."

"Honest."

"How do you like my bathing suit?"

"Ve-ery slinky. From a distance it might not be there at all."

"Ooh, you're so witty! You'll have me in stitches..."

"You really made it yourself?"

"Of course. You don't mind if I keep it on, do you? And you take off your jacket. It's crazy to be wearing that inside in this weather, you'll be sweating like a pig!"

"I'm used to it, Tonya."

"Well, I'm not having it. Your face is all hot and shiny. I'll take it off if you won't."

"Tonya, don't!"

"Still trying to keep me off, are you? I try to look after him, and he won't let me! I'm taking that jacket off now! Hands up! What're you doing, d'you want a fight or some... Oh!"

"There."

"Glebbie... Oh my God! They're so hard... Glebbie, what are they?"

"I'm growing wings, Tonya."

She put her hands over her mouth in amazement and stood there for a few seconds, swaying her head gently from side to side.

"Poor thing... What are you going to do now?"

"I don't know."

"So that's why you have to go to the cottage?"

"Yes. I might not even have time to say goodbye to them, Tonya. I can't even imagine how they're going to manage in this mess..."

"Oh I'm so sorry. Oh what a cow I am! I'm sorry!"

"What for?"

"I'll tell you later... They stick out so. Not much time left, is there?"

"They grow quickly. As if they'd been building up to it for ages and then finally burst out. Why did it have to happen to me, Tonya?"

"Does it hurt?"

"Not much now. But it's weird. They feel stiff and numb."

"Can I kiss them?"

"Why them?"

"Because they hurt."

"You're so gentle, Tonya. I feel so sorry for you..."

"And I feel sorry for you... I've heard so much about it, I read about it in the paper once... But I've never seen it. None of our lot... What is it?"

"No-one knows."

"And where will you...?"

"No-one knows."

"I'd fly off anywhere with you... But how can I? How much do you weigh?"

"Sixty-three kilos, I think."

"Well I'm almost seventy! My tits on their own are getting on for four, every time I'm in a queue some dirty old sod jogs them with his elbow as though by accident... Glebbie, oh Glebbie... I'll never see you again either. Let me make the bed up. Please..."

There was nothing I could say. She waited, staring at me imploringly, and then the bathing suite seemed to be swept off her by a gust of wind.

I made love to her.

But however I embraced her or lay across her, as if to protect her from bullets whistling past, I couldn't defend her or shut her off from her real poverty, from that oppressive and stuffy little room; from the truck-driver raising his dumper; from the queues with their joggling elbows; from sweaty hands feeling up her skirt in overcrowded buses until she pushed them away with her bag, then scraping around for small change in it; from the endless rumble of the constantly broken foul-smelling washing machines; from the musty fumes of the dim, intestinally twisted communal apartment; from the cries "Tonya's brought a new one back!"; from the stink of the rubbish bins festering in the heat right below her window in the blistering chasms of the well-shafts, and of the swill running out onto the cracked asphalt, buzzing with swarms of gigantic flies; from the legitimized poison in the potatoes and cutlets she cooked so lovingly; not from anything, even my own imminent departure... These embraces were a deception and pretence. They promised protection, more than that — by definition they had to involve protection as their basic meaning — but they did not provide it, so that no matter how the girl beneath me laid herself open, oblivious of herself, no matter how she cried with happiness, feeling the eruption of my infertile, unprotective tenderness deep within her — I didn't feel like a man, I was a eunuch, the order of life had castrated me.

But if I learned to forget, to drive away these thoughts and make love out of a concern for the functional relief of the organism — that would make me a lecherous bastard. Our life forces us to choose between being a lecherous bastard and a eunuch; there is no other choice.

"Oh that was so good, Glebbie. I never thought anyone could be as tender as that... You know, I'd give ten years of my life to have you like that just once more. Did you like it?"

I just smiled.

"You're smiling, lovey. Want me to guess what you thought when you saw me in the bathing suit?"

"Go on then."

"You weren't thinking about me at all."

"Oh no?"

"No. It was after that you thought about me and what you could do with this shameless tart pushing herself on you."

"Tonya!"

"But first of all you thought about how nice it'd be to give your wife a bathing suit like that. Did I guess right? Don't say anything, I know I did. Want me to make you one? Tell me the size and I'll have it for you in three days."

"Tonya, you're an angel."

"No way. Do angels screw?"

"Everyone does the same thing, they just feel different things."

"No, Glebbie. You know, I lied to you. I really wanted to see you, you're going to kill me for this. My brother can't help us, they've been trying to elect a new deputy chief of Technical Control for the last four days, God knows how much longer they'll go on yelling and shouting about it. They're all worked up over it, no one's working and the garage is locked up. See what a cow I am? And I'm not sorry. Because this was the best evening of my life. And if you come back in three days I really will make your wife a bathing suit like that, and maybe all that palaver will have finished by then and we can go. Will you, Glebbie, will you?"

"I don't know... How can I promise anything now? Give me a break..."

"You didn't like it. I'll get dressed then."

"You sound very cold suddenly..."

"Don't worry. I'll have a good cry tonight, then in the

evening I'll go to see Semyon. He's just put his wife and kid into hospital and he asked me over for a bit of rumpy-pumpy while the house is empty..."

"Why, Tonya?"

"It's my problem. You just fly away. Go on, fuck off♦"

"Tonya..." Sucking on a heart pill, I wandered home over the soft asphalt. After its thorough boiling, the town was slowly cooling on its unwashed asphalt still seeming to sizzle slightly as the occasional vehicle passed. The haze was trembling, and houses swayed in the murk along the receding sight lines of the streets. I didn't know what to do. Should I really go tomorrow — or today, rather — to the first train and try to grease someone's palm? It wouldn't work... Anyway I should be careful with money, things would be tight for my wife when I... went away. That was another thing: tomorrow, or today rather, I had to draw all my money out of the bank and leave it at home, or take it with me if I managed to go. Or maybe send a postal order? But then there were charges... All of a sudden, like the crowning mockery, the title of the book I hadn't written loomed up before my eyes — I'd had it all in my head for ages, just never got around to writing it, formulating it, giving the text a structure.

It was a little cooler at home. I swept the cockroaches from the table and mindlessly, without thinking, I began to write out the numbers from my hands on a separate sheet of paper, indicating which queues they were for and — in brackets — the next dates for signing on. It was very strange writing down the dates, knowing for sure I wouldn't be around when they came; totally absurd... ninth of June for the pressure cooker — I'd manage that, then the twelfth — well it would probably be over by then, and my wife would be left without scouring powder for the autumn. What a shambles... How would they manage without me?!

By the time I'd finished it was about two in the morning, and a thick grey light was glowing behind the curtains. My eyes were red and inflamed, but there was no question of sleep; and anyway I had to get to the Finland Station by five and do something. Maybe I could buy someone's ticket from them? But who would sell one? Or they'd ask so much for it that all my savings would evaporate and my wife would be left without anything in reserve, and after all my salary would be gone anyway as soon as I disappeared — my mind was going round in circles.

When I finished I just sat there for a while, then I got a packet of old photos from the back of the lower drawer of the desk and began slowly going through them. They were five, seven, eight years old — everything seemed such a short time ago, but how everything had changed. I loved looking at them when it was quiet, when I felt especially bad from this soulless and brainless rat-race, they gave me strength, no, not just strength, something more — feelings. I looked at my wife's young faces — which actually looked more or less the same as she did today, and felt as though I was transported in spirit back to this recent past, which felt at once strangely close and strangely impossible: in a Karelian forest, among the fresh golden pines, or the transparent sunny expanses of the Crimea... This is us, I felt, this is how we really are — happy, fun-loving, free, hungry for each other and caring for each other; and everything else which had now grown over us like a mould, was simply the result of tiredness and worry, it was a kind of surface scum; we only needed to wash it away somehow just for one evening, and this was how we'd shine then!

There's no way to get to the Crimea now — there aren't any tickets for the train or the plane, although trains and planes apparently do go there. People have more money now, but there aren't any more flights than there used to be; I've heard you can go for hard currency, but I've never had any in my life. And I haven't been all that keen on going there ever since a government commission was so quick to prove that there wouldn't be any more serious earth tremors in the Crimea, and commissioned an atomic power station ahead of schedule, obviously afraid that the government would change its mind after having poured in a hundred and seventy billion roubles extra above the projected cost — so you could pick up about seven hundred rads from a dip in the crystal clear water, and as usual the doctor would say you'd got sunburn and give you three days off work... And what if you had your kid with you? Never mind the rads, even, to hell with them, there was no drinking water at all. Everything provided by the canal dug through the arid steppe was swallowed up by the cooling circuit, and the shoreline from Kerch to Sudak, overheated by effluent, was soured by algae. That was announced quite openly at the Congress.

My wife was jealous of her own photographs. "Why drag up the past? I'm not interested in the past, it's past — I'm interested in now and what comes next." That's what she said to me a couple of years ago when I suggested we reminisce together for a while, take a stroll arm in arm around our common roots which were sinking irresistibly in the quagmire of days; once it even went as far as a row. It was her birthday and the guests had already left. Absolutely shattered after all the cooking, she bundled an over-excited Kir off to bed, then collapsed herself. By two in the morning I'd done all the washing up, after boiling the kettle five times — as usual in the summer there was no hot water because of the seasonal check on the mains. It was hot enough to wash in your own sweat if you sprinkled yourself with a little Pemoxol washing powder, or, if worse came to worst, something cheaper like Surzha. If you got a rash then it served you right for having delicate skin.

When I was sure that she was asleep, I retired to my study and played an invigorating game of patience. The door opened abruptly behind my back. The photographs on the table fluttered from the sudden slap of the draught. Still drunk, she asked from the doorway: "Masturbating again? You've got a real woman lying in bed there for you and here you are fingering these cold flat pictures..." The cognac was gurgling through the blood vessels in my brain too; the neurons, like tipsy yokels, harmonicas at the ready, stood up to their knees in it without boots — I didn't even attempt to hide away the dried up petals of my withered life, when I could wear a shirt for five·seasons and, even though it faded, it wouldn't disintegrate after the first wash; when a bunch of grapes and a tin of sardines was enough to make us happy for a whole glorious, sunny day by the sea, and they cost only seventy kopecks instead of forty-three roubles with a temporary residence stamp, for which you had to queue for twenty-four hours under a sign saying "Citizens of the USSR have the right to a holiday" and then pay a two hundred and seventy-three rouble state levy and a little over thirty roubles commission; when I was I sure that the well-being of my family depended on my honesty, my talent, my ability to work and the fact that they could be proud of me — after all I was discovering and inventing things that no-one in the world apart from me could discover... and effortlessly, of their own accord, these ideas blossomed as though in the hot sun, and bubbled as though they were boiling over a hearth, in my head, and pages by the dozen — the ones I later used to make the pram — were covered with words that were astonishingly intelligent and precise... Not taking very kindly this rather rude intrusion tipped me over the edge, and I quietly replied:

"But look how many of them there are, and anyway they're of someone I used to love..."

She got hysterical. She wept. She shouted: "Get out if you can't stand it any more! You think I'm washed out, don't you? Well just take a look at yourself. Get out — go wherever you like, even to your librarian girlfriend, if you think she's still waiting for you! Go on! Then we'll die! A woman on her own can't earn enough and find things to spend it on! I'll go crazy, or I'll drop dead, or get crushed to death in some crowd, and your son'll starve to death in an empty flat! Go on! Go and get on with your scribbling, one day you might be a professor!"

The well-being of one's family depends only on how quickly the numbers on one's arm become lower.

I put away the photos and went over to the window. I stood very straight but still felt as though my back was hunched under an unbearable weight. A hard damp log had swollen inside me and was choking the air out of my lungs; I couldn't draw breath; I couldn't forget even for a moment. I opened the window and the clamminess of the street met the clamminess of the flat and came to a standstill on the windowsill. The silent, sleeping houses hovered in the clear darkness. The empty streets, strangely wide, wound around below like grey ribbons. Nothing moving.

A couple came out of the house opposite.

It was a young man and a girl, both wearing trousers and topless. They were holding hands. They had only a few minutes left. The girl's wings were tensed, extended in a huge glittering cross — even from here you could see the underwing stirring in the thick still air, rippling in velvet waves and finding its bearings. They noticed me, the young man said something softly, and the girl laughed musically in the infinite silence of the night, waved a white hand at me and cried:

"Have a good time!" "Enjoy yourself, man!" shouted the bloke. He wasn't quite so far gone, and a huge shapeless trunk seemed to dangle from his shoulders down to the ground. They didn't turn my way again. The girl pressed her breast up against the man's elbow. They stood and waited, looking into each other's eyes.

Somewhere in the distance, beyond the district Party committee building, an empty lorry rumbled, the loose metal of its body clattering over the ripped up asphalt. Then everything was still and quiet again.

It's difficult to say exactly when the epidemic started. At first, when there were only isolated cases, the flights were dismissed as mystical fantasy or idle gossip, like the Bermuda Triangle or flying saucers — but now according to UNESCO figures, there were as many as a hundred and fifty throughout the country on some days. The new mystery had caught everyone out. Some talked about nitrates and the chemicalization of daily life in general; others mentioned the long-term effects of Chernobyl and Karachai, or else genetic mutation caused by the seemingly half forgotten and archive-bound traces of the nuclear tests of the fifties. Sometimes, in a whisper, people said it was most likely some kind of psychogenic effect. Was there any causative agent? If so, how was it transmitted? If not, on what principle did the illness select its victims? What exactly were the wing embryos? How did they attach themselves and take root? How did they sprout and what fed the process? What provided the lifting force and the energy for horizontal motion, which didn't follow the wind, it was no secret that the direction of flight, as far as could be gathered from the tardily compiled statistics, had never been into the centre of the country. Several ideologists had therefore alleged quite convincingly that the Slavic race had at last generated some kind of pressurised cleansing bioenergy field which squeezed all the pampered, thin-skinned, nervous half-breeds out to the backyards of the world... How and why did the

163

wings wither away painlessly within a few hours after the flight? There were no answers to these questions.

But it was impossible to prevent the consequences of the infection. Attempts were made, especially in the early days, haphazardly, to look out for sufferers about to take off and hold them down with something heavy — bulldozer tracks, excavators' buckets, concrete beams or railway sleepers... but physical injury was never avoided. Attempts were made to isolate sufferers in totally sealed rooms without windows — but the strength of the fully-fledged embryos was such that they either broke through the roof and shot the shredded individual into the sky like grapeshot from a cannon, or squashed them to death against the wall, themselves bursting and covering the room with blood and a strange shiny lymph... Attempts were made to amputate the embryos at various stages of maturity. One of these was carried out by an old school friend of mine, an outstanding cancer surgeon. At the categorical demand of her parents, who didn't want their child to be a pampered half-breed and thereby cast doubt on them, he tried to remove the seven-hour-old embryos from a happy, bubbling twelve-year-girl who was passionately fond of books... Her mother gassed herself afterwards. My friend gave up surgery forever, he turned grey, and his fingers would begin to tremble at the mere sight of any instruments. The girl took three days to die, screaming almost non-stop, the anaesthetic didn't work and no painkillers could counter the shock. The stitches on her back burst inexplicably time after time with a distinct snap — as if exploding from within, belching out on to the sheets and the wall of the ward blood that would not clot and fibrous lumps of some black substance, fragments of shoulder-blades and vertebrae, disintegrating like rotten wood...

The down on the girl's wings stood on end, bristling. The

girl soared gently upwards — the young man held her by the hand, clearly shaken. She said something, he made no reply and dragged her back down towards him with an effort. The trunk behind his back quivered. The girl laughed again, bent down beneath the flat, elastic roof of her wings and — now I couldn't see their heads very well behind the wings — she must have kissed him.

That seemed to be what he needed. The ugly lump on his back suddenly snapped open with a mighty hollow clap, thrusting out the vanes of two vast wings to the sides; the instantly tensed down was swept by a rapid wave of glittering sparks. Still holding hands, the two of them began to rise up like a candle-flame, slowly at first, then faster and faster. The young man started laughing and hooting — fit to wake up half the city; as they flew past my window, he put his hand in his pocket and, still howling triumphantly, hurled something at me. Two small flat shadows, like bats, fluttered past my face and fell limply to the floor.

It was their internal passports.

When I looked out again, all that could be seen in the ashen pre-dawn sky was the longish shape of two spots linked into one.

I put two heart pills in my mouth at once and crushed them between my teeth so they would dissolve more quickly.

And then — then I almost jumped out of my skin when my disconnected phone began ringing.

A Saviour

"Hello, Poimanov. Do you recognise my voice?"
"Of course, Alexander Yevgrafovich," I replied, as my limp legs gave way and I collapsed into an armchair. "Good morning."

"Very tactful of you," he said. "It's a long time till morning. But I couldn't get hold of you in the evening — to start with the phone was engaged, then there was no one home... So I made up my mind to bother you at night — as you know even better than I do, time is precious."

"Why is it?" I asked, pretending, with the insolence of a dying man, that I didn't know what he was talking about.

"We know all about your problems," he said.

An animal terror pummelled into my DNA spirals by so many, many master-torturers of the secret police blacked out the dawn for a second.

"How?" I wheezed.

"Oh, don't worry, no one's been informing on you this time," I could tell from his tone that he was smiling. "Your boss told me you were in a difficult spot. He couldn't get through on the phone and as he was rushing for his plane he passed the matter over to me, remembering how long we've known each other. I'd like to meet you as soon as possible — there's a chance we might be able to help you. Would you like me to come over?"

"Yes," I said. We really had known each other a long time. As far back as 1980, in my post-grad days, Alexander Yevgrafovich, then a captain I believe, was in charge of a little group which terrorised my mother into a heart attack when they politely turned my house upside down and removed a whole load of material which has now been published by all the best journals in a spirit of rivalry. There were no fatal consequences — I was even allowed to defend my thesis, but now and then, once every two years or so, Alexander Yevgrafovich would call me as a friend to ask me a question or give me some advice. The first few times I was nervous, then I got used to answering the questions with meaningless advice and responding to the advice with meaningless questions.

Fastidiously brushing aside the cockroaches with a newspaper, he sat down opposite me. The armchair gave a strangled squeak, as though the entire thousand-tonne State apparatus, complete with all its boilers, shafts, clutches, pistons and bolts, forged at ancient weapons factories, had been lowered into its fragile wickerwork hollow.

The State had come to me again. He had aged too.

"Nothing's changed," he said, looking around and lighting up a cigarette. "Everything's just as it used to be. Even this chair... Lots more books, though. Do you have time to read?"

"It depends."

"I know what you mean... I don't often get the chance either. I've only just read *The Gulag Archipelago* properly... we used to have to hand it in straight away for inventory. The old chap distorted the details a bit, but on the whole it's a sound piece of prose."

"Somehow I still haven't got around to rereading it."

"I see, if it's permitted, it's not interesting, is that it?" he grinned, holding his cigarette away to one side. The smoke rose almost straight up, without twisting. Like a candle flame. I said nothing. "Of course it's nothing new for you... although, I do seem to recall that in those days you flatly denied having read Solzhenitsyn. Well anyway, I'm sorry, but now it's mass entertainment." He took a drag, screwed up his eyes and became serious again. The chair squeaked. "So you'll be leaving us soon?"

I said nothing.

"Most unbecoming, my dear professor, most unbecoming, leaving the country at a time like this, abandoning it, when every decent citizen counts! And your family, your three-year-old son — will you toss him under the wheels of the locomotive of history?"

I said nothing.

"You've made a career. You're not badly paid for a scholar, and your wife, as a doctor, must bring something back to the nest. You're not exactly living in poverty. You're in the boss's good books. We've never interfered with you — you take part in symposiums, you defend the honour of Soviet science... So what's upset you? It's time you finished sowing your wild oats!"

"I'm no use to anyone," I said suddenly.

He even grunted. "What made you think you were? Of course you're not! These aren't the times for sitting in ivory towers! You won't feed the country on the fine arts. But imagine you're taken off somewhere where someone manages to find a use for you! Your articles are translated, you will have pupils coming here in awe of you... people write to you glowing letters from abroad! Although, between you and me, I think it's because they've nothing better to do... I can't imagine any normal healthy person being seriously interested in socio-structural ethics... But let's say they do find a use for you. Isn't that a slap in the face to us? Write here! Write for the desk drawer and for Christ's sake, maybe they'll come in useful some day!" He was getting excited: this was clearly a topic close to his heart. "Malevich's works rotted in the storerooms for fifty years — now it's one exhibition after another, and all raking in the dollars for the country! When Bulgakov was dying, he couldn't even get people to read his brilliant novel — and now look! It's been translated into every language in the world — that's Soviet literature for you, not that piss-artist Fadeyev! Or take that ... well, that guy who compiled the first dictionary of oriental swiggles... he happened to be executed as a Japanese spy, but now forty world-famous universities bow down before his musty manuscripts! And as for you?! You want everything handed to you on a plate while you're still alive! How pathetic!"

"Bulgakov's wife loved him," I said. "She saved his manuscripts. She went round all the publishers..."

"Well what can I say," he shrugged. "A romantic nature, a pre-revolutionary upbringing. Perhaps he was just, forgive me, a bit better in bed than you? Try eating more vitamins... instead of wasting your strength on those wings of yours. A little cognac always helps too — a shot before you... well, you know."

"Stop bothering me, Alexander Yevgrafovich. You think I'm doing it on purpose or something? Don't you know this is an illness?"

"Illnesses should be treated, Gleb Vsevolodovich."

"Yes," I agreed. Then suddenly burst out: "I'd sell my soul to the devil to get this hump cut off!... Do you understand? My soul!..." I swallowed hard. The day had been too hard — my nerves were in shreds, and once again my eyes were stung by tears welling up from inside like acid.

He began to go a bit easier.

"Well, that's fair enough. So I wasn't wrong about you."

"Let's have a smoke."

He offered me a fat packet of Rothmans glittering with blue and gold. He gave me a light.

I wished I could also feel at ease like that, with a cigarette dangling from my hand. That outburst had been intolerable and humiliating. But the cigarette didn't help. It shook in the air along with my fingers, and the smoke rose in a timid blur, not straight like a candle-flame. It just made my head spin more.

"I think we can help you," said Alexander Yevgrafovich.

"And how exactly?" I asked coldly, crossing my legs and trying to relax. Again I couldn't manage a relaxed pose appropriate to a conversation between equals — I had forgotten my hump; it thrust against the back of the chair and left me stooped forward.

"With therapy."

"I don't want to die either," I said. "Especially in agony."

"I'm not talking about an operation. We've developed a new method." Alexander Yevgrafovich took a long drag and waited a moment, carefully flicking his ash into the pencil stand. "Of course there's a risk, but... Basically we need a volunteer. When your boss phoned me I knew it was a stroke of luck. I had faith in you and even vouched for you to the general. For some reason... for some reason people who are critical of the country are more inclined to sacrifice themselves for it when the hour of reckoning comes."

We both inhaled deeply. Like equals. The ash sprinkled on my knees in a miniature snow shower.

"So what is this new method?"

"Halting the growth of the embryos. The hump, of course, will remain, but... you've seen hunchbacks, surely. Intelligent, well-mannered people, just physically handicapped. You must have plenty of other things wrong with you, physically. But you could stay here, with your friends and family!... But I don't need to explain that to you... The sooner we start, the smaller the hump will be, that's why I was in such a hurry. Otherwise it'll swell up at a terrible rate."

"Who developed the method?"

Alexander Yevgrafovich paused for a moment, then, with another precise flick of his ash, said:

"Experienced specialists."

"If the embryos are killed, the tissue could rot, causing infection... gangrene... I'm very skeptical."

"You'll be monitored."

He paused. Again we simultaneously inhaled.

"Of course there's a risk," he repeated. "It's not something we can test on animals."

A crimson wisp of dawn drifted gently into the room through a narrow gap between the houses opposite. The first tram of the day rumbled in the distance.

"You have the right to refuse," Alexander Yevgrafovich went on. "If you want to fly away, then fly. But if that's the case be man enough to admit to yourself that you want to go. And no-one will blame you..." His cheeks twitched, he suddenly slammed his hand down on the table, and with an agonized cry said: "But we must stop this hemorrhage, we must! If it carries on like this, there could be no one left, apart from hopeless alcoholics and top management!"

"I have one condition," I said hoarsely.

"I'm listening."

"I have to see my family."

He nodded.

"I see... I understand... Of course, Gleb Vsevolodovich. There's a Volga waiting with a driver in the yard. It's all yours."

I turned round. A stifling ashen sun was looming over the rooftops.

"In case of... undesirable consequences," said Alexander Yevgrafovich, "your family will be looked after. You can be sure of that, comrade Poimanov."

"I hope so," I said, and got up.

I couldn't take a single step. My legs seemed to be rooted to the spot.

Alexander Yevgrafovich understood; I could hear him raising himself ponderously from the chair behind my back. The chair squeaked in relief. It squeaked in just the same way, whether he was lowering his weight into it or taking off the strain.

"I'll be waiting in the car," said Alexander Evgrafovich, sighing heavily. Without looking at me he left the room, stooping slightly. A second later a door clanged in the corridor and there was absolute silence. Only the rising buzz of the distant city streets as they awoke.

I glanced round the study. I desperately wanted to look at

the photos. I straightened out the papers on the table, tied the strings on the folder containing the thesis I hadn't finished reading. Everything was in its place — the shelves and the books; and the pencil stand was still smoking slightly. Pink light flooded the walls. I picked up the receiver and put it straight back down on its silent stand. The phone was disconnected again.

The Volga drove along the rapidly filling streets, neatly overtaking packed trams and trolleybuses, slowing politely at narrow sections and flying across the bridges like a bird. Alexander Yevgrafovich tried to light up again, but blasts of air from the half open window kept putting out the lighter flame. Alexander Yevgrafovich clicked the lighter a couple of times and wound up the window with a sour expression.

"I'll have one too," I said, as if my rank already required him to offer me one. He held out the packet and offered me a light. We inhaled simultaneously.

"Been smoking long, Gleb Vsevolodovich?" he asked, without looking at me. It was awkward trying to smoke — the car jolted over the patchy asphalt, the back of the seat kept bashing against my humps like a boxer pounding his punching bag, and I kept missing my mouth with the filter.

"Anyone who breathes this air smokes," I replied. "The smell of cheap fags in your mouth day and night."

"So you don't like it here, after all," said Alexander Yevgrafovich bitterly.

I said nothing. We were jerked to the right in our seats as the Volga flew over Ushakovsky Bridge, hurtled through an amber light, and turned on to Primorsky Avenue almost without braking. This place, this very turning, meant so much to me — here rest was always just up ahead, the gulf, the endless sandy beaches scattered with boulders, the clean forest... To the left the green islands stretching out beyond the narrow mirror-like strip of the Little Neva drowning in floods of lilac; a seaside pavilion with an echo flashed past — my wife showed it to me. As the night progressed, the pavilion drifted along, slowly cleaving the grey water from the grey sky, while I broke off branches of blossom and said "Oh!" to which the pavilion's ceiling replied "Oh!" and my wife replied "Ooh!"

We flew past the Buddhist temple. The driver swung the wheel sharply to avoid something, but he was too late and we bounced up onto a warped and badly adjusted manhole.

"Does it hurt, your...?" Alexander Yevgrafovich asked wearily.

"No, it's completely numb. It's just awkward, that's all."

He opened the window a little, stuck his cigarette out, and the wind licked away the grey trail of ash.

"We have to hurry."

"I'm doing the best I can," said the driver. This was the first time I'd heard his voice.

"Not you, Volodya. You carry on." He turned to me," I'll give you an hour."

"Three," I said.

"I think haggling is inappropriate in these circumstances," said Alexander Yevgrafovich. I gave a wry chuckle, and Volodya suddenly burst out laughing and swung round to us, revealing a cheerful, swarthy face.

"Not many cars," I said. "Strange. There used to be a constant stream in weather like this..."

"There's not really anywhere to go any more," muttered Alexander Yevgrafovich gloomily. "The gulf's polluted, there's hepatitis in the lakes, or else meningococcus..."

"That's got nothing to do with it, Alexader Yevgrafovich," Volodya put in. "People go swimming in the LWR, at Pine Grove, and nothing happens to them."

"What's that?" I asked.

"The Liquid Wastes' Reservoir," replied Alexander Yevgrafovich. "A radioactive dump."

"That's the place! People even like it, they say it's warm... But now the road tax has gone through the roof again! Who can shell out that much except the mafia? And it's all just money down the drain! Just look at that road surface! That's a death trap, not a road surface! Private car owners are getting rid of their cars..."

We inhaled simultaneously.

"The only more or less convincing theory," said Alexander Yevgrafovich suddenly, "is that these flights are some kind of adaptive reaction. Our medics believe that the people who are falling ill are the ones whose adaptive capacity has been exhausted. If it's hot, a person sweats involuntarily. If it's cold, his teeth start to chatter and he jumps around. But if he is totally bugged, he involuntarily goes flying off God knows where... Something like that."

"Interesting," I muttered.

"Interesting as hell," he said gloomily; he lit a second cigarette and this time, without asking or waiting for me to ask, he offered me the packet. I lit up. My mouth stung and burned. "It's just beyond me. The Tsar oppressed and starved the population — they just sat there quietly and worked away. Stalin oppressed and starved the population — they still sat there and built communism, foaming at the mouth as they worked. And now, when they should all be really putting their backs into it... they've started flying off. Like little birds!"

"Maybe it's like radiation exposure," I suggested gloomily. "The doses go on building up... the strontium goes on settling in your bones, and you even start to get used to it, you think it's quite normal: as if you couldn't manage without strontium... and then it suddenly hits you.

"Well now," said Alexander Yevgrafovich slower and

somehow more softly, turning his entire frame towards me. "Tell me honestly. Off the record, as they say. Do you really think... our life is like... strontium?"

I said nothing.

"Let me tell you this!" he almost shouted when he realised he wasn't going to get an answer. "Over there they have other theories! In April a group of doctors from Los Angeles published an article in which they tried to prove that our flights were the beginning of some vast global process of intermigration. The species' genetic stock has supposedly sensed a regional stagnation of genetic information and is trying to counteract it. They claim that in the conditions of our rapidly changing technogenic world, man is not able to develop at the same pace as his own creations and adapt to them fast enough, so the adaptation has to be accelerated by strengthening the gene mutation factor, How? By intermingling the races and nations as quickly and chaotically as possible..."

"That's interesting too," I said, "but very complicated."

"For you it is," said Alexander Yevgrafovich, almost maliciously. "But those bourgeois philistines soon got things sorted out. Self-satisfied bastards! Just let them wait till they start flying off from their Iowas and New Zealands and coming down on the poorer land in Russia, or the Kulanda steppe... They'd be frightened out of their bloody skulls! They keep well clear of our flyers over there now — afraid of infection. The day before yesterday" — his face darkened visibly and he literally gnawed at his filter — "the day before yesterday there was the first reliably documented case of lynching. A lad came down near Caltagiron, his wings hadn't even come off yet. Those brutes... from a distance of forty metres, they burnt him to death with army flame-throwers, then spent ten minutes incinerating the body and the ground around it till the bones were burnt to a crisp! We happened to film it from a satellite..."

I said nothing. I thought of the young couple flying away today, so carefree in the early morning. Then I thought of Kirill.

"And I'll tell you something else," he went on. "The World Health Organization has recently made representations to our government twice already. Asking us to protect them somehow... They even went so far as to hint..." he shook his head, so angry that he couldn't find the right words. "Basically, that the Anti-Aircraft Defences should shoot the migrants down over the border. They don't want to dirty their own hands at the state level — the cowards! You see what they want — they want us to shoot down our own people with our own MIGs! In order to strengthen trust between East and West... And I'm not sure that our people have the guts to keep on refusing."

I was thinking about Kirill, and could think of nothing else. And then suddenly for some reason I remembered — with my whole physical being — how sweet and easy it was with Tonya the day before.

For a moment my heart slipped from the spit on which it had been transfixed in constant agony — into the dancing flames. In Sestroretsk we got stuck in a crowd of people. We couldn't understand what had got into them — some were laughing excitedly, some were sobbing, some were talking heatedly... In the distance a thickset, bearded man had got up on an urn and was shouting something, but we could hardly hear him.

"What's going on?" asked Alexander Yevgrafovich sharply, putting his head out through the open window as the Volga, zigzagging a little, made its way between the reluctantly separating people.

"We've strangled an AIDS carrier!" a dishevelled, unshaven youth cried with cretinous joy. He wore shorts and a torn T-shirt, on which a hastily affixed crucifix dangled upside down.

"What?" cried Alexander Yevgrafovich. The veins on his neck swelled and turned purple. The youth slammed his fist against the bonnet of the Volga ecstatically. Volodya, concentrating on his driving, shuddered and swore under his breath as if he'd been punched himself — but didn't even turn his head.

"Seemed decent enough, had a ring on her finger," a tidily dressed woman clucked readily as she trailed along beside us, one hand pushing a pram containing an indifferently staring child. "But she came out of the laboratory where they take the samples — crying! It's obvious, isn't it — she's positive! And our lads here've organized a watch in the bushes — twenty-four hours we're on the lookout!"

The bearded man in the distance was going at full throttle, shouting above the rumpus and waving his hand triumphantly — we caught snatches of what he said: "The physical and moral health of the Russian nation go hand in hand! The crisis demands drastic measures, and any will be justified because the stakes could not be higher! The Kremlin fawns on foreigners, and cannot be relied on for effective help! We have the right to ask: 'Gorbachev, where are the condoms you promised us? You gave them all to the Kazakhs!' The deadly AIDS virus, bred in secret Masonic laboratories in the days of Loris-Melikov, whose real name, we all know, was Leiba Meyerson..."

We broke through. Making up for lost time, Volodya took the car up to the limit. The asphalt flew beneath the hissing wheels as they hobbled over the potholes in the road.

"He's right, there aren't any condoms," observed Volodya. "That's the problem," Alexander Yevgrafovich replied with a heavy sigh.

"Are you doing anything at all about that lot?" I asked, pointing back at the crowd with my thumb.

Volodya guffawed bitterly. Alexander Yevgrafovich gazed straight ahead in silence.

"Gleb Vsevolodovich," he said after a while in a hopeless voice, "we just can't manage everything... What can I say!" his voice trembled with suppressed grief. "They've even frozen our tape stocks. We can only work on people we're already listening to. If you want to do a bit of extra bugging nowadays, then it's at your own expense..."

"What's life coming to?" said Volodya without turning round.

We spoke no more until we reached Roshchino.

The Meeting

This was heaven. The wooden hut was wallowing in the fresh greenery of June and the morning air was fragrant; real ordinary winged birds were twittering to each other in the silence. Kirill was standing on tiptoe, his chin resting on the edge of a brimming water butt. Holding a pinecone in his outstretched hand, he swished it around in the water with intense concentration.

"Kirill," I said, "hi."

He turned towards me.

"The cone's swimming," he informed me, as if we'd only parted half an hour ago. At first I froze in horror, thinking he'd had a fall and scraped the skin off his face. But it was his allergy. So much for the fresh air.

"Great," I said, "nice for the cone. But your sleeves are wet."

"No, they're not," he objected earnestly.

"Don't you want to do anything else?"

"Nope!"

His sleeves were wet through. I rolled them up. He had no numbers on his arms, so it didn't matter.

My wife was sitting by the gas stove with her legs crossed and her back to the door. She was reading something. Something was bubbling on the stove, and steam was rising from the slightly skewed lid of a saucepan. The gas was very low even though it was on full blast. The cylinder needed changing.

"Hello," I said. She turned round. As if we'd only parted half an hour ago.

"Hi," she said pleasantly without closing her book. "What brings you here?"

"I thought I'd drop in and see how you were," I explained, trying to stand bolt upright and somehow pull in the humps on my shoulder blades which threatened to betray me by stretching out my jacket. "A friend dropped me off... just for a little while. He's got some business here, he has a car. I'm going back in an hour."

"Fine friends you've acquired while we're away. With cars too. A man or a woman?"

She had got a bit of a tan. But she looked terribly tired, simply exhausted. She had dark bags under her eyes, her lips were pale...

"A man, believe it or not. How're you getting on? Are you well?"

"No worse than usual," she replied. "My throat's bad, especially in the mornings. If I have a warm drink it feels alright for a while... But Kirill's not sleeping. And he won't let me either, of course... Same as usual, I suppose."

"Poor thing... Are the mosquitoes biting?"

"Beginning to. The landlord says it's nothing yet, just wait a week or so..."

179

"What are you reading?"

She closed the book and stuck it into a pile of dishes on the table."

"I've no time to read here. Wash-cook-walk, walk-wash-cook..."

"Are you making soup?"

"Three days we've been using the same packet," she reached into the bucket behind the stove and showed me a packet of Novelty soup. The shop's absolutely bare. It was okay at first, but now they're coming in in their droves to their summer-houses. Have you brought anything?"

"No, I didn't think of it somehow."

"Oh great!" she rapped her knuckles on the table to show how thick I was. "There's a chicken in the freezer!"

"You know, I didn't even look in there."

"Bring something. We'll be eating grass soon."

"Tree bark."

"Goosefoot."

"Do you know what goosefoot looks like?"

"I'll ask the landlady."

"How do they get food?"

"God knows. I don't like to ask. You know yourself: everyone has their own little tricks... They gave me a bit a couple of times. They're not exactly eating well, either, you know..."

Kirill trudged by under the window, peddled with something on the bench by the door and glanced in at us.

"The cone's sunbathing," he said, walked up to his mother and climbed up into her arms with his shoes still on. She pushed him away listlessly. I got him by the shoulders.

"Don't, Kirill darling. Mummy's very tired."

"Mummy's very not tired."

"Mummy's very tired," I repeated convincingly, holding him facing me and looking him in the eye. He blinked and pursed his lips; he listened obediently. "Mummy spends all her time looking after us, and that takes a lot of strength. Don't bother her, she's making us yummy soup, she's so good at it..." When Kirill was still on the way, my wife and I spoke a lot about how beneficial it would be, right from birth, to say only good things about each other, in front of the child, as much and as often as possible, and be obvious in giving each other the tastiest morsels of food or the best place in front of the television... I stuck to this religiously and my wife tried her best too — but with a few modifications. She'd say:

"Daddy's very clever, only he's cack-handed," and leer at me slyly, or "Daddy's very good, but he's hassled." She gave a new meaning to the words about the tastiest morsels as well: "Daddy's deserved that nice piece of meat today..." or "Daddy earned that lovely slice honestly..." At first I used to get upset, but soon I got used to it; and I couldn't start a row every time over quips like that, especially since they came out quickly, innocently... and, to be perfectly honest, they were often justified.

Kirill listened patiently, got fed up and went outside, shutting the fragile door carefully behind him.

"He's talking more clearly now," I remarked, "I can make out almost all the words. A change of scenery certainly encourages development, it's good we decided to take this cottage..."

I stopped short. It was no time to be talking about the benefits of a change of scenery.

But my wife didn't take any notice of what I said. She had unbuttoned her dressing gown to the waist and dropped it off her shoulders. She wasn't wearing a bra.

"You've certainly got a bit of a suntan," I said. "Now I can see it properly."

"Look at this though," she said, lifting her left breast on

181

her palm. "A little lump. It's been painful to touch for three days, and I can't get a proper look at it, Kirill and I broke the mirror."

I looked.

"It's a blackhead. It's a bit inflamed. Your bathing-suit must have made it sore."

"Yuck, that's disgusting... Squeeze it out."

"No, I can't. I'd be afraid to hurt you."

She bit her lip and pulled her dressing gown back on to her shoulders.

"Okay," she said, fastening her buttons. "I can't ask you to do anything... I'll try to beg a mirror from the landlord. Stay here and make sure the soup doesn't boil over... Anyway, it's good you came. Look, the cylinder's almost run out. Could you nip down to get a new one? You can use the car."

"I'll have a try," I said. "I can ask anyway."

"There's an empty one over there in the corner. There's the coupon, there's the user's license." She got up wearily and walked to the door. "Enjoy yourself."

"I'll try."

"What a stoop you've got," she remarked as she passed me. "I keep telling you..."

I smiled.

She snorted. The door gave a protracted creak, the badly fixed glass in the window rattled.

I lay down on the stove-bench. The sun was shining brightly through the foliage and joyous patches of light lay motionless on the wall, undisturbed by any wind. The saucepan murmured gently to itself. It was so cosy, so peaceful and quiet, that I thought I might even be able to go to sleep. I'd got there anyway. My legs throbbed gently. My head buzzed. I seemed to feel a faint trickling or rippling sensation in the depths of my spine. Kirill came in, but I didn't even have the strength to turn my head to face him. He stomped up to me and stood beside the bench, sniffling as he looked me tenderly in the eye."

"Ooh!" I said.

He laughed and answered:

"Ooh!"

"Ee-ee!" I said, sticking out my jaw and tickling his tummy with two fingers. It peeped out from his shirt like the moon through the clouds. He squirmed away. He bent over me; he grinned, and slowly stuck his nose against mine. When our noses touched, he said tenderly:

"Daff."

"Daff," I replied delightedly. That was our greeting. His nose was small and smooth, his eyes were large. But his cheeks and chin looked as if they had scalded. You could make a great discovery, you could hang yourself, you could go out onto the square with damning slogans — but that won't cure a skin allergy. It can only be cured by reducing the quantity of numbers on our arms. Kirill climbed onto the bench — I gave him a hand up. He snuggled under my armpit. I heard my wife's obsequious voice from the yard: "I just don't know how to thank you... You've saved my life..." I was about to sit up on my elbow and look through the window to see what it was she was so pleased about — but I lay back down, suddenly realising that I wasn't interested. What did it matter! Maybe someone had squeezed out the blackhead. Kirill sat there, propping me up with one shoe and happily making faces at me. The thought that I was most likely sitting with him for the last time was unbearable: I tried to forget it and smother my feelings in making faces back at him.

My wife came in with a plastic bag and flopped down heavily on to a rickety chair.

"Aagh," she said, then suddenly gave me a suspicious glance and smiled almost guiltily. "I'm at the end of my tether...

My knee's aching. I can't remember banging it on anything...
Oh well. The owners let me have a dozen potatoes. A treat
for the man I love."

"Oh no thanks, you have them..."

"If you say so." She stood the bag against the wall, and
its contents rumbled and bumped as it slumped on the floor.
"They'll come in handy... But next time you must bring that
chicken."

"Okay."

"How are you managing? All right?"

"Sure," I replied. "I'm very busy."

"Get anything useful done yet?"

"No..."

"We're not there and you still can't get anything done.
Pity," she sighed, then, wiping her knee, looked anxiously at
the stove. "It was my teenage dream — to wipe the sweat
from the brow of my genius."

"Well there was something... Those Frenchmen are arri..."

"We're right out of gas. Are you going to fill the cylinder?"

"Nope," said Kirill, for some reason deciding the question
was aimed at him.

"Yep," I said and got up.

Volodya slouched with his backside against the bonnet,
smoking slowly, and looking serenely round at the tranquil green
countryside. Alexander Yevgrafovich was dozing silently with
his head resting on the back of the rear seat and his mouth
slightly open. But he was dozing professionally — he heard
me from about five paces away, shut his mouth, opened his
eyes, and stepped lightly.

I felt a complete idiot.

"Well, how is she?" he asked tactfully.

"Not too bad," I replied.

"Brave woman."

"Volodya chucked away his fag end, looked at me respectfully and climbed into his seat.

"The thing is," I mumbled, holding out the red, slightly peeling cylinder. "They're out of gas, so I need to get this cylinder filled first. And you know... since we've got the car... an hour or so either way won't make any difference, the hump doesn't bother me. I need to get them a chicken from town — I left it in the fridge at home."

Volodya's hands slipped from the steering wheel. Alexander Yevgrafovich swallowed painfully.

"Are you serious?"

"They've got nothing to eat!" I shouted, shaking the cylinder.

"What's the matter with her, can't she buy a chicken herself?" shouted Alexander Yevgrafovich, turning purple and reaching into his pocket nervously for his cigarettes.

"Have you been in the local shop? All they've got there is imitation flowers, hand-made candles from cooperatives and cheap cigarettes!"

"We should at least be grateful for the cigarettes!" Alexander Yevgrafovich muttered, puffing on a Rothman. His hands were shaking with indignation.

"Give me a cigarette."

He hid his packet away in his pocket. He peered fixedly at me through narrowed eyes and exhaled. As he did once before.

"Listen, Poimanov, You remember those books we took off you?"

God knows why I didn't clock him one with the cylinder there and then. Probably because I was very tired.

"I remember," I said. The issues of *Continent* with Grossman, Zamyatin, both the Orwell novels in the Posev edition... *Darkness at Noon* in typescript... A couple of excerpts from Roy Medvedev..."

"All fine works of literature!" cried Alexander Yevgrafovich, waving his cigarette right under my nose. "Intelligent and honest! And you were drawn to it! You took risks, conscious risks — but you were drawn, you wanted understanding, truth, something higher! Something substantial! I remember you when you were brought in — a young pup, shaking all over, but you were proud! Every step, you were in control — a hundred per cent, even your voice didn't tremble. And it was written all over your face: now they're going to torture me! And the next day The Voice of America will tell the entire country about me — a prisoner of conscience, the final humanist in the evil empire... I respected you, I swear! And you never said where you got those books! Turned yourself inside out but never breathed a word! I was going to write a report on you! That would've brought you down, it always does... But your boss put in a word for you. He's such a talented lad, he said, he'd think better of it. And look where you are now! You've got everything: talent, status... all the books you could possibly want. You've been given freedom, freedom! You should be sweating blood for your country! And what's on your mind? Chickens, chickens!" he taunted in a nasal voice. "It makes me want to throw up."

He stopped and inhaled again greedily. I followed every movement of his cigarette. I don't know what for. Probably because he didn't let me have one.

"So that's it, Poimanov," he said, and trod his fag end under foot. He grabbed the door-handle. "You can go to hell. Nobody'll ever be able to use you anywhere. You're finished."

"Why should anyone have to use me? I'm a living being!"

Taking advantage of his boss not being able to see him, Volodya gave me a meaningful look and tapped the side of his head. "Until you've proved your value to your country," said Alexander Yevgrafovich harshly, "whether you're alive or not is nobody's concern but your own. First heroism, and then chickens, if the authorities can find some to spare or consider it worthwhile taking them away from someone. But you want it the other way round: first chickens, then, if you're just happy to feel like it — heroism. That won't keep us a great power. We don't have enough chickens to go round. Nor should we have."

There was something amazingly familiar about those words: "Today Daddy earned this piece of meat honestly."

How alike they are, people who do not love, but use. Who despise, but need. They're so harassed and emotionally brutalised that they can't help trying to live like parasites.

At one time I used to repeat over and over to myself every day that we are always responsible for those we have tamed. These words of Saint-Exupery's, which had made such an impression on me as a child, used to cheer me up a bit. But in real life things turned out to be different: we were always responsible for those who had tamed us.

"But doesn't it worry you, Alexander Yevgrafovich, that instead of being heroes everyone's either ripping off everything they can, or snatching everybody else's stuff?"

His eyes narrowed, as if he were taking aim.

"We'll sort things out," he said with conviction.

"Have you," I looked at the Volga, the driver, who'd been frantically giving me warning signals, and the fag end, its golden strip gleaming handsomely, "done many heroic things?"

He shrugged and replied in a deadpan voice:

"My whole job is heroism..."

"I see," I said.

"What do you see?" he flared up again. "You don't see anything? The cistern in my toilet's been overflowing for five days! All the pipes are rotten... And the plumber, the bastard, doesn't listen to the radio, not even Soviet radio, doesn't read

187

the papers and hasn't touched a book since school... He boozes on vodka and does bugger all. You can't frighten him with anything..." He sighed a long hoarse sigh as he got into the car. "What a bloody life... to the office," he said with a completely different, steely voice, and slammed the car door viciously.

And than I realised what had happened.

Something seemed to snap inside me. I ran after them. I was too weak to run, the cylinder banged against my thigh, and the humps under my jacket shook like the humps of a galloping camel.

"Stop!" I cried. "Please stop! I don't want to leave! They'll be finished without me, finished! Never mind the chicken, let's just get the gas! CURE ME!!!"

Its suspension rocking and clattering on the sandy ruts of the village, the State drove away from me. Of its own accord. The dust settled. I stopped to get my breath back.

The lilacs were in bloom.

The lilacs were in bloom around the seaside pavilion too. "Oh!" I said. "Oh!" replied the echo from the dome. "Oooh!" replied my wife, and buried her happy face in the fragrant bushes...

Got to pull myself together. And fast.

It was 60 kilometres to town, I could walk it in a day and a half. And a day and a half back. I should just about make it. Only the chicken could go off on the way back, and I couldn't carry the whole fridge. Bloody hell, even if I could, where could I plug it in on the way? Well, if it goes off that's too bad. I'll roast it before I leave.

And then there's the cylinder.

They'll take out the phone. There's no way I can get to Sinopskaya Street today, so they'll take it out, the bastards. How's my family going to manage then? If they have to call an ambulance, say..."

I'd definitely have to take all the money out of my account. Leave some at home and bring the rest here.

Put all my notes in order. Someone might find them useful sometime.

I wonder how high I'll fly? I'd like to go really high, into the stratosphere, where I'd suffocate...

Mustn't forget the coupon for the tickets.

Vyacheslav RYBAKOV (b. 1954) is a resident of St Petersburg. A graduate of the Department of Oriental Studies at Leningrad University he is mostly known for his philosophical science fiction. He could only start publishing in post-Soviet years although his earlier stories were available in samizdat. A prolific writer Rybakov has a number of prize-winning sci-fi novels to his name and numerous short stories.

Remembering
the Soviet Past

Georgy VLADIMOV

A General and His Army

excerpt from the novel and summary

Translated by Arch Tait

What picture did the words "General Headquarters" conjure up in the mind of a driver sitting numbly in his seat, peering dully at the road ahead, blinking his red eyelids and trying periodically with the doggedness of a man who has not slept for a long time to drag the cigarette butt glued to his lip back to life? Probably in the very words he heard and imagined something high and enduring, soaring above the Moscow rooftops like a fairy-tale turret, while at its foot would sprawl the long-anticipated car park, a courtyard surrounded by a wall and covered with vehicles like the court of a coaching inn which he had once read something about. Somebody would constantly be arriving or taking their leave, and the endless chit-chat between the drivers would be well up to the level of that which their bosses the generals would be exchanging in quiet, dimly lit chambers behind heavy blinds on the eighth floor. To venture in imagination beyond the eighth was beyond the reach of Driver Sirotin, his own life having been lived hitherto at the ground (and only) floor level, but neither would he have the brass located any lower. They must surely be allowed a view of a good half of Moscow from their windows.

How cruelly disappointed Sirotin would have been to learn that General Headquarters was buried away deep underground at Kirovskaya metro station, that mere plywood partitions divided off its cramped offices, while its lunchrooms and cloakrooms were tucked away in railway carriages. It would have seemed reprehensible, meaning as it did that it was deeper underground than Hitler's bunker. It would have been quite wrong for our Soviet Headquarters to be thus tucked away because the German HQ was justly derided precisely for being in a bunker. In any case, how could a bunker inspire the same trepidation with which our generals would proceed into the entrance hall, their knees half giving way beneath them.

It was there, at the foot of the turret where he would

have positioned himself and his jeep, that Sirotin anticipated discovering what fate now held in store for him, perhaps again welding his destiny with that of his General, or just as possibly decreeing it a separate course. If he kept his ears open he might well pick up some useful intelligence from the other drivers, just as he had picked up on this journey ahead of time from a colleague in Headquarters' motor transport division. Settling down for a lengthy smoking session while they waited for a conference to end, they had first talked of abstract matters. Sirotin recalled expressing the view that if you were to mount the engine from an eight-seater Dodge in a jeep you would get a great little buggy you couldn't wish to better. His colleague had not denied this but observed that the engine of a Dodge was on the large side and might well not fit under the hood of a jeep. You would have to make a special panel to cover it, and they then jointly concluded that things were best left as they were. From here the conversation moved on to changes in general and whether they were all that good a thing. Here, too, his colleague pronounced himself a believer in tradition, in which connection he hinted that they in the Army could expect some changes too, literally in the next few days, and the only question was whether they would be for the better or for the worse. What precisely these changes might be his colleague did not let slip, saying only that a final decision had yet to be taken, but from the way he lowered his voice you could gather that the decision when it came would issue not even from Front-line Headquarters but from a higher level, perhaps indeed from such a height as the two of them were never destined to see. "Although," his colleague suddenly said, "you just might. If you get to Moscow, tell the old girl hello from me." To register astonishment at the idea that he could possibly find himself in Moscow in the middle of the present push would not have been commensurate with Sirotin's status as the Commander-in-Chief's driver. He just nodded, while secretly resolving that his colleague couldn't have any hard information, had heard some distant echo, and might indeed have been the origin of it himself. But it had proved to be no echo, and he was ordered to Moscow for good and real! Being a prudent sort, Sirotin had already started making preparations on the off chance: he fitted new tyres, "Mother's own", American tyres which he had been keeping until they would drive into Europe, and welded on a bracket for an extra fuel canister, handy on a long journey. He even pulled on the tarpaulin they usually left behind whatever the weather because the General disliked it: "It's as muggy as a dog kennel under that thing," he said, "and it hinders dispersal," that is, jumping out over the sides at the double if you came under fire or were being bombed. So, all in all, it was not that great a surprise when the General suddenly ordered, "Harness her up, Sirotin. Let's have a bite to eat and then we're off to Moscow!"

Sirotin had never once seen Moscow, and was both delighted at having his long held, indeed pre-war ambition realized, and at the same time apprehensive for his General abruptly recalled to GHQ, to say nothing of himself. Who else might he end up driving, and might he not do better to ask to transfer to driving a thirty-hundred-weight truck, where you got less hassle, and there was also a slightly better chance of staying alive in an enclosed cabin, which would keep out at least some of the shrapnel. He also had a strange sense of relief and even of a kind of deliverance which he did not care to admit even to himself.

He was not the General's first. Two earlier drivers had come to a bad end if you counted from Voronezh, and that after all was where the Army's history began. Before that, in Sirotin's opinion, there had been no Army and no history, just sheer wretched chaos. So then, since Voronezh the General himself had not suffered a scratch but two jeeps had, as they said in the Army, been shot from under him, on both occasions along with their drivers, and one time also with his aide. A persistent legend had grown up that the General had a charmed life, and confirmation of this was seen in the deaths of those who had been right next to him, literally a couple of paces away. Admittedly a more detailed account revealed a slightly different picture: the jeeps had not exactly been shot from under him. The first time his vehicle had suffered a direct hit from a long-distance high explosive shell. The General was not actually in the jeep when it happened, having been held up for a minute at the divisional command post. He emerged to find everything a shambles. And the second time, when the vehicle was wrecked by an anti-tank mine, he had just got out to walk along the road and check how satisfactorily the self-propelled artillery was camouflaged before an attack. He ordered the driver to move away out of the open, and the idiot went and drove off into a grove of trees. The road had been cleared of mines but the sappers had left the grove as no traffic was projected to pass through it... What difference did it make, Sirotin wondered, whether the General was too early or too late to get himself blown up: that was all part of the charm. The trouble was, it did not extend to those accompanying him, only took their common sense away. When you thought about it, his invulnerability had been the cause of their death. The experts had already worked out that almost ten tons of metal went into killing a single soldier in this war. Sirotin did not need them or their calculations to know how difficult it is to kill a man at the front. You had only to last out three months or so to know not to listen to the shrapnel or bullets, but to listen to yourself, to that inexplicable chill which warned you, and the more inexplicable it was the more you could rely on it, to get the hell out of somewhere. It might root you out of the world's

197

safest dug-out with seven layers of logs in its roofing, and send you instead to some totally useless ditch to shelter behind an insignificant clump of grass, and the dug-out would promptly be reduced to a log pile, while the tuft of grass protected you from harm. He knew that this crucial survival mechanism lost its edge if not constantly used, if you were away from the front line for as little as a week, but while this General of his was not obsessive about being at the front, he certainly had no aversion to it. Sirotin's predecessors could not have got used to it. So it must have been their own silly faults. They had not listened to themselves.

As far as the mine incident was concerned, you didn't know whether to laugh or cry. It was against regulations and against common sense. Could he imagine himself driving off the road into a grove of birch trees for cover? He could not, even if every shrub had a notice stuck in front of it proclaiming: "Checked for Mines: Clear". There might well be none for the guy who had checked the area out, he would be well out of harm's way by now; but you could bet your bottom dollar that in his haste he had left just one little anti-tank mine specially for you. But supposing he had swept the grove from end to end with his belly button, everyone knew that once in a while even an unloaded rifle goes off. The shell took more explaining. Choosing to argue with a mine was something you did yourself, but a shell chose you. Some unknown hand traced its trajectory beneath the heavens, corrected a slight error with a rippling of the breeze, deflecting it two or three thousandths to the right or to the left, and all in just a few seconds. How were you to sense that your one and only, the one chosen for you by destiny herself, had already left the barrel and was rushing towards you, whistling, droning, except that you heard nothing while other men needlessly ducked their heads. But why would you have stayed in the open when something held the General up at that command post? It was that same inexplicable sixth sense that would have made you stay, that was what had to be recognized.

In these musings Sirotin was invariably conscious of his superiority over his two predecessors, but who was to say that this was any more than the eternal dubious sense of superiority of the man who is still alive over the man who is dead. That did occur to him too. The trouble was that it was something you were not allowed to feel. It could disorientate you even worse, driving away that saving chill. The science of survival demanded that you be always humble and never weary of begging to be spared and then, maybe, you might be all right. The main thing, however, that the chill whispered constantly to him was that he would not see out the war with this General. Why not? If you could have put a name to the reasons there would, of course, be nothing inexplicable about it... Somewhere, some time it would happen, there were no two ways about that. It was always at the back of his mind, and was why he was so often morose and depressed. Only a very experienced eye would have seen behind his bravado, behind the extravagantly dashing, gallant appearance, to that concealed presentiment. Somewhere the rope must have an end, he told himself. It had been winding round and round for a long time now; he had been too lucky, and how he longed to be let off with just a wounding, and after his hospitalisation to start afresh with a different general who did not have such a powerful charm protecting him.

These were basically the misgivings, there was nothing else that Driver Sirotin imparted to Major Svetlookov from the army counter-intelligence unit, Smersh, when the latter called him in for a talk or, as he preferred to put it, "for a bit of a gossip about one or two things." "Only, you know what," he said to Sirotin, "you can't have a proper talk with anyone in the unit. Somebody's bound to come charging in with some crap. Let's see if we can't find a better spot. But in the meantime, not a word to anyone, because you never can tell, eh?" Their meeting took place in a small wood not far from headquarters. Major Svetlookov sat himself down on a fallen pine tree and took his peaked cap off, turned his stern, bulging forehead with the red line left by the cap-band towards the autumn sun, and seemed thereby to neutralize his superior rank, disposing one to honest and open conversation. For all that, he motioned to Sirotin to sit down on a lower level than himself, on the grass.

"Come on then," he said. "Tell me all about what's on your mind, and why our soldier boy is sad at heart? I can see something's bugging you, not much gets past me..."

It was not wise for Sirotin to be talking about things, which the science of survival bade you keep silent about, but Major Svetlookov immediately saw his problem and was sympathetic.

"Never mind, never mind," he said without a trace of irony, vigorously tossing his flaxen locks as far back as he could. "We quite understand all this mysticism. We are all superstitious, not just you, the Commander-in-Chief is too. And I can tell you a secret: his life is not all that charmed. He does not care to remember it and does not wear the badges he was awarded for being wounded, but he was, as the result of his own stupidity, in "forty-one, near Solnechnogorsk. He earned himself eight bullets in the stomach. You didn't know? His orderly didn't tell you? He was there when it happened. And there was I thinking you had no secrets from each other. Ah well, I expect Fotii Ivanovich ordered him to keep it quiet. So we'll keep quiet about it too, eh? Here, listen," he suddenly glanced down at Sirotin with a merry but piercing gaze. "I don't suppose you are, you know, holding out on me? Keeping back the one thing that really matters about Fotii Ivanovich?"

"What would I have to keep back?"

"You haven't noticed him behaving strangely lately? I should mention that one or two people have. But you haven't, nothing at all?"

Sirotin shrugged, which could equally well have meant that he had not noticed anything, or that he did not see it was a matter for the likes of him. He had, however, detected a danger, as yet unclear, which threatened the General, and his first impulse was to distance himself if only for a moment in order to understand what threat there might be to himself. Major Svetlookov was peering straight at him, and it was not easy to meet the gaze of those piercing blue eyes. He had evidently figured what was behind Sirotin's confusion, and this gaze was to put him back in his place as a member of the entourage of the Commander-in-Chief, which was the place of a devoted servant who trusted his chief implicitly.

"Don't tell me about sundry doubts or suspicions or miscellaneous other nonsense," the Major said firmly. "I only want facts. If there are facts, it is your duty to alert me to them. The Commander is an important man. He has done a lot of good things, he is valuable, and that puts us under an even greater obligation to do our utmost to support him if he has stumbled in some respect. Perhaps he is tired. Perhaps right now he needs special care and attention. He is not going to ask us for it himself, is he, and we might not notice, we might miss an opportunity, and then we would kick ourselves afterwards. It is, after all, our job to look after every man in the Army, and as for the Commander, well, it's obvious, isn't it?"

Who precisely this "we" was who had to look after every man in the Army, he and the Major or the whole of the Army's Smersh in whose eyes the General had evidently somehow "stumbled", Sirotin did not know and, for some reason, did not feel he could ask. Their talk was ever more obviously drawing him in a particular direction, towards something mightily unpleasant, and the thought vaguely occurred to him that he had already taken a small step towards treachery in having agreed to come here to "gossip".

From the depths of the forest there came the damp freshness of the breeze that preceded evening, and into it a cloying sickly stench insinuated itself. That wretched burial detail, Sirotin thought, they had collected our own dead but not bothered to pick up the Germans. It would have to be reported to the General, he would teach them not to fall down on the job. They hadn't felt like picking up the corpses while they were fresh, and now everyone else had to hold their noses.

"Tell me one thing, though," Major Svetlookov said, "what do you think his attitude is towards death?"

Sirotin looked up at him in astonishment.

"Same as the rest of us, I suppose."

"You do not know," the Major said severely. "The reason I ask is that just now the protection of our command personnel is very high on the agenda. There has been a special, classified directive from GHQ, and the Supreme Commander has stressed on more than one occasion that commanding officers are not to put themselves at risk. Thank God, this is not 1941, we have worked out how to force a river crossing, and that there is no reason for the commanding officer to be there in person. What was the point of Fotii Ivanovich making the crossing along with everybody else under fire? Perhaps he was deliberately placing himself at risk? From desperation of some kind, from fear of failing to cope with the operation? Or maybe, you know, he might have gone a bit odd. Who's to say. To some extent it would be understandable, this is after all a very complex operation..."

It might not have seemed to Sirotin that the operation was actually that much more complicated than any other, and it seemed to be going perfectly smoothly, however those up there at the great height from which Major Svetlookov had condescended to him might well have considerations of their own.

"A one-off incident perhaps," the Major was meanwhile wondering aloud. "No, there is a pattern behind it all. When the Commander-in-Chief of the Army moves his command post ahead of the divisional posts, what option does the divisional commander have? He moves even closer to the Germans; and the regimental commander has to move in right under their noses. Are we trying to show off to each other how brave we are? Or take another example: you often drive up to the frontline without an escort, not using an armoured car, without even taking a radio operator with you. You're asking to be ambushed, or you might be trying to cross over into German lines. How are we to establish afterwards that there was no treachery going on, and that it was all just a mistake? We have to foresee these possibilities, and head them off. And that means you and I first and foremost."

"What can I do about it all?" Sirotin asked with some relief. The subject of their talk had finally become clear to him and was close to his own anxieties. "It's not up to a driver what route he chooses."

"It certainly isn't for you to give instructions to the Commander-in-Chief! But it is within your competence to know in advance where you're making for, isn't it? Fotii Ivanovich does say to you, doesn't he, 'Harness her up, Sirotin, we are heading over to the hundred and eighth?' Doesn't he?"

Sirotin was properly impressed by such knowledgeability, but objected,

"Not always. Sometimes he gets in first and then tells me where we are going."

"Quite true, but you don't just have one destination in the course of a day, you inspect three or four positions: half an hour in one then, maybe, a good two hours somewhere else. There's nothing to stop you asking him whether you are going to be there long and where you are going next, as if you want to be sure you are going to have enough gas. And there's your opportunity to ring through."

"Ring through where?"

"To me, of course. We'll exercise general oversight, and contact the position that you are heading for at any particular time so they can send someone out to meet you. Of course, I realize there are times when the Commander-in-Chief wants just to turn up unannounced, to catch everyone with their pants down. One thing does not need to get in the way of the other. We have our own job to do. The divisional commander will not know when Fotii Ivanovich is going to show up, but we will."

"I thought," Sirotin said smiling uneasily, "that your job was catching spies."

"Our job takes in everything," the Major said. "The main thing is that we should always know what is happening and that the Commander should never be left without our protection. Will you promise me that?"

Sirotin furrowed his brow, stalling for time. There seemed nothing wrong if every time, no matter where he and the General were heading, Major Svetlookov should be in the know, but he didn't at all like the idea that he would be having to report behind the General's back. Sirotin asked straight out:

"What do you mean, keep it secret from Fotii Ivanovich?"

"Uh-huh," the Major mocked him. "You don't like the idea, but the whole point is to keep it secret. Why trouble the Commander with it?"

"I don't know," Sirotin said. "It doesn't seem right, somehow."

Major Svetlookov heaved a long sad sigh.

"And I don't know either, but I do know that's how it has

to be. So there we are. There used to be political commissars in the army and it was all so simple. What I have been trying to get out of you for an hour already the commissar would have promised me without a second thought. Nobody would have found it strange in the least. The commissar and counter-intelligence worked hand and glove. Now military commanders are trusted more, and it has become infinitely more difficult to do our job. You can't just drop in on a member of the Military Council. He is a general too, and values that more than being a commissar. You're not going to get him to waste his time with this sort of nonsense. But we lesser mortals have to get on with it and work away on the quiet. Yes, our Supreme Commander has made life difficult for us, but he has not let us off doing our duty."

The sadness and concern in the Major's voice and his openness and also the burdensomeness of the task designated by none other than the Supreme Commander all came together to leave Sirotin feeling he did not have a leg to stand on.

"Yes, but phoning through, you know... The signaller's line is nearly always busy, and when it is free he's not just going to let you use it. And you have to tell him where you are phoning to, and before you know it, it will get back to Fotii Ivanovich. No, it's..."

"What do you mean, `No'?" Major Svetlookov thrust his face towards him, instantly amused at such naivety on Sirotin's part. "What a funny fellow you are! Are you really going to go and say, `Please put me through to Major Svetlookov in Smersh?' That really would land us in the soup. The simplest way is to play the lovesick soldier phoning his lady. That line works every time. Do you know Kalmykova in the military police? The senior typist?"

Sirotin had a vague recollection of a bosomy, flabby and, in his twenty-six-year-old eyes, ancient old bag with an unrelentingly bossy expression and thin, pursed lips yelling authoritatively at the two girls junior to her.

"What, not your type?" The Major smiled, a blush rapidly suffusing his cheeks. "She has her admirers, you know. They even say she's dynamite in the sack. Let's face it, love is blind. In any case we are not running a convent. When we do move into Europe, this year or next, they have monasteries there specially for women. More precisely, for virgins, being as how these lady monks, `Carmelites' they are called, give a vow to stay virgins till the day they die. Think of the sacrifice! So their purity is guaranteed. Choose whichever one you fancy, you can't go wrong."

The austere Carmelites somehow got associated in Sirotin's mind with caramels, and seemed very enticing and sexy indeed. For all that he just couldn't see himself making a pass at Flabby Breasts, or even chatting her up over the telephone.

"Sehr gut," the Major conceded. "Let's think of an alternative. How do you fancy Zoechka? Not that one that works for the MPs, the one who's a telephone operator at headquarters. With the curls."

Now those ash-blond curls spiralling down from her forage cap on to the curve of her little porcelain forehead, the surprised look in her little eyes which yet sparkled so brightly, the neatly taken in tunic with a single button undone (never two, which might have got her into trouble), the little custom-made chamois boots, and the slender manicured fingers, that was all much closer to his heart.

"Zoechka," Sirotin repeated dubiously. "I thought she was going with that bloke from the operations section, practically married to him."

"That `practically' has just one secret obstacle, a lawful wedded wife in Barnaul who is already bombarding the political section with letters. And two dearly beloved offspring. We'll have to do something about that. So... You wouldn't turn up your nose at Zoechka? I suggest you get stuck in straight away. Roll along to see her, start building bridges — and then phone from wherever you can. You think the signaller isn't going to connect you, the driver of the Commander-in-Chief? All right. You just don't need to be a shrinking violet, remember your status in the army. Just give Zoechka the old `How I miss you, long to kiss you' routine, and then drop in in passing something along the lines of, `I've got to go now, sweetheart. Ring you again within the hour from Ivanovo.' There's a lot of loose talk goes through signals, one more slip won't make any difference. But we can even get round that — we'll work out a code later, a password for each position. Anything you don't understand?"

"No, but somehow..."

"What do you mean, `No but somehow...' Eh?" The Major was suddenly irate. Somehow it did not seem in the least surprising to Sirotin that the Major already had the right to get angry with him for being slow and tear him off a strip. "Do you think I'm doing all this for my own benefit? I'm doing it to safeguard the life of the Commander-in-Chief of the Soviet Army! And yours, incidentally, also. Or are you seeking death too?"

He heatedly slashed at his boot with a stick which whistled as he brought it down. God knows where that had come from. The sound it made was nothing, but for some reason Sirotin cringed inwardly and got a sinking feeling in his belly, the same dismal, anguished feeling produced by the whistling of a shell after it has left the barrel of an artillery piece and splashes down into marshy ground. The sounds are all the more significant and terrifying precisely because the roar of splintering steel and the splash as a fountain of brackish water rises in the air and the rending of branches severed by shrapnel are by now no longer any threat to you. You have been missed again. This meticulous, limpet-like Major Svetlookov who could see everything, had recognized what was bugging Sirotin and making his life a misery, but he had also intuited something more important, and that was that there really was something up with the General too, something dangerous and leading ineluctably to his destruction and the destruction of those around him. When he had stood up full height during the river crossing in his conspicuous leather coat so picturesquely exposing himself to the bullets coming from the right bank and from the swooping Fokker aircraft, it was not bravado or "setting a personal example of bravery," but that same mysterious thing which Sirotin was sure he had seen from time to time afflicting certain other men: he was seeking death. Sirotin wanted only in every way possible to help this concerned, omnipotent Major, to give him as much detail as he could about the oddities of the General's behaviour in order that he should be able to build them in to whatever calculations these were that he was working on.

Summary of the novel

Vladimov began writing *A General and His Army* after ghost writing the memoirs of leading Soviet generals about the conduct of the Second World War. The KGB soon took an interest, and his manuscripts were confiscated. Persistent rumours were spread that his novel would attempt to rehabilitate General Vlasov, commander of the Russian Liberation Army which fought on the German side against Stalin. In fact, he describes the main concern of his novel as being the phenomenon of large numbers of Russians, variously estimated at between 400,000 and two million, taking up arms against their own country.

Vladimov is a skilled writer in the style of classical Russian realism, and Tolstoy influences the characters directly and indirectly, from Major Donskoy, General Kobrisov's adjutant, who tries unsuccessfully to model himself on Prince Andrey Bolkonsky, to the German tank commander Heinz Guderian, his headquarters based at Tolstoy's estate of Yasnaya Polyana, who reads and re-reads *War and Peace*, trying to fathom the mentality of his Russian foe.

A major theme of the novel is the relationship between the mentality of rebellious Russians and the despotism of Stalin and his secret police in the context of war. Khrushchev is present as a prominent Party representative on the Ukrainian front, and Brezhnev figures as a character so insignificant that no one can remember his name.

The novel is densely written, with constant allusion to events past and future, and a completely original perspective on the Russian conduct of the Second World War as an ambiguous history of criminal brutality, incompetence, and heroism. At the same time, Vladimov concedes great shrewdness to Stalin in his understanding of the people over whom he ruled.

The novel is framed by the fictitious General Kobrisov's never accomplished return to GHQ in Moscow after his recall from the Ukrainian front.

Travelling with him in his jeep are his driver Sirotin, his batman Shesterikov, and his aide Donskoy. All three of them have been questioned by Major Svetlookov of Smersh (the Army's secret police) and made to inform on their boss. The naive driver Sirotin is a reluctant but ultimately easy prey. The batman Shesterikov, who once saved Kobrisov's life, gives nothing away but fails to warn his boss. The ineffectual Major Donskoy finds Tolstoyan morality no defence against the plebeian brutality of Smersh.

There is a flashback to the day when Kobrisov accidentally blunders into a village occupied by the Germans, gets himself shot in the stomach, and is dragged to safety by Shesterikov. Shesterikov then has to find a way of getting the wounded general to hospital in Moscow, along a road flooded with demoralised Russian deserters who are heading into town ahead of the (in fact no less demoralised) Germans. His contact with Vlasov comes when the latter hijacks fresh Siberian troops intended to reinforce his own army, and drives the Germans back with them, breaking the encirclement of Moscow. Vlasov's disciplined troops enable the wounded general to be put on a sleigh back to the capital.

This same day Heinz Guderian, commander of the tank army moving on Moscow from the south, finds himself humiliatingly stranded when his tank falls into a shallow ravine. Hitler's decision to divert the Blitzkrieg towards Kiev (captured) and Leningrad (unsuccessfully besieged), delays the advance on Moscow until the cold of winter wreaks havoc on the ill-equipped and supplied German troops. Finally returning to his headquarters at Tolstoy's estate, Guderian writes out the order for his troops to retreat from Moscow for the winter.

The next flashback is to the autumn of 1943 when Kobrisov, who has now formed the 38th Army, has established a bridgehead on the right bank of the Dnieper in the Ukraine. He finds himself outmanoeuvred at a war council chaired by Marshal Zhukov, where it is decided that a Ukrainian general should liberate the first major Ukrainian city to be recaptured, Predslavl. Unlike Zhukov or his fellow generals he has an acute awareness of the value of human lives and cannot reconcile himself to the "four-layer theory" of Russian warfare, whereby three armies pave the way for a fourth to advance over their corpses. (Zhukov was to sacrifice 300,000 Russian lives in the attempt to get to Berlin by May Day 1945 and without the aid of Eisenhower.)

In order to delay Kobrisov's advance on Predslavl he is instructed to encircle and capture Myriatin, a town he has been leaving alone because he knows most of its defenders to be Russians fighting against Stalin. He fails to present a plan of campaign to his superior and is sent back to Moscow to "recuperate". Just as he reaches the capital the radio broadcasts news of the fall of Myriatin to the 38th Army and of the decoration of Kobrisov and his promotion to Lieutenant-General. He gets very drunk as he looks down on Moscow, recalls how, just before the outbreak of war he was arrested by the GPU on a charge of attempting to assassinate Stalin (two of his tanks had broken down in front of Lenin's Tomb during the

Revolution parade), but was saved by the outbreak of war. He imagines the mass executions which Smersh will now be instigating in Myriatin. The mistake in decorating him as commander of the 38th Army (or has Stalin deliberately disregarded the decision to send him away?) allows him now to turn away from Moscow and return to the front to fight on.

Georgy VLADIMOV (1931-2003), winner of the Russian Booker Prize for his novel *The General and his Army,* is known in the West mainly for his novel *Faithful Ruslan*, published in many languages. His other major novel, *Three Minutes of Silence* (1969) was greeted with a barrage of official criticism in the USSR. In 1977 Vladimov resigned from the Writers' Union and assumed the leadership of the Moscow chapter of Amnesty International. He was forced to emigrate to the West in 1983, and edited the émigré journal *Grani* from 1984-6.

Vassily
GROSSMAN
The Commissar

Translated by James Escomb

It was strange to see the blush come to Vavilova's dark, weather-beaten cheeks.

"What's so funny?" she said after a moment. "Don't be silly."

Kozyrev lifted her application from the table, looked it over and, shaking his head, again began to chuckle.

"No, I just can't..." he laughed. "Leave permit... for the Commissar of the First Battalion... for forty days on grounds of pregnancy."

He grew serious.

"Well, there we are. Now who can replace you? Perlmutter, do you think, from the Political Division?"

"Perlmutter's a sound communist," said Vavilova.

"You're all sound," said Kozyrev and, lowering his voice to suit the delicacy of the situation, asked:

"When is the birth expected, soon?"

"Soon," replied Vavilova and, taking off her sheepskin hat, wiped sweat from her brow. "I'd have had it aborted," she said in a deep voice, "but I let things drag on. You know I was hardly out of the saddle for three months down by Grubeshov. By the time I got to the hospital, the doctor wouldn't do it."

She wrinkled her nose, as though on the point of tears.

"I even threatened the bastard with my revolver, but he still refused, said it was too late."

After she left the room Kozyrev remained seated at the table, scrutinising the application.

"That's Vavilova for you," he thought. "She's scarcely a woman at all, goes around with a pistol, wears leather pants. How many times has she led the battalion into attack? Even her voice isn't a woman's, but there, Nature has the last word."

For some reason this thought seemed to sadden him.

He wrote on the application:

"The bearer is permitted to..."

He sat there, frowning and irresolutely twiddling the end of his pen above the paper. What should he write?

"...to take 40 days leave." He thought further and added "on grounds of sickness", then inserted the word "female", cursed himself, and crossed it out.

"How can you fight a war with women?" he said, and shouted for the orderly. "Have you heard about our Vavilova?" he said gruffly, angrily. "She's a fine one."

"I heard," said the orderly, shook his head and spat on the floor.

Together they damned Vavilova to perdition, and all women with her, exchanged lewd jokes and had a laugh before Kozyrev summoned the chief of staff and told him:

"You'll have to go and see her tomorrow, find out if she's having it at home or in hospital, and check that everything's O.K."

Then he and the chief of staff sat till morning, poring over the one-inch map and speaking hardly at all — the Poles were coming.

Vavilova was to lodge in a requisitioned room.

The little house stood at the Yakti, as the market-place in the small town was called, and belonged to Chaim-Abraham Libovich Magazanik, known to his neighbours and even his own wife as Chaim Tooter, meaning Tatar.

Vavilova's arrival caused much commotion. She arrived accompanied by a tall, gangling lad in a leather jacket and uniform cap, who worked for the Community Department. Magazanik cursed him in Yiddish. The departmental representative remained silent and shrugged. Magazanik switched to Russian.

"The cheek of these snotty bastards," he shouted at Vavilova, as though she ought to be a party to his indignation.

"Can't they even think? As if there weren't any bourgeois left in this town. The only room the Soviets can take has to be in poor old Magazanik's house. The one and only room has to be in the house of a worker with seven kids. What about Litvak the baker? Or Khodorov the haberdasher? And what about Ashkenazy, our leading millionaire?"

The Magazanik children stood beside him: seven ragged, curly-haired cherubs, watching Vavilova with eyes as black as night. She was as tall as a house, taller than their father.

Magazanik was finally pushed aside and Vavilova proceeded to her room.

It smelt so overpoweringly of human habitation, from the tired-out eiderdowns, the sideboard and the sagging chairs with their gaping holes, that before she dared enter she took a deep breath as if diving into water.

She could not sleep that night. Behind the partition, the Magazanik family snored like an orchestra, from the droning of a double bass to the high notes of flute and violin. She felt suffocated by the stuffiness of the summer night and the all-pervading smells. The room smelled of everything imaginable — paraffin, garlic, sweat, goose-fat, dirty underwear. A truly human habitation!

She touched her ripening, swollen belly. Now and then the being living within her kicked and squirmed.

She had fought it, fairly and stubbornly, for many months. She had jumped down heavily from her horse. Silently, fiercely, on her Saturdays working in the town, she had heaved great blocks of pine around. In the villages she had drunk potions and herbal draughts and drawn so much iodine from the regimental chemist that the medic had been ready to write a complaint to the brigade medical department. In the bath-house she had scalded herself till she came out in blisters.

But the child had stubbornly gone on growing, hampering

her movements, making it hard to ride on horseback. She had been sick, felt heavy and earthbound. At first she had laid all the blame on the sad, morose man who had found his way through her thick leather jerkin and coarse uniform tunic to conquer her woman's heart. She had seen him lead the way across a frighteningly makeshift wooden bridge. There had been a burst of Polish machine-gun fire and he had seemed to vanish. An empty greatcoat threw up its arms, fell and lay hanging above the stream.

She had ridden headlong above him on her maddened horse, and behind her the battalion had hurtled forwards, forcing her on.

After that all that remained was the child, and it had to carry all the blame. Now Vavilova lay there vanquished, and victoriously it beat its little hoofs and lived within her.

Next morning, when Magazanik was getting ready to go to his work and his wife was giving him breakfast and he was shooing the flies and the children and the cat, he nodded towards the wall of the requisitioned room and said, quietly:

"Give her some tea — may the cholera take her."

He sat bathed in the dusty pillars of sunshine, surrounded by the cries of children, the miaowing of the cat and the cooing of the samovar, and he did not want to go to the workshop. He loved his wife, his kids, his old mother, and his home. With a sigh he went out, and only the women and children remained in the house.

The Yakti bubbled like a cauldron all day long. Peasants were trading birch-logs white as chalk. Women rustled strings of onions, and old Jewish ladies presided over downy piles of geese, tied together by their feet. Buyers blew into the down between their legs and pinched the yellow fat beneath the soft warm skin. Girls in colourful skirts, with sunburnt legs, carried tall red pots brimming with wild strawberries. They looked nervously at the buyers, as if getting ready to run away. Carts carried butter for sale, golden sweating pats wrapped in plump dock-leaves. A blind beggar with the white beard of a wizard was uttering tragic prayers of lamentation, holding out his hands, but his grief touched nobody's heart — they passed him by indifferently. One woman, taking the smallest onion from her string, threw it into the old man's tin bowl. He felt the onion and, interrupting his prayer, angrily scolded: "May your own children give you as little when you are old" — and again sang out his keening prayer, as old as the people of Israel.

People were buying and selling, probing, tasting, and raising their eyes towards heaven as if waiting for someone to advise them from the gentle blue sky above whether to buy the pike, or better take the carp. And all the time they shouted and swore, cursed each other and laughed.

Vavilova swept and tidied her room. She put away her greatcoat, her sheepskin hat, and her riding boots. Her head was buzzing with the noise from the street, and indoors the little Tooters were shrieking. She felt she was sleeping through a bad dream.

Magazanik came home from his work in the evening and stopped at the door dumbfounded. His wife Beyla was sitting at the table beside a large woman who was wearing an ample dress, bedroom slippers on her bare feet and a brightly coloured scarf over her hair. They were laughing quietly and chatting, trying the size of tiny baby jackets in their great clumsy hands.

Beyla had gone into Vavilova's room earlier in the day. Vavilova was standing by the window, and Beyla's sharp womanly eye detected the swollen belly her tallness concealed.

"You must excuse me," said Beyla resolutely, "but you look to be pregnant." Then throwing up her arms, laughing and crying, Beyla began to fuss around her.

"Children," she said, "children. What a business they are!" She cuddled and pressed the youngest Tooter to her bosom. "Such trouble, such constant bother. Every day they want to eat and not a week goes by without one getting a rash and another a fever or a boil. And Doctor Baraban, God grant him health, takes ten pounds of baking flour for every visit."

She stroked the little Tooter's head.

"And every single one of mine survives, not one will die."

She soon discovered Vavilova didn't know anything about babies. She immediately deferred to the wisdom of Beyla. She listened, asked questions, and Beyla, laughing with pleasure at finding that the Commissar was quite clueless, told her all there was to know. How to feed the baby, how to bathe and powder it, what to do to stop it crying at night, how many nappies and baby-jackets she would need, how new-born babies wear themselves out crying, turn blue, and your heart nearly bursts from fear that they are going to die. How to cure diarrhoea, how they catch nappy rash, how you know when the spoon begins to rattle in the baby's mouth that it's teething.

A complicated world with rules, customs, joys and sorrows all its own. Vavilova knew nothing of this world, and Beyla indulgently, like an elder sister, led her into it.

"Get out from under my feet," she yelled at the children. "Out, into the yard!" And when they were alone together in the room Beyla, lowering her voice to a confidential whisper, told her about childbirth. "Oh, that's no laughing matter."

Beyla like an old soldier, told the new recruit about the tortures and bliss of childbirth.

"You think having a baby is as simple as making war. Pif, paf, and it's over! I'm sorry to say, it's not as easy as that."

Vavilova listened. For the first time in her entire pregnancy she had met someone who talked to her about her absurd and embarrassing accident as a happy event, and perhaps even the most important thing in her life.

The discussion, now including Tooter, continued that evening. There was no time to be lost. After supper Tooter climbed up into the attic and with much clattering brought down a metal cradle and a tub for bathing the new baby.

"You need have no fear, comrade Commissar," he laughed, his eyes shining. "It's a going concern you're joining."

"Be quiet, you clod," his wife retorted. "You're not known as the Tatar without good reason."

That night Vavilova lay in her bed. The stifling smells no longer oppressed her as they had the night before. She no longer even noticed them. She didn't want to think about anything.

She imagined horses neighing, their chestnut heads in a long row, all of them with a white blaze on the forehead, moving restively, nodding, snorting, and baring their teeth. She thought of the battalion and remembered Kirpichov, the political officer of the second company. There was a lull in the fighting. Who could give them a talk on the July uprising? The quartermaster should be hauled over the coals for delaying the delivery of boots. And they should be told to cut up the cloth themselves for puttees. There were some disaffected elements in the second company, especially that curly-headed man from the Don who was forever singing songs. Vavilova yawned and closed her eyes. The battalion moved, far away, into a rosy corridor of early sunshine between wet hayricks, and her thoughts about it seemed somehow beside the point.

The child gave her an impatient jab with its little hoofs. Vavilova opened her eyes and sat up in bed.

"A boy or a girl?" she asked herself out loud, and suddenly

felt her heart surge within her breast, warm and powerful. "A boy or a girl?"

The contractions began that day.

"Ow!" cried Vavilova hoarsely, like a peasant woman, feeling the sharp, piercing pain take hold of her.

Beyla helped her to the bed. One of the little Tooters ran gleefully off to fetch the midwife. Vavilova grasped Beyla's hand and kept saying in a low, hurried voice:

"It's started, Beyla — I thought it wouldn't be for another ten days or so. It's started, Beyla!"

Then the pains stopped and Vavilova thought there had been no need to send for the midwife, but half an hour later they started again. Vavilova's face turned white as a death mask under her tan. She clenched her teeth, and from her expression she seemed in an agony of embarrassment, as if she were about to rise up in her bed and cry "What have I done, what have I done?" and cover her face with her hands in despair.

The children kept peeping into the room. Their blind grandmother was boiling a big saucepan of water on the stove. Beyla kept looking towards the door, alarmed by Vavilova's anguished expression. The midwife came at last. Her name was Rosalia Samoilovna, and she was stocky and red-faced and had her hair cropped very short. The house was suddenly filled with her shrewish, piercing voice. She barked orders at Beyla, the children and grandmother soon had them all bustling around her. The primus started hissing in the kitchen, the table and chairs were carried from the room, and Beyla hastily mopped the floor as if putting out a fire. Rosalia Samoilovna personally shooed the flies out with a tea towel. Vavilova looked at her and thought how similar it all was to the army commander visiting their headquarters. He too was stocky and red-faced, with a peevish voice, and he only came when the enemy had broken through the front. Everybody would be reading the official releases, exchanging anxious looks and whispering as if there were a dead body or someone gravely ill there. The commander would gruffly cast this web of mystery and silence aside, shouting and swearing, issuing orders amidst roars of laughter, as if he couldn't care less about cut-off transports or surrounded regiments.

She did as Rosalia Samoilovna's authoritative voice commanded, answered her questions and turned herself over. Now and then her mind became clouded, the surfaces and angles of the walls and ceiling seemed to blur and break up and move in on her like waves. The midwife's strident voice brought her round and Vavilova became aware again of her red, perspiring face and the ends of her white kerchief knotted round her neck. At such moments her mind was a blank. She just wanted to howl wildly like a wolf and bite the pillow. She imagined her bones straining and cracking, and sticky, sickly sweat broke out on her brow. But she did not cry out, only ground her teeth and, convulsively jerking her head, gulped for air. Sometimes the pain went away and it was as if there had never been any, and she looked around in wonder, listening to the sounds from the market, gazing in wonderment at the glass on the bedside table and the picture on the wall.

As the child again began to struggle, desperately striving to begin its own life, she felt terror at the imminent contractions, but at the same time a confused happiness. Since it must be, let it come quickly.

Rosalia Samoilovna murmured to Beyla: "You wouldn't catch me wanting to have my first at thirty-six, I can tell you, Beyla."

Vavilova didn't catch the words and was frightened by the midwife's low voice.

"What, shan't I live?" she asked.

Beyla stood by the door, pale and distraught. She shrugged her shoulders and said: "What on earth's the point of all this suffering? It does no good to her, or the baby, or the father (God rot him!), or God himself in His heaven. Oh, whoever was the wise man who brought all this on us women?"

The birth took a long, long time.

When Magazanik came home, he sat on the front steps as anxious as if his Beyla herself were giving birth. The shadows deepened, lights came on in the windows.

Jews were coming home from the synagogue, carrying their rolled-up prayer-cloths under their arms. By the light of the moon the empty square, the little houses and streets took on a beautiful and mysterious aspect. Troops in riding breeches, their spurs jingling, strolled along the brick pavements. Girls were nibbling sunflower seeds and laughing in the direction of the Red Army soldiers. One girl was rattling on:

"I was eating sugar-lumps and throwing the wrappers at him, eating them and throwing the wrappers..."

"Ah, women are just trouble," said Magazanik. "As if I don't have trouble enough with my own, I have to have the whole partisan brigade coming to give birth in my house."

Suddenly he pricked up his ears and got up. From inside came a hoarse male voice which shouted such strong oaths that Magazanik shook his head and spat on the ground. Vavilova, crazed with pain and in the final throes of giving birth, was taking issue with God and the accursed destiny of women.

"That's more like it," said Magazanik. "That's more like it. That's a commissar giving birth. All my Beyla can manage is "Oh, mother, oh my dear mother, oh mother!""

Rosalia Samoilovna smacked the newborn baby on its soft, wrinkled bottom and announced: "It's a boy!"

"What did I say?" said Beyla triumphantly, and, opening the door, she crowed victoriously "Chaim, children, it's a boy!"

The entire family gathered at the door, excitedly chattering with Beyla. Even the blind old granny fumbled her way over to her son and smiled at the great miracle of life, smiled and whispered inaudibly. The children were pushing her away from the door, but she craned her neck and drew closer, wanting to hear the voice of ever-victorious life.

Vavilova gazed at her newborn, amazed that this tiny scrap of red and blue flesh should have been the cause of such agony.

She had imagined that her baby would be born already a big boy, with freckles, a snub nose, and a mop of red hair, and that he would be naughty from the outset, yelling deafeningly and in a great rush to be off somewhere. Instead he was as puny as a stalk of oats grown in a cellar. He couldn't hold his little head up, his little bent legs twitched as if they were withered, his whitish blue eyes were unseeing, and his piping cry was scarcely to be heard. It seemed that if you opened the door suddenly, he would blow out, like the thin sagging candle Beyla had fixed above the edge of the cupboard.

Although the room was as hot as a bath-house, she stretched out her arms and said: "He's cold, let me hold him."

The new little person squealed, rolling his head from side to side. Vavilova followed him with her eyes, squinting, afraid to move.

"Drink, drink, my little son," she said, and began to cry. "My son, my own little son," she murmured, and the tears welled up in her eyes and rolled in clear droplets down her cheeks to be absorbed by the pillow.

She remembered him, her stern lover, and she wept for both of them, filled with the grief and pain of a mother. For the first time she wept for her lover, killed in the battle for Korosten, who would never see his son.

"And this tiny, helpless child will never have a father," she thought grief-stricken, and covered him with the blanket, so that he shouldn't be cold.

Perhaps, however, she wept for quite another reason. At least, Rosalia Samoilovna, lighting up a cigarette and fanning the smoke out through the window, said: "Let her cry if she wants to. It'll calm her nerves better than bromide. All my mothers cry after the birth."

On the third day after the birth Vavilova got up. She could feel her strength streaming back to her and walked about a lot, helping Beyla with the housework. When there was no one else in the house she sang quietly to her little boy, who now had a name: Alyosha.

"You should see her," said Beyla to her husband. "That goy woman's quite mad. Three times already she's run with him to the doctor. You can't open a door in the house for fear he'll wake up, or catch a fever. In fact, she's just like a good Jewish mother!"

"What did you think?" answered Magazanik. "You think if a woman wears leather pants she turns into a man?" He shrugged his shoulders and closed his eyes.

Kozyrev and his chief of staff came to visit Vavilova a week later. They smelt of leather, tobacco and horse sweat. Alyosha was asleep in his cradle, shielded from the flies by a swathe of gauze. Squeaking deafeningly like two new riding boots, they approached the cradle and gazed at the wizened little face of the sleeping baby. In his dreams, the baby's face moved, seeming now to express grief, now petulance, now a smile. The officers looked at each other.

"Well, well," said Kozyrev.

"You're right," replied the chief of staff.

They sat down on two chairs and started bringing Vavilova

up to date. The Poles had gone on the offensive and our units were withdrawing. Temporarily, of course. The Fourteenth Army was grouping at Zhmerinka. Divisions were coming in from the Urals. The Ukraine would be ours. We could expect the breakthrough in a month, but meanwhile the Poles were putting on the pressure. Kozyrev swore roundly.

"Shhh," said Vavilova. "Don't make so much noise, you'll wake the baby."

"Yes, they've given us a nose bleed," said the chief of staff, and laughed.

"You and your jokes," said Vavilova, and added in a pained tone, "You might stop smoking. You're puffing away like a steam engine."

The officers suddenly felt bored. Kozyrev yawned. The chief of staff looked at his watch and said:

"We mustn't be late. We still have to get to Bald Hill."

"I wonder where he got that gold watch from," thought Vavilova irritably.

"Well, time to say good-bye, Vavilova," Kozyrev announced, standing up. "I've given orders for you to be given a sack of flour, some sugar and salt pork. They'll bring it round on the cart later today."

They went out onto the street. The little Magazaniks were clustered round the horses. Kozyrev lumbered into the saddle, while the chief of staff clicked his tongue and mounted with rather more agility.

As they reached the corner of the street they unexpectedly pulled up, as if by prior agreement.

"Well, well," said Kozyrev.

"You're right," replied the other officer.

They laughed, whipped the horses, and rode off at a gallop in the direction of Bald Hill.

The two-wheeled cart arrived that evening. Having

dragged the sacks of provisions inside, Magazanik went into Vavilova's room and said in a conspiratorial whisper:

"What are you going to think of this, comrade Vavilova? The merchant Tsesarsky's brother-in-law came to see me at my workshop." He looked round and, as though apologising to Vavilova, said incredulously: "The Poles are at Chudnov, and Chudnov's only twenty-five miles from here."

Beyla had come in. She listened awhile, and said decisively: "There's no two ways about it, the Poles will be here tomorrow. Anyway, they're not the Poles, they're Austrians, Galicians or whatever, but you can stay here with us. God be praised, with all the stuff they've brought you — there's enough food for three months."

Vavilova said nothing. For the first time in her life, she had no idea what to do.

"Beyla..." she said, and fell silent.

"I'm not afraid," said Beyla. "You don't think I'm afraid, do you? I could look after five little babies like that if I had to. But whoever heard of a mother abandoning her baby when he was just a week and a half old?"

All night long the neighing of horses, the creaking of wheels, and angry, excited voices could be heard outside the windows. The transport wagons were on their way from Shepetovka to Kazatin.

Vavilova sat by the cradle. The baby slept. She looked at his little yellow face. In the long run it didn't matter all that much. Kozyrev had said they'd be back in a month, which was exactly when she was due back off leave. But what if they were cut off for a long time? Well, that didn't frighten her either.

When Alyosha was a bit stronger, they would find their way across the frontline.

Who would touch them — a peasant woman with a baby

at her breast? She imagined herself walking through open country early one summer's morning, a coloured kerchief round her head. Alyosha would be looking all around and holding out his little hands. Wonderful! She sang softly:

"Sleep, my little one, sleep," and herself fell into a light sleep rocking the cradle.

In the morning the market was as busy as ever. The people seemed especially excited. Some, watching the unending chain of transport wagons, were laughing happily. Finally the last of the wagons had gone. The streets were full of people. The townsfolk stood by the gates — "the civilian population" — as they were referred to in the Commandants' orders. They were all talking among themselves in excited whispers, looking around anxiously. The Poles were said already to have taken Pyatka, a hamlet ten miles from the town. Magazanik did not go to work; he sat in Vavilova's room and indulged his bent for philosophising to the full.

An armoured car rumbled past in the direction of the railway station, covered in a thick layer of dust. Its steel bodywork seemed to have turned grey from weariness and long sleepless nights.

"To tell you the truth," said Magazanik, "this is the best time for us civilians. One government has left, and the other hasn't yet got here. No requisitions, no forced contributions, no pogroms."

"He's only this pert during daylight," said Beyla. "Come nightfall, when the whole town's in an uproar at being ravaged by bandits, he sits there looking like death and scared witless."

"Let me carry on an intelligent conversation, will you?" retorted Magazanik angrily.

He kept running out into the street and coming back with some new item of news. The Revolutionary Committee had evacuated the town last night, the District Party Committee left right behind them, and the military headquarters had left this morning. The station was deserted: the last army train had already departed.

Suddenly there was shouting in the street. An aeroplane was flying overhead. Vavilova went over to the window. The plane was flying at a great height, but the white and red roundels on its wings could be seen clearly — it was Polish air reconnaissance. It circled over the town, and flew off towards the station. Then, from the direction of Bald Hill, came the sound of cannon-fire. Shells flew over the town, and the rumble of explosions reached them from far away beyond the level-crossing.

First came the shells, howling like a blizzard, then the low sighing of the guns, and a few seconds later the explosions rang out joyfully. This was the Bolsheviks slowing down the Polish advance on the town. The Poles soon began to respond, their shells landing here and there within the town.

Vaaam! The air was torn by deafening explosions; bricks crumbled, smoke and dust danced above the overturned wall of a house. The streets fell silent, austere, empty as a deserted stage set. After each explosion there was an eerie silence, and all the while the sun shone down from a cloudless sky, flooding the town with light as though it were a spread-eagled corpse.

To a man townsfolk were cowering in basements and cellars with bated breath, moaning and groaning in terror and keeping their eyes shut.

Everybody, even the children, knew that this bombardment was known as "softening up", and that before taking the town the troops would fire a few dozen more shells. Then, as they knew, it would grow incredibly quiet, until suddenly, with a clatter of hooves, a cavalry reconnaissance patrol would gallop down the wide street from the direction of the level-crossing. Thrilled with terror and devoured by curiosity, everybody would peer out from their gates or their curtains and, drenched in sweat, would creep out into the courtyards.

The patrol would ride into the town square. The horses would prance and snort, their riders excitedly shouting to one another in amazingly simple, human language, and their captain, delighted at the meek surrender of the conquered town lying flat on its back, would give a drunken yell and fire his pistol into the empty silence, lifted high on his rearing horse.

Then from all directions the infantry and cavalry units would flood in while tired and dusty soldiers would run from house to house, good-natured peasant lads but capable of murder, in their blue greatcoats, greedy for the locals' chickens, their embroidered towels, and their boots.

Everybody knew this. The town had already changed hands fourteen times, and been held by Petlyura, Denikin, the Bolsheviks, Galicians, Poles, the private armies of chieftains Tyutyunik and Marusya, and even by the wildly unpredictable irregular Ninth Regiment. Each time was like the last.

"They're singing," Magazanik called. "They're singing!"

His fear forgotten, he ran out onto the front steps. Vavilova followed him. After the stuffiness of her darkened room, it gave her special pleasure to breathe in the light and the warmth of the summer day. She had been expecting the Poles in the same spirit as she had awaited the birth — since it must be, let them come quickly. The explosions had frightened her, she was afraid they would waken Alyosha, and she had brushed aside the screaming of the shells like flies.

"Take it easy, will you?" she had crooned over the cradle. "You'll wake Alyosha."

She had tried to think of nothing at that moment. Everything was, after all, decided. In a month's time, either the Bolsheviks would return, or she and her baby would go to them over the frontline.

"What on earth's going on?" Magazanik said. "Just look at that."

A column of Bolshevik cadets dressed in white canvas trousers and tunics was marching along the broad empty street in the direction of the crossing from which the Poles were expected.

"May the Red Flag embody the hopes of the workers," they sang, slowly and somehow mournfully.

They were marching towards the Poles.

"Why? Whatever for?"

Vavilova gazed at them. Suddenly she remembered — a huge Moscow square, several thousand workers who had volunteered for the front thronging round a hastily erected wooden platform. A bald man, gesticulating with his peaked cap, was addressing them. Vavilova was standing very close to him, so excited that she could not make out half of what he was saying, spoken in a clear voice with a mild speech defect. The people round her had hung on his words, and an old man in a cotton-wadded jacket had wept for some reason. She had experienced a strange exhilaration on that Moscow square.

One night she had wanted to talk about it to him, her silent lover, thinking he would understand, but the words wouldn't come. When they had left Red Square for Bryansk Station, they had been singing this same song.

Looking at the faces of the singing cadets, she felt again what she had felt two years before.

The Magazaniks saw a woman in a sheepskin hat and greatcoat running down the road after the cadets, slipping a cartridge-clip into her big, dull-coloured Mauser as she ran.

Magazanik looked after her in complete amazement.

Alyosha had woken and was crying, his little legs

pumping as he tried to escape from his nappy. Recovering herself, Beyla said to her husband:

"Listen, the baby's woken up. You'd do better to light the primus. We've got milk to warm."

The platoon disappeared round a turn in the road.

Vassily GROSSMAN (1905-1964) grew up in the town of Berdichev in the "Jewish Pale". He graduated from the Chemistry Department of Moscow University and worked for a while at the Donbass coal mines as a chemical engineer. There he began writing stories based on his first-hand impressions of pogroms and workers' living conditions. In 1933 he moved to Moscow on the invitation of Maxim Gorky, who was particularly impressed with Grossman's story "This Happened in Berdichev" ("The Commissar"). Grossman spent the Second World War as a frontline correspondent for the *Red Star* army daily. His war impressions made the basis for his novel *Life and Fate*. In 1949, together with Ilya Ehrenburg, he wrote the *Black Book* about the extermination of Jews on Nazi-occupied territories. The book was banned as part of the campaign against cosmopolitanism. He stopped being published and was severely criticised for underrating Russian heroism in the war and other "ideological errors". His major novels *Life and Fate* and *Forever Flowing* were known in samizdat, but in 1961 the manuscripts were "arrested", drafts and all. Two decades later they resurfaced and were published in Russia and many other countries.

Friedrich
GORENSTEIN

Bag in Hand

Translated by Andrew Bromfield

A vdotya woke up in the early hours and immediately remembered about her little bag.

"Oh, my, my..." Avdotya began keening, "Oh, oh... Carrying that can of milk yesterday, the handle broke, it's all worn out... I have to stitch it up before the shops open."

She glanced at her old alarm clock. Once upon a time that alarm clock used to get Avdotya up out of bed together with the others... Who? What's it matter... What personal history has Avdotya got nowadays?

Soviet citizens remember all the detailed ramifications of their personal history, thanks to the innumerable forms they have to fill in so very often. But it was a long time since Avdotya had filled in any forms, and of all the various state institutions her interest was reserved for the grocery stores. For Avdotya was a typical grocery-store granny, a social type unrecognised by socialist statistical science, but actively involved in the consumption of the product of socialist society.

Before the weary working population comes pouring out of its workshops, factories and institutions in the evening; before, worn to a frazzle by rush-hour travel on public transport, it squeezes itself into the hot, cramped gas-chambers of the shops, Avdotya has time to dart around them all, like a mouse... She'll pick up a few Bulgarian eggs in one place, a little bit of Polish ham in another, a Dutch chicken in yet another, a bit of Finnish butter somewhere else — the topography of the food-hunt, as it were. She never even thinks any more about the taste of a good Russian apple from Vladimir or a sweet dark red cherry, and she gathers berries outside Moscow to eke out her pension, not for eating.

Off she'll go, bag in hand, into the woods that are still left alive — as if she's just going to another grocery store to buy a few raspberries and strawberries from old Mother Nature — getting there before the alcoholics who follow Michurin in expecting no favours from nature and are collecting raspberries to make drink. They'll strip the woods so bare there'll be nothing left for a bird to peck at or a squirrel to gnaw on. They'll plunder their younger brethren and then squat heavily on the shoulders of their brothers and sisters among the working people.

Our Avdotya will sell a little bagful of raspberries from the Moscow woods — a rouble for a fifty-gram glass — then she'll buy a kilo of bananas from Peru at a rouble ten kopecks a kilo. She'll sell a few bilberries at a rouble fifty a glass, and buy some Moroccan oranges at a rouble forty a kilo. It's a fine life under socialism. The western peace fighters are quite right. It's just a pity their visual propaganda doesn't make use of our Avdotya's weighing scales and Avdotya's added value.

Avdotya the grocery-store granny was an old hand at shop-plundering, she was experienced, and her weapon was her little bag. Old Avdotya loved her little bag, and as she made ready for the working day she would croon to it:

"Ah, my little provider, my own little Daisy-Cow!"

Her plan was all drawn up in advance. First to "our shop" — that's the one next door to her house. After that to the bread shop. After that to the big department store. After that to the milk shop. After that to the "deli." After that to the shop run by the Tatars. After that to the vegetable stall. After that to the bread shop opposite the stall. After that to the shop beside the post office...

It was never calm in the big shop. When you plunged in there, the waves grabbed you and bore you away... From the grocery section to the delicatessen, from the delicatessen to the meat section... And always elbows on every side, elbows and shoulders, more elbows... The good thing was they couldn't nudge you here — there was nowhere to fall. But an elbow to the face, the "mug" — nothing could be simpler.

Now they've wheeled out a trolley piled high with flat tins of herring. This kind of situation is manna from heaven to Avdotya... No queue or order of any kind, straightforward pillage. Free-for-all grabbing. It's not the cunning of the fox Avdotya requires here, but the cunning of the mouse. Just like a circus act: hup, one, two — and the trolley's empty. People look around to see who's holding what. The men have grabbed one or two... Some folk have grabbed nothing but empty air, they're furious. The leaders of the pack are the strong, skilled housewives, with three or four tins. A few little old women are up there with them. Avdotya has three tins in her little bag.

If the grocery store grannies ever combine forces, then they're formidable. Once seven old women, including our Avdotya, stormed a counter in chain formation. The leader, Matveevna, who's in hospital with a fracture just at present, was holding herself up with a crutch. They pushed everyone aside and they got their Polish ham. Of course, you always have to assess the situation in advance. For instance, it's pointless getting involved in that kind of situation over there in the meat section... Something's just been wheeled out, but just what isn't clear. Something between a scrum and a scrimmage. A few people smiling stiffly — the ones who try to make a joke of their brutality. But most of the faces are seriously vicious. This is work...

Ooh, you get away from there, Avdotya. You've grabbed your herring, now get out. Herring's not like nice smooth broth, it tickles as it slips through your guts, and it hurts when it makes you belch... But you still want it anyway. You can't always be doing what the doctors tell you, you have to please yourself. Some potato will fix the salt, and a sip of sweet tea will settle everything down. Now you've got your fatty herring, you get out of there, Avdotya, while you're still in one piece. Get out, Avdotya...

But it was a bad day, nothing going right... Avdotya realised the situation too late. There was no space left to turn around, not even room to draw breath... And there was a new smell — home-grown coarse tobacco and tar, tar from new roads in the satellite towns...

They've arrived... There are the tourist buses outside the supermarket. Every bus a requisitioning detachment's mobile headquarters to which the plundered purchases are carried back. The entire bus weighed down with bundles, sacks and string bags. The troops move off in various directions — men and women with fine strong arms: and the scouts are nimble boys and girls. A freckle-faced girl comes running up.

"Uncle Parshin, aunty Vasilchuk said to tell you they're selling vegetable oil."

"What kind of oil's that, lop-ears?"

"Yellow," says freckle-face, nodding gleefully. "I got inside and saw them giving it out... And someone gave aunty Vasilchuk a shove with his shoulder..."

But uncle Parshin's not listening anymore:

"Vaniukhin, Sakhnenko! Get the milk-churn!"

Off runs the combat crew with a forty-litre churn... Oh, so many of them... Oh, it's just too much... And now they've shoved in another churn.

"Ooh, he... help. Help!"

The satellite towns work smartly. Transporting sausage, cheese and grains through the air. It's harvest-time. If you don't reap, you don't eat. And if you don't eat, when you pick up the Party newspaper, you get annoyed. And ideological wavering is not a good thing. And who are the satellite towns anyway? They're the best fighters in Russia... "Just as long as we're fed, we'll give anyone a thrashing... Just whistle for us, Central Committee, just give us the order, 'Comrades, stand to!' But we can't do nothing if there's nothing to eat, Central Committee. The satellite towns is your support, father Central Committee, and there you go feeding that rotten whore Moscow... And even in Moscow you can't always find vodka to put some lead in your pencil."

Our Avdotya made her escape. And she saved her little bag too... Avdotya's lived a long time on this earth, she knows a thing or two. It's not the truth she seeks, it's groceries. But this day's not going to go according to plan. She called into a "delicatessen". Quiet, calm, the air's clean and the counters are neat and empty. Could at least have put something on them for appearance's sake. Even if it was only a bone for a dog. The sales-girl sits there with her cheek propped up in her hand. People come in, swear and spit. But our Avdotya went in and stood there, taking a pause for breath, then spoke.

"Have you got any nice fresh fillet steak, love? Or some nice tender sirloin?"

"I think you're in the wrong place, granny," the sales-girl answered. "It's not a delicatessen you need, it's an eye doctor... Can't you see what's on the counter?"

Our Avdotya didn't take offence.

"Thanks for the advice," she said.

Off she went to another delicatessen, and when she went in, — there was something there! She snatched a pair of kidneys from under the nose of some dimwit. The kidneys were lying on a dish in damp isolation, like anatomical specimens, and the dimwit was studying and sniffing them. Taking off his glasses and putting them back on again. Avdotya dashed across to the cash-desk and paid for the kidneys.

"That's not right," cried the intellectual, "I was first."

"You were just sniffing them, but the granny here paid," replied the retail trade worker.

"What about some more?"

"There aren't any more... Buy some of the specials, they're not in very often."

The intellectual took a look and couldn't make out what they were. He read the label — "Egg with caviar." He looked closely, and it was indeed a hard-boiled egg, not too fresh, cut in half. And the sulphurous surface was dotted with black sparrow's droppings.

"Where's the caviar?"

"That's as much as there should be. Thirty grams. What d'you expect for that price?"

It's a price for which under that voluntarist Khruschev, on the eve of the historical October 1964 Party plenary session, which marked a turning point in the development of agriculture, you could buy two hundred grams of fine caviar in any delicatessen. Russia moves on apace, as though there were dogs barking at its heels... But where are we going in such a hurry? Why not sit down and take time to draw breath and think, wipe the sweat from our brow? Just you try suggesting it. The political columnists will make you a laughing-stock.

So this is the life of Avdotya, the little old grocery-store granny without any personal history. She's adapted to it. She peers at the political commentators on her little television and regales herself with kidneys. The political commentator's face twists and warps and his voice roars distortedly, because her television's been out of order for ages. But what can she do about it? They've forbidden the consumption of caviar and fresh-smoked sausage, but at least they still let you chew on kidneys. And there's other food that hasn't been totally requisitioned yet. Russia's abundance is unlimited. In one place they queue for Indian tea, in another they queue for Bulgarian eggs, in yet another they queue for Rumanian tomatoes. Just stand there long enough and you get them.

Our Avdotya went into the milk shop. That calm and peaceful food-product — milk, the non-alcoholic drink. Children drink it, and people on strict diets. Sometimes the queues in here are calm too. But not today, when they're selling pre-packed Finnish butter...

Avdotya goes in and listens: the queue's buzzing like a circular saw that's hit a stone when it's running at full speed... The queue's face is hyper-tense, white with red blotches. A rosy blood-and-milk complexion... Avdotya pushes in backwards, into the Tatar's shop, where the manager is a Tatar and his wife is a sales attendant...

The Tatars are under siege by plundering hordes from the Ukrainian steppes... Makhno's anarchists... All in the same uniform — neck-scarves and double-breasted fur-trimmed plush jackets. Beefy scarlet hands, crimson faces and garlic breath...

But then just recently Russians, especially the policemen for some reason, have garlic breath too... Perhaps it's from the sausage, perhaps they're trying to kill the taste of the poor food with garlic?

The anarchists shout at each other:

"Teklia, ver's Tern?"

"Gonfa shompine wiz Gorpyna."

While the satelliters plunder the basic products, Makhno's warriors plunder the luxury items. They bring their sacks of pumpkin seeds or early pears to the market, stuff the sacks full of money, and then fill the sacks up with delicacies.

There's Gorpyna helping Teklia lift a bag full of champagne on to her shoulders. There's Tern clutching rucksacks bulging with bars and boxes of chocolate in both hands. It brings back memories of the old partisan gun-carts loaded with plundered landlords' property. But this is a different kind of pillage. Inspired not by Bakunin, but by Marx. Goods — money — goods...

The Soviet shop is an object lesson on the history and economy of the state — and on politics and morals and social relations...

"How much they giving?"

"Still won't be enough for everyone..."

"Two kilos each..."

"You in the queue?"

"Nah, I'm just standing here to take some air."

"What?"

"Shove off..."

The permanent cold war for hot-smoked sausage shows no signs of settling down. This is where the fighters for peace could have a real field day! This is where the foreign diplomats should study our problems. Pick up a string bag, stuff it with empty yoghurt and wine and vodka bottles, put on a dirty shirt, stand in front of the radiator for a while till you start sweating, then go off to the grocery store. You have to be able to shove with your elbows, glare viciously, and know just one word in Russian:

"Otvali" ("Shove off...")

You can add anything extra in your own language. Everyone gets the meaning anyway. But a foreigner in Russia is a privileged individual. He goes either to the Beriozka foreign currency shops or the Central Market. At the Central Market there is an abundance of high-quality foodstuffs and foreign cars. The country is capable of producing firm sun-ripened tomatoes and cool fragrant cucumbers, sweet dessert pears with succulent flesh and aromatic peaches so lovely that they are as good as flowers for decorating any festive table. The country is capable of covering counters with the delicate yellowish-white carcasses of geese, ducks, chickens and turkeys. Mounds of fresh meat. Chunks of lightly-salted, mouth-watering pork fat, spicy fish, full-fat off-white cream cheese, thick sour-cream... Here at the Central Market it's still the NEP period, there's no onward march towards communism here, no over-fulfilment of the plan, no grandiose space-flights or struggle for peace.

The Central Market is a good place.

But where's our Avdotya got to? We've completely lost sight of her... There she is in an itinerant queue — there are some like that. A shop-porter in a blue overall is dragging along a trolley, and on the trolley there are foreign cardboard boxes. No one knows what's in the boxes, but a queue forms anyway and runs after the trolley. New people keep on joining. Avdotya's somewhere in the first third of this long-distance queue... She should get some. Avdotya's grey hair is soaking wet and itchy under her headscarf, her heart is in her mouth, her stomach is squashing her bladder, and there's a rasping ache from her liver somewhere in the small of her back. But she mustn't fall behind. Fall behind and you lose your place in the queue. The shop-porter has a hangover and he wants to clear his head with a breath of fresh air, so he drags the trolley along without stopping. Someone in the queue, exhausted, calls out:

"Can't you stop now, we're tired, start selling the stuff..."

Then the woman from the retail organisation, following behind the trolley with her fat backside and short dirty overall, tells them:

"You make any fuss, and I won't sell anything."

The queue turns on the timid rebel sniping at him:

"If you're not happy, you can go home and cool off... What a fine gentleman — can't even stand a walk in the fresh air!

They know better than us where they're supposed to sell the stuff. Maybe they've got instructions from their boss."

Our Avdotya runs on after the others. The drunken shop-porter deliberately swings this way and that. Over towards the tram-stop, then back towards the bus-stop... And the woman with the fat backside is laughing... She's been drinking too... They're just taunting everybody, the monsters...

Under the present state structure they share direct power over the people with the local policeman, the house-manager and the other "public servants". Avdotya once arrived in the offices of the Moscow energy corporation, after some kind people told her how to find it, in tears. The kind young girls working there, their characters still unspoilt, asked her:

"Why're you crying, granny?"

"I've no paper left to pay the 'lectricity. They say they'll turn off the 'lectricity. What'll I do without 'lectricity? I can't cook and wash in the dark." And she held out her old payment book, all used up now, the one that a kind neighbour filled out for her.

"Oh, your payment book's finished? Here, take another one." And they gave her a nice new one, didn't even take a single kopeck for it. How Avdotya thanked them and wished them good health. And how much mockery she must have suffered in her life in various offices for her to be so afraid of all civil servants! These weren't just clerks, they were her providers.

Avdotya runs on, although she already has black spots in front of her eyes. The porter turns this way, the porter turns that way. And whichever way he turns, the queue follows him, like a tail. On one steep turn the engineer Fishelevich dropped out of the queue with its clanking of yoghurt bottles and a crunching of bones. Couldn't stand the pace. But the rest stick with it, even though they're almost out of energy. Then luckily the porter tried to be too clever, turned too sharply, and the cardboard boxes tumbled off right in the middle of the pavement... A few burst, and egg white and yolk came running out. The queue was delighted — they were going to get eggs. They felt better already. Something they needed, and they didn't need to run after it any more. The queue stood there, breathing heavily, resting while the porter and the woman with the fat backside conferred in obscene language. Volunteers were even found to carry the boxes from the middle of the pavement over to the wall of the building. Selling began...

The Russian heart and the Russified heart is easily appeased... difficulties and injuries are quickly forgotten — too quickly forgotten. Following the catastrophe the porter and the woman with the fat backside have decided in consultation that at the request of the people they will allow each purchaser ten whole eggs and ten cracked ones... And instead of calling them "culinary eggs," they will dub them "dietary eggs" and increase the price shown on the label. But at the same time they will give out plastic bags free of charge. Good. Our Avdotya took her ten whole eggs in one plastic bag, and her ten cracked ones in another, paid the new price, put everything in her little bag and went away happy. She called into the bakery and bought some bread — half a black loaf and a long white one. No queue for bread in Moscow yet. If ever there's a queue for bread, it'll mean the beginning of a new stage of advanced socialism. To advance the struggle against cosmopolitanism they'll ban the consumption of American, Canadian, Argentine, and other foreign grain. For the time being this question remains in the province of peaceful co-existence. International flour bakes good bread. A bit of meat to go with it would be good. Since she didn't get any nice young chicken, a little bit of meat would do nicely... And there's the meat shop, right in front of our Avdotya. The meat shop's buzzing, the meat shop's humming. That means they're selling. Our Avdotya goes inside.

The queue is by no means small, but there's no violence. Meat queues are usually some of the most violent. Maybe the smell transports people back to the times of our ancestors when the leaders of various caves fought each other for a prime cut of mammoth sirloin? A human being can turn wild as easy as drinking a glass of beer...

Those are the kind of thoughts that come to you in a Moscow meat queue, as your nostrils are assailed by the smell of tormented flesh. Our Avdotya began sniffing too, our toothless predator. She spotted something... That little piece lying over there... Not too big, not too small... Ah, if she just could get that one... Our Avdotya would pamper it like a child, wash it first in cold, cold water, and then in lukewarm water, clean out all the little bits of tough tissue and tendons, cut out the marrow bone to make a bit of soup. And she'd use the soft meat for a nice matching set of meatballs, like twins. She could try begging the queue for that piece in the name of Christ the Lord. The queue didn't look vicious.

Just as she thought it, she took a closer look — and she froze... Standing there in the queue is Kudriashova, Avdotya's old enemy... Kudriashova is a hardened bread-winner, the backbone of a large family of voracious children, and our Avdotya has often beaten her to the goods... Kudriashova has sloping shoulders and hands like meat-hooks. Kudriashova can carry two bags that our Avdotya couldn't even lift for long distances, as long as the load consists of foodstuffs. And Kudriashova is a fine child-bearer. Her eldest is already in the army, and her youngest is still crawling. Kudriashova is a strong woman, well adapted to queues. She can take on the average male at fisticuffs on equal terms. But when it comes to grabbing — and as we know, that's sometimes what's needed in the retail sector — then our Avdotya is quicker and smarter than Kudriashova, just as a sparrow is quicker than a crow. She might easily grab a little head of cabbage or a wrapped piece of Tambov gammon out from under Kudriashova's hand.

"You just wait, you witch," Kudriashova threatens and abuses her, "you just wait till I nudge you."

"I'll call a policeman," Avdotya replies. "You and your nudging."

But she's still afraid: "Oh, she's going to nudge me. Oh, she's going to nudge me."

Now seems like the right moment to explain what this word "nudge" means. It comes from an old Slavonic form *pikhat'*, the meaning of which is still preserved in a modern Ukrainian word. In modern Russian it translates as "to shove", but it's not quite that. A different intonation can change the meaning of a word, so that in usage, if not in grammar, there are actually two words. To shove means to push or move someone away from oneself. Sometimes someone who's shoved you will say sorry, beg your pardon. But if they "nudge" you, then there won't be any apology. Because when they nudge someone they try to make sure he gets smashed good and proper.

"Oh, she's going to nudge me," thinks our Avdotya, "she's going to nudge me." But the queue is calm, not at all belligerent, and Kudriashova is calm too. She glowers at Avdotya, but she doesn't say anything. What reason could there be for that? The reason's not the meat — it's the butcher.

An unusual butcher has appeared at this trade outlet. An intellectual butcher, looking more like a broad-boned professor of surgery with a white cap set on his greying hair, with his firmly moulded, well-fed face, wearing glasses. A butcher as merry and cynical as a surgeon, not gloomy and dirty like a butcher. For him a queue is an object of jolly mockery, not an occasion for neurotic altercation. He is above the queue. With his immense but clean hands he takes the pieces of meat and sets them on the meat tray in the display counter. And he replies to the murmuring in the queue when it demands quicker service with a faultless rendition from Pushkin's *Eugene Onegin...*

"What's going on?" grumbles a woman with a tired face, who's obviously not standing in her first queue of the day. "What's going on? You're put there to serve the customers."

"Chapter Two," replies the butcher: "The village where our Eugene suffered so / Was really quite a charming little spot, / Where a simple pleasure-seeker might well go / And thank the heavens for his pleasant lot... "

A strange picture and one, which summons up strange thoughts. A picture, which leads to unexpected conclusions. The first conclusion is that Pushkin should be recited to the meat queue by a butcher. This is actually the most important conclusion, well worth a few moments reflection in the oppressive heat of the shop. The butcher jangles Pushkin's lyre with a cynical and vulgar hand, but nonetheless he soothes the savage beast. The people remain silent, in line with the final stage direction in Pushkin's play *Boris Godunov*. They stand there quiet, not actually listening to Pushkin, but hearing him. Just let some great Pushkin specialist or famous actor try reciting Pushkin to a meat queue. They'll be lucky if the response is no more than mockery. Viciously expressed hatred is more likely. No, culture must be brought to the people by the authorities. Then what kind of culture is it? What kind of Pushkin? We can answer that question by starting from a different angle. Answer a question with a question. Have you ever watched the sunrise? Not over luxuriant subtropical greenery that knows all about the sun and consciously lives by it and waits with academic assurance for it to rise. And not over a calm, grass-covered forest glade, which is itself a particle of sunlight, which believes in the sun and lives through the sunrise as an intimate experience of its own.

We're thinking of the sunrise over lifeless northern cliffs, where you ask yourself: what good is life to the dead? What good is the sun to the cold rocks? The rocks lie there calm and heavy and dull in the remoteness of night, covered with ice and snow, the stones greet the short grey day with indifference, accepting on their unfeeling breasts its barbed blasts of wind. But the sun does rise over them, a weak imitation of the hot, fructifying sun or the gentle, caressing sun that we know. And suddenly the cliffs are transformed. The rocks turn pink, moss and lichens appear, and an unprepossessing insect crawls out of a cleft to greet the brief holiday. It's probably not even aware of where the light has come from or why the wind has died down, why the indifference to cold is no more, or what this new feeling, or rather sensation, of warmth and peace really is. But let the southern sun, or even the gentle temperate sun, rise over the rocks of the north, and it would be a disaster. The cold rocks would split, the lichen would dry out, the unprepossessing insect would shrivel up and die. The cold north needs a cold sun.

The butcher picks up a piece of meat in his huge white hands. A really fine, juicy piece. And a bone like loaf-sugar. Our Avdotya just can't believe her eyes. What happiness!

"Happy holiday!" she says, trying to flatter the butcher's feelings, so he won't change his mind.

"Thank you very much," answers the butcher. "Which holiday's that now? The Party holiday or the church holiday?"

The rumbling subsides. The people are in happy mood, even though the queue is packed in tight. And with merriment comes awareness.

"It's tough enough for us," someone says, "but what about the lonely old folk?"

Our Avdotya reaches out for the meat. The butcher doesn't give it to her. Avdotya is even a bit alarmed. But she needn't be.

"Let me put it in your bag for you," says the butcher.

The meat's in the bag. Avdotya, happy, has turned to leave, but the butcher calls after her:

"Thank you for your custom."

"God grant you good health," Avdotya replies.

Avdotya has gone outside and she walks along with a smile on her face. She goes round the corner, takes the piece of meat out of her bag, jogs it up and down like a child, kisses it. Some nice young chicken might be better, but Avdotya doesn't have any chicken, she didn't get any, and this meat is all her own. Our Avdotya's day started badly, but it's turned out well. While she's in luck she might as well make the best of it. Avdotya decides to visit the shop a long way away, one she rarely goes to. "Never mind, there's a little bench on the way, I'll sit down for a bit and then go on. Maybe I'll pick something up..."

Off goes our Avdotya. She walks, rests, walks on again. Suddenly she sees the town fool coming towards her. She knows his face to look at, but not his name.

This fool was no longer young. He's had a bad burn on his head, so he always wears a cap. This sharp-nosed fool travelled around on the public transport and cut silhouettes of people out of paper. They caught a good likeness, and they cost money. At one time the fool used to work as an artist in a tannery. Then one day, instead of the slogan "We shall fulfil the five-year plan in four years," he wrote "We shall fulfil the five-year plan in six years." What could he have been thinking of? But then, the fool's own brother, a colonel and a hero — medals, four-room flat, honoured veteran of the Great Patriotic War — suddenly announced one day in public: "Today, by order of the Supreme Commander-in-Chief, Comrade Stalin, snow fell in the city." And at that time not only was comrade Stalin no longer in this world, he was no longer even in the mausoleum. How could he have ordered the snow? They thought it was just a poor joke on the colonel's part, but when they looked closer they saw he was quite sincere, and there was an unhealthy gleam in his eyes. In short — bad genes. Maybe it's true and he is a real fool, but they do say that in some district quite a long way from his own, where people don't know him very well, the colonel's younger brother, the artist, approached the very jaws of a raging, bloodthirsty hours-long queue standing in the baking sun at a kiosk where they were selling early strawberries and declared: "In the name of the Supreme Soviet of the USSR I propose that you serve me three kilos of strawberries." As he spoke he extended his right hand with the palm upwards. The palm was empty, but the people did as he asked, and he took his three kilos of strawberries... There's a fine fool for you...

The fool sees our Avdotya and he says:

"Granny, they're selling Soviet sausage in the Store No. 15. And there's no one in there."

A man who happens to be walking beside her and overhears the fool's words, says:

"What kind of nonsense is that... All our sausage is Soviet, Jewish sausage is what we don't have here."

"It's nice sausage," answers the fool. "Smells good. Haven't seen any like it for ages."

"He's a bit... y'know," our Avdotya whispers to the man, and taps a finger against her headscarf.

"Ah," says the anti-Semite, and goes on his way. Store No. 15 is the one Avdotya was going to. She gets there. The

shop is as long as a narrow hose and dirtier than dirt itself...
Even for the Moscow suburbs it's far too dirty. A shop, you
might say, just begging to be satirised in the *Moscow News*.
The sales-assistants are all dirty, crumpled and unkempt,
standing behind the counter as though they're just out of bed
and they had vodka instead of coffee for breakfast. The cashier
is drunk too, and she's facing a drunken customer. They babble
at each other, but they can't come to any agreement. She's
speaking Ryazan dialect, he's speaking Yaroslavl dialect. And
all the shop-porters have tattoos on their bony arms and on
their sunken alcohol-corroded chests... One has Stalin tucked
away in his bosom, peeking out from behind a dirty undershirt
as though from behind a curtain, another has a grinning eagle,
a third has a naval chest — a sailor with the inscription "Port
Arthur."

Avdotya knew about this shop, and rarely came here. But
here she is today. Avdotya goes in, looking around her, sees the
picture described above and already feels like backing out. But
then she glanced into the far corner, with the "Delicatessen"
sign. She glanced, and she couldn't believe her eyes. The fool
was telling the truth. Lying there on the counter was beautiful
sausage, such as Avdotya hadn't even thought of in an age.
Firm as dark-red marble, but you could see at a glance that it
would taste juicy, with a white pattern of firm pork fat. A miracle,
that's what it was. How had several cases of smoked, Party-
standard, delicatessen sausage turned up here, as though they'd
come straight out of the stocks in the Kremlin? And why hadn't
the shop staff plundered it all themselves? They must have been
really drunk to put it on sale to the general public. And the label
hanging there said "Soviet Sausage". The fool hadn't lied. The
price was no joke, but the other cheap stuff there was full of
starch and garlic. Matveevna said that they put the meat of
water-rats in sausage when they used their skins to make fur

caps. But this was prime meat, pork and beef. And the meat smelt of Madeira... The closer Advotya came, the stronger the smell. If you sliced it fine and put it on bread, you could dine on it in fine style at breakfast and supper for a long time.

There was once a time when Avdotya didn't take her supper alone. There was a boiling samovar of pure gold, and Fillipov's breadrolls. He was handsome. And Avdotya had a long tawny braid. 1925 it was... No, '23... Half a pound of sausage in a crackling paper bag. The sausage had a different name then, but it was the same one... When he brought it he'd say: "Try this, Avdotya Titovna. It's made with Madeira." And he used to bring a little bit of smoked sturgeon... "Try a bit," he used to say.

"Well then, old girl," the drunken unkempt sales-assistant behind the counter says to Avdotya, "you buying any sausage? Be another ten years before you can get sausage like that."

But Avdotya doesn't answer. There's a lump in her throat. "Which one d'you want?" asks the sales assistant, "This one?" And she lifts up a fine firm stick of smoked sausage. But Avdotya can't see, her eyes are full of tears.

"What you cryin' for?" asks the sales assistant. "Son-in-law thrown you out, has he?"

"I haven't got a son-in-law," Avdotya scarcely manages to answer, and she sobs and sobs.

"Must've had something stolen," suggested the shop-porter with the naval chest. "You had something stolen, old girl?"

"Yes, stolen," Avdotya answers through her tears.

"D'you do it, Mikita?" The question is for the one with Stalin peeping out from behind the curtain of his undershirt...

"Never even laid eyes on her," answers Mikita. "All you could steal from an old crow like that is her piles."

"Stolen," says Avdotya, and the tears keep on and on pouring down... It's a long time since she's cried like that.

"If you've had something stolen, go to the police, don't stop the shop working," says the sales assistant, and puts the stick of sausage on the scales to weigh it for the anti-Semite.

The anti-Semite has clearly come to his senses and come back, having decided to believe the fool. And more and more people keep turning up. The fool has obviously done a good job spreading the word about the Soviet sausage.

Soviet sausage deserves a special mention of its own. Sausage queues and orange queues form the main axis of the trade war between the State and the people. You and I have not stood in any real sausage or orange queues, because Avdotya avoids them. Our Avdotya is cunning, and so too are the satellite-towners. And Makhno's Ukrainian anarchists are not often found there either. They stick more to the outlying districts, where the goods in short supply turn up. Then just who does stand and fight in those queues? The railway stations. And what exactly are the railway stations? They are the USSR. But the USSR only stands in line for oranges against its own will. Instead of pears and apples the USSR grows Kalashnikov automatic rifles in abundance, and the Third World grows oranges. A natural exchange unrelated to Marx's *Capital*. The orange is a strange foreign product. It gives the USSR bitter acid indigestion. The orange is not a serious product, it doesn't go with vodka — only good for giving to children to chew on. But sausage is a different matter...

The sausage shops of Moscow are filled with the spirit of the railway stations, the stuffy air of the railway stations... In the Moscow sausage shops you have the feeling that any moment your head will be set spinning by a barked announcement:

"Attention, boarding is beginning for train number..."

And then the trains will set out directly from the Moscow sausage shops for the Urals, Tashkent, Novosibirsk, Kishinev... The railway station people are not violent. The satellite towns

253

are cunning, but the stations are patient. Cunning is elastic, but patience is strong as iron...

Iron knows how to wait. And iron has its own reasons. It knows how far which products can be transported. After all, education has made great strides in the USSR. There's a high percentage of educated people in the queues. There are engineers standing there, physicists and chemists... Standing there and calculating... Meat and butter will travel as far as Gorky. But meat goes bad before it reaches Kazan, while sausage survives. You can take smoked foods, tea and tinned foods out beyond the Urals. And those oranges to amuse the kids. But there's nothing better than genuine smoked sausage. And the iron stands patiently in line. The USSR queues up for sausage. "Ah, sweetheart, a bit of you with a little bit of butter and some bread, and it's just like the good old days."

Then our Avdotya came to her senses. "I'm first," she yells, "I was the first in the queue."

Useless, they'd crossed her off the list. Avdotya got angry, she got really angry: "People nowadays are no better than scavengers, people nowadays are just rotten swindlers." Our Avdotya got really carried away in her resentment. Her scarf slipped off her head. She bruised her fist on someone, she bruised her elbow on someone else. Avdotya even heaved and strained and tried to "nudge" someone. But then she got nudged herself. Some man nudged her with his backside, without even bothering to turn round. And his backside was a progressive, Young Communist League, reinforced concrete backside.

Avdotya comes to in hospital. She comes to and her first thought is for her little bag.

"Where's my bag?"

"What bag?" asks the nurse. "You'd do better to worry whether your bones will knit. Old bones are brittle."

But Avdotya mourns and can't be comforted.

"There was meat in it, and three tins of herring, and bread, and two lots of eggs... But most of all I want the bag back..."

Getting treatment in the same hospital as Avdotya was the engineer Fishelevich, a low-paid cyberneticist. Hospital is like jail — people get to know each other quickly.

"Yury Semenovich."

"Avdotya Titovna."

"What's wrong with you, Avdotya Titovna?"

"I got nudged."

"What kind of illness is that?" Fishelevich asked ironically. "I, for instance, have a fracture of the right arm."

Avdotya took a close look.

"That's right," she said, "they shoved you out of the queue on the right hand side, I remember that. But don't you be upset. Going without eggs isn't nearly as bad as going without sausage."

But then one day the nurse said:

"Rodionova, there's a package for you."

Rodionova is our Avdotya's surname. Avdotya looked — it was her little bag... She looked again — it really was her little bag, she wasn't dreaming... No meat, of course, and no eggs, and only one of the three tins of herring. But someone had put in a bottle of yoghurt, a bag of honey-cakes and about a kilo of apples...

Then how Avdotya set about hugging her little bag, how she stroked and cuddled her Daisy-cow... And then she suddenly thought — who brought the package? Avdotya had no-one at all. She reached into the bag and there was a note in the bottom written in a crooked hand: "Eat and drink, granny, get well soon." It was signed: "Terenty." What Terenty?

Terenty was that shop-porter with the naval tattoos, the one with "Port Arthur" on his chest.

Which goes to show that even in the very darkest of souls the spark of God's light is not entirely extinguished. And therein lies our only cause for hope.

Friedrich GORENSTEIN (1932-2002) was born in Kiev. His father, a professor of economics, was arrested in 1935 and died in a prison camp. Fearing arrest, his mother moved to the provinces but she was imprisoned anyway. Friedrich lived in an orphanage before his relatives adopted him. In 1962, he went to Moscow to enrol as a student of scriptwriting. He became famous as the scriptwriter for the films "Solaris" and "Slave of Love". He wrote 17 film-scripts in all.

Gorenstein was forced to emigrate to West Berlin after the unsuccessful publication of the dissident almanac *Metropol* in which he took an active part, one more of the countless victims of the Soviet "cultural" policy.

His better known novels include *Atonement* (1967), *Psalm* (1975), *No Place* (1976), *Fellow-Travellers* (1983). His plays *Discussing Dostoevsky*, *Berdychev*, and *Child-killer* have been staged in Moscow theatres.

Evgeny Popov

Popov

Pork Kebabs

Translated by Rachel Osorio

A ll sorts of people used to go to the cosy little restaurant at Poddelkovo station on the line to Moscow. All sorts of people used to sit there for a few minutes, hours or days. All sorts, yes, but good people.

It was such a lovely, lovely station too — a real little gem. The station had a clean, polished, medium-sized, bronze bell that had never been rung. An old-fashioned clock with stiff hands and staring numbers marked out the time. There was also the stationmaster in his red hat — a severe unsociable character. And the station policeman who was the exact opposite. Yashka Blue-Cap was a simple chap and everyone liked him: he even used to crack walnuts for the children with the butt of his revolver.

The Moscow-Volga canal flowed so close to the station that in the summer you could see the deck of the steam boat, full of cheerful, enthusiastic holiday-makers, and the empty expanse of the tops of passing barges, where the sailors' washing fluttered in the wind as barefoot figures lounged about among the stacks of timber and played popular dance tunes on concertinas.

The suburban trains buzzed past like long, grey rats, their grey shadows clinging to the grey asphalt platform: hiss-s-s-s the rubber-edged doors opened, and tu-tu-tu bu-bu-bu-vu-vu — they set off for Moscow.

That's right. Only towards Moscow, not in any other direction, because it was the last station on the local line. Anyone who wanted to go further from Moscow had to get on an ordinary train with a conductor, a boiler in each carriage, a steam engine, and a lot of smoke. And that's what people did. They would get on those trains, carrying their cheap suitcases or rucksacks — and head off to some unknown destination — maybe Petersburg or Vorkuta, since the railway headed north, not south towards the warmer weather.

So there we are. The area around the station was itself rooted in those wild, ancient times when the Tatars were more powerful than the Russians, and fortresses were built around monasteries, surrounded by earthworks, moats and strong gates. They had obviously not been much good as fortresses, even though several centuries later they had acquired a new function as medieval monuments — "Poddelkovo fortified monastery is protected by the state" — and this was clearly reflected in the racial composition of the population in the Poddelkovo region, which confirmed, at least in part, the contentious theory proposed by certain individuals which goes as follows: there are no Russians left in Russia — we are all mongrels. And anyone who claims to be Russian and says that his mother was Russian is either a barefaced liar or confused as a result of not having examined the question closely enough, or possibly not having paid any attention to it at all.

Clearly an area containing such a large number of old Russian monuments could not claim to lead the world in terms of industrial development, but our region was known for its erudition. In addition to the research institutes located in the basements of churches, where graduates of the Moscow Historical Archives Institute rummaged through archives, there was also a massive nuclear station (for peaceful purposes), which did away with the need for peat, coal, petrol, solar energy and firewood, and used only water, graphite and a little bit of Uranium-235. And the biological centre with its guinea pigs, dolphins, tortoises and dogs was so famous that the streets of the ancient and somewhat boring little town were frequently enlivened by foreign visitors. They looked just like you or me, but they didn't understand a word of Russian.

There's no point in telling you all about the technical colleges, institutes and polytechnics — except to say that there were quite a few of them. Before I get on to the main events

259

of my sad story I should just mention one more point of interest in the region — a psychiatric hospital for 1,200 patients. It was renowned throughout Russia as a place where new drugs and methods of treatment were tried out. And that suburban Moscow air, with its unique, health-giving properties, the forest and the nearby tranquil water helped to straighten out the twisted minds of people suffering from ailments which have, alas, become very common in this intellectual era.

As for the methods of treatment they used, the latest to be thought up by the scholarly doctors was the PSC — or Patients' Social Committee.

The patients were so delighted by this, that they immediately undertook to produce a wall-newspaper, which came out in two copies. It was entitled "Towards a Healthy Mind", and contained discreet but bold criticisms of particularly unacceptable behaviour on the part of certain nurses. After the newspaper they went even further. The patients themselves, singing cheerfully the while, renovated the entire hospital and painted the walls a brilliant shade of azure, so that the psychiatric home became one of the most eye-catching and beautiful buildings in town. But that wasn't the most important thing. The most important thing was that working on the project completely cured many of the long-term patients. To such an extent that their numbers fell to rather fewer than 1,200, and there were even some vacant beds in the hospital. Those who remained acquired, through the work they had done, a certain wisdom and peace of mind, which helped them to bear their affliction. Such were the curative processes effected by the Patients' Social Committee!

Whether or not you are kindly disposed towards me, I am sure you now realise, dear reader, what a wealth of themes and subject matter is afforded to the fledgling writer by Poddelkovo station and the environs. But I am not going to write about the magical properties of the atom, nor about the guinea pigs, nor about ancient times, nor about the lunatics. So far, unfortunately, many sad incidents such as the one which follows have yet to be recounted. When they have all been told I shall start to write about archivists and happy students. So please don't grow impatient as you read the sad story of the manager of the Poddelkovo restaurant at Poddelkovo station. The story of the dramatic events, which took place within its walls and during a session of the local court of assizes in the presence of a public prosecutor, three reporters from various newspapers, and a large, excited audience.

This restaurant was right at the railway station. You had to push open the stiff station door and cross the waiting room where passengers dozed on yellow benches, and where, in addition, there was a pay phone from which, for only 15 kopecks, you could phone direct to Moscow, right to the very heart of Russia. And then you had to open another door — a glass one guarded by a doorman — go across to a table, sit down and inhale the fragrance of the dish whose reputation was what brought people here in the first place — "pork kebabs" — an invention of which the restaurant, or to be precise, its manager, was extremely proud. Oleg Alexandrovich Svidersky was a person of unique talent. I'll tell you all about him in due course, but first I must tell you about the kebabs, as they were the cause of the whole rumpus.

The kebabs were notable for a whole range of special qualities, but of these, two were outstanding: their moderate price and their unforgettable flavour. Judge for yourselves, my friends: where else within striking distance of Moscow would sixty-four kopecks buy you such a tempting and delicious-smelling plateful of fresh meat. Not only was the portion large, it was garnished with spicy orange sauce, not to mention spring onions, and even a slice of lemon! Ah! My mouth fills with deliciously thick saliva as I recall those savoury sensations, at the very attempt to convey the experience on paper.

"The best thing about this place is that they give you a decent-sized portion. Oh yes! You get a very decent-sized portion," the afficionados would say nervously watching, their eyes glistening avidly, to check that Nellie the waitress was taking care as she unloaded the metal dishes from her metal tray onto the elegant table with its array of beer bottles and SMP (salt, mustard, pepper) pots.

The knowing faces of the regular clients appeared nervous not for any reason, but because they were drinking vodka bought in a state shop, not in the restaurant. As everyone knows, vodka is outrageously expensive if you buy it in a restaurant. And if a representative of the restaurant administration, in the person of a waiter, was to notice that the restaurant's interests were being infringed in favour of the interests of the state, he would immediately, albeit inconspicuously, demand payment, to the tune of fifty kopecks or even a whole rouble, for his continued neutrality.

Ah vodka! It makes me sad to think about it. I'd rather write about those kebabs: they gave off a subtle, earthy, meaty fragrance, they melted on the tongue: they were the perfect incarnation of cooked pork. On more than one occasion the tipsy kebab-worshippers broke into spontaneous applause, trying to summon Svidersky, the restaurant manager and kebab-inventor extraordinaire, to take a bow, chat and share a drink with the simple workers, who spent their leisure hours in his restaurant, solving at a single stroke the vexing question of what to do in their spare time. But they never managed to persuade Svidersky to come out. He lived for his work, hidden away somewhere in the depths of the restaurant, behind the cauldrons, hot-plates, saucepans, automatic chopping machines, trunks, rattling abacuses, bills, with his certificates, safes and a red pennant awarded to the restaurant for first place in a competition.

You used to see all the staff — the waitresses, Nellie, Rimma, Shura, Tanya and Natasha; Esther Ivanovna who stood behind the counter; the two doormen, Kempendyayev and Kozlov; even occasionally the cooks; but you never laid eyes on the manager.

Well, never mind. That's the way it was.

The clients knew it as a calm, well-run establishment. Who could know, who could even guess at the terrible disaster hanging over this friendly operation, which always seemed to run as smoothly as clockwork.

The real cause of the disaster was the restaurant drivers at Poddelkovo. They were a shower of foul-mouthed drunkards, thieves and womanizers; a selection of the most worthless specimens of humanity you could hope to find.

The last to arrive, a fellow called Ordasov, managed to outperform his ten predecessors in the outrageousness of his behaviour. His horse was so hungry and had been beaten so hard that it turned a greenish colour and began to sway from side to side. This Ordasov would storm into the kitchen and seize the very first skewer of kebabs he could lay his hands on. He would demand a bottle of beer, then a second and a third. And when the dishwasher or any of the other women working in the kitchen had to go out into the yard to satisfy a call of nature, Ordasov immediately started grabbing at them and making unambiguous proposals concerning the loft above the restaurant stables and the hay which was stored up there, and how very nice and soft that hay was. And if by any chance his seductive charms failed to convince, Ordasov immediately unleashed a volley of abuse, calling the women all kinds of names.

Some people might not like to admit it, but there is no

doubt that the entire staff of the restaurant sighed with relief when they heard that Ordasov had illegally sold someone a lump of restaurant butter. He drank himself into a stupour on the proceeds, got picked up by the citizens' watch committee, then broke down sobbing at the interrogation and admitted everything. He was promptly packed off to where he belonged.

And one bright, beautiful morning, at the time when nature is waking up, the birds are just beginning to chirp, and the dew is still glistening on the asphalt, when they had already begun to boil up the stock in the restaurant kitchen, and Victor the sauce-chef had fastened the yellow buttons of his white overall, when everything was just beginning, a young man nobody knew suddenly appeared in the yard. Everyone noticed him. He was tall and sad, his clothes were rather strange: Texas blue jeans made in Moscow, a sturdy pair of cheap hiking boots, and a grey terylene shirt, the right sleeve of which was unbuttoned.

While everyone was wondering who this sad stranger was he dug in his trouser pocket, pulled out a whip, rapped on the kitchen window with its handle and said:

"Ahh? Uhu!"

They all froze on hearing these strange sounds, but the young man circled once more round the yard, then with a kick of his sturdy boot he opened the heavy stable door, led out the horse Rogneda and tipped the cart back on its axle. The next moment he set the collar on the horse's neck and harnessed her to the cart — the restaurant's running gear was now ready for use.

"He's the new driver!" shouted the sauce-chef, whereupon his colleagues all trickled out into the yard.

The grass was green, and the dandelions were yellow, and Rogneda's shit was steaming gently. And the new carter was getting to know his workmates.

"I — Anikusa, I — new driver, I drive horse, I go 'chk chk — woah'. Ahha?"

"Uhu!" the onlookers answered, deeply moved.

Then the new driver did something very strange.

He pulled the collar of his shirt down onto his right shoulder, so that the unbuttoned sleeve completely covered his right hand, stamped his feet and began to sing:

"Where the ship goes nobody knows!"

"He's a bit simple, that's what. We've got a simpleton this time." The waitresses felt pity for the young man as they watched his strange behaviour.

"Right then, Anikusha, time to get down to work" — the voice was kindly but firm.

And everyone began to whirl and bustle about. They ran to their cauldrons and chopping machines, to their saucepans, skewers and frying pans, their potato peelers, graters, siphons, sauce pots, mincers and collanders... because Oleg Alexandrovich Svidersky, the manager himself, had appeared on the concrete porch at the back of the restaurant.

With firm steps he walked up to Anikusha and said to him:

"Anikusha! If you work hard and keep your nose clean, you'll have a good life here."

That's what he said, and Anikusha lowered his bead and looked solemn; but only for a moment. After a second he cheered up, loaded his cart with empty crates and with a solemn air he drove out through the green gates to begin work.

That was the time when the restaurant really reached its peak: the staff was fully primed with the addition of that final cartridge — a cartridge with a good percussion cap and the right amount of powder. A small cartridge, maybe, but ever ready for action.

The kebabs began to taste better, even more perfect. And the circle of devotees increased steadily, so that within a short time a huge number of people had visited the restaurant at Poddelkovo station.

There were physicists from the nearby nuclear station, severe-looking men in glasses. In reality they were completely ordinary lads: they used to tell jokes, and one of them, he must have been one of those yuppies, sang a rather risqué song, even though his fine eyes expressed his faith in our ideals. He was just a young lad who hadn't really settled down yet... They ate and enthused about the food...

There were biologists, who for some reason didn't seem to smell of animals at all, even though they had such intimate relations with all kinds of tortoises. They were nice people, but somehow painfully soft and tender; it was one of the women in their group who said:

"It's incredible. Just imagine, comrades! Vie, Alex — here we are at the back of beyond, eighty kilometres from Moscow, to find such cooking, such wonderful service! As you know I'm a Russian, but I came to Moscow from Baku, and we used to eat kebabs there. And now I can sit here and remember my sun-soaked home, and it almost makes me weep. I feel like a lily in the rain."

And her friends, Vie, bald-pated Alex, Emma and Emmanuel clinked their glasses filled with Moskovskaya vodka from a state shop, ate and enthused about the food.

There were also students who came out from Moscow, representatives of the new generation gap. They tasted the kebabs, they gasped, ate and enthused. Then they tuned up their electric guitars. They were the next generation who no longer had beards, but were long-haired and wore bell-bottoms and bright Japanese sweaters. But when they sang their big beat songs, all in harmony, everyone realised that they should not be criticised and that it is not just trousers and haircuts that determine the quality of a human being, as the poet Yevtushenko once wrote. And that jazz is a very good thing too, certainly it isn't harmful, and of course we know about classical music too, and respect it, but in terms of its particular relevance to modernity. Oh no, you mustn't think that these categories are being turned inside out, no, that's not it at all, of course we live in an age of innovation and physicists and mathematicians who understand everything and take an ironic attitude to it all. That was how they played, the students who came out from Moscow — geology students, they turned out to be. People gathered round, little by little, to hear them play. And everyone ate and enthused about the food.

One warm summer evening, when a sympathetic doctor allowed Lysov, chairman of the PSC and inventor of a perpetual motion machine, out of the hospital to go for a walk on his own, Lysov ran straight to the restaurant and sat down at a table in the corner. He chatted with some physicist he had never met before about the future prospects and past history of his invention... Lysov himself was small and balding, with the tired face of an idiot. He only ended up in the mental hospital because of a sheepskin jacket he stole at the market. He was prepared to go on working on his invention until he dropped dead, and he could produce philosophical proof of its existence, on the basis of his interpretation of life itself as a perpetual motion machine. All that remained was to discover what kind of engine kept such a machine in motion. Lysov worked on his model in his free time — he was a good craftsman. But then he stole the sheepskin jacket at the market and got sent down for a few months. And while he was in prison he started ranting and carrying on; in particular he insisted on telling everyone about his machine, so the prison administration sent him off for compulsory treatment, pardoning him for the theft. Once he was in the mental hospital Lysov began his real career, the pinnacle of which was achieved when he became chairman of the Patients' Social Committee — a pleasant and honourable position.

The madman and the physicist were engaged in heated debate, and at one point the physicist said to Lysov:

"Listen here, old chap, you're a clever fellow, and you know perfectly well that a perpetual motion machine is an impossible idea. It has baffled the most brilliant minds — why can't you acknowledge your own puniness in the face of the whole of the scientific world!"

Chairman Lysov burst into tears, flung his arms around the physicist and admitted everything — that he was still determined to build his machine, but that even he himself had no real faith in its durability for one simple reason: certain parts, including the drive belt, would eventually wear out and have to be replaced — so while the machine would of course work it could not be claimed to be perpetual. But they also continued to eat and to enthuse over the food.

While all this was going on Anikusha the driver was sitting in the kitchen, uttering profound ideas to anyone curious enough to listen, about how much he loved cats and dogs, fish and birds, to say nothing of the flowers and the grass. When he had nothing to do he would whirl around the premises, leaping and cavorting, making bleating noises, and creeping into parts of the restaurant which should have been strictly out of bounds — the pantry, the fridge — yes, even the fridge: he even found his way into that holy of holies, the manager's office, where he also leapt and cavorted about, even when Svidersky had a visitor with him — and strangely enough the manager didn't get particularly angry with this holy fool, but on the contrary praised him and spoke gently to him. In this way one insignificant person may help society at large understand another, more important person. Suddenly everyone realised that Svidersky was simply a very good-natured, weary, middle-aged man —

a man who had seen a great deal in his life and suffered as a result; who had become wise and unsociable, but remained true to himself and to his native talent.

Anikusha worked from morning till night, with a zeal that was most unlike the attitude of his predecessors. Even when he settled down for the night in his stable, there was no drinking or monkey business. He didn't steal or play cards, or sprinkle pepper on the hot stove, or skulk in corners. It was almost strange to see an ordinary, run-of-the-mill half-wit behaving so extremely well.

More than that. They noticed that occasionally a strange glow seemed to emanate from Anikusha. Not the kind of permanent halo you see round the heads of Christ or the saints. More intermittent than that. It didn't come from his head but from his belly button. It would flash on and off. Honestly! A kind of intermittent flashing, coming from somewhere lower — somewhere around his navel, more or less. But they didn't take notice of this phenomenon. Anything can happen when you have a holy fool about the place — and what's more you never know what you might imagine when you've spent the whole day leaning over a scorching stove, turning those blasted pork kebabs on their skewers, and washing mountains of dishes. There's no denying that it's hard work, and anything can happen if a person's tired enough.

Everyone was totally amazed when the whole thing came to an abrupt end — with a very simple explanation.

The police arrived. They sealed off the restaurant, and poor, pale, white-faced Svidersky, with a farewell backward glance at his creation, stepped into the impenetrable gloom of a Black Maria, where someone with a revolver at his side was already waiting. The Black Maria drove him through the sleepy streets, straight to a solitary cell, where they shaved his head, dressed him in prison garb and unmasked him as the villain he

269

was: Svidersky, born 1915, Russian nationality, no children, unmarried, did not fight in World War II. He was brought to trial and condemned of a most loathsome crime, to whit: it turned out that those kebabs, famous throughout the region, were not made from pork at all, but from dog meat. Rufuses and Rovers, Sheps, Rexes, Jacks, Spots, Goldies — one and all were transformed by Svidersky into chunks of meat.

You cannot imagine, dear reader, the vileness of this abomination.

It was the talk of the town — that in the nth year of Soviet power, this bastard, this grey-haired scoundrel and his team of equally foul, loathsome villains, were able to install themselves in that dear little restaurant outside Moscow, start taking the skins off our Rufuses and Rexes and turning them into — I can hardly bring myself to say it — dog meat!

And to add to the shame of it — our local gourmets, in their quest for the pleasures of the palate, were deluded by those delectable kebabs. No doubt they would have been just as happy to dig into cat kebabs if they had been served up. Even connoisseurs were unable to tell pig from dog.

To reassure the public that had been so wickedly deceived, I would have liked to recount a little story that I heard from an old woman at the market in the town of K. She told me how, one winter, she cured five people of consumption using the lard from her puppy Kutka, and how dog fat was widely used as a cure for T.B. But when I got to the court and saw the looks on the faces of those turncoat witnesses, I instantly abandoned any such idea. I wasn't going to risk ridicule, or maybe even a beating from such strong people, who had been fed on dog kebabs and knew no fear.

Anikusha disappeared as well. At first the word was that he had been the kebab-maestro's right-hand man. But then it became clear that he had caught Svidersky red-handed and then throttled him in his steely police grip. He turned out to be Senior Police Lieutenant Vzglyadov. He had discovered, photographed and exposed a number of dark deeds on microfilm, using his micro-flash. That would account for the mysterious glow, which baffled the kitchen crooks.

There was of course a memorable trial, held in the old courthouse, on an old street, presided over by an old prosecutor. Half of Poddelkovo turned out for it — and even kebab lovers from other towns came along.

Svidersky repented in the dock, weeping villainous tears. But not a shadow of sympathy was to be seen in the eyes of the audience. Someone even demanded capital punishment, and although it was obvious from the outset that the criminal would not actually get the chop — however many dogs he had murdered — the idea was extremely popular.

Even the defence lawyer continually picked his teeth with a sharpened match. We cannot be sure what he wanted to imply by this gesture, but if we think about it we may hazard a fair guess. He was really saying: "I will defend you, Svidersky, to the very best of my ability, but only because it is my job. It has fallen to my lot to try to save miserable scum like you from the punishment you so richly deserve." In the end Svidersky got a sentence, which was neither particularly heavy nor particularly light, in accordance with the laws of the land. The fraudulent culinary innovator disappeared from view amidst a storm of outrage, having sown the seeds of discord and skepticism in the hitherto carefree hearts of innocent gourmets.

While all this was going on, the restaurant had long since been reopened and renovated by a stalwart workforce. There was Boris, a waiter, born in 1945 and exempt from military service, who liked to tell the customers about how he tried to enrol in the Moscow Geological College for three years running.

There was a new clerk, a new cashier, a new driver, and of course there had to be a new manager — a man by the name of Zvorikin. Utterly unlike his predecessor, he was a noisy, jolly man. He liked to loosen his trousers so his paunch hung out, and sit down with clients or particularly honoured guests, regaling them with stories of his life.

But under Zvorikin's tutelage the kebabs went into total decline. They became too grey or too brown, and considerably smaller, as though they had shrivelled up in shame at their own unappealing appearance. You didn't really want to put one in your mouth — but what was to be done? After Svidersky, the local people couldn't bear to go a single day without eating a kebab.

The new manager didn't last long either — which is rather strange, because they say lightning never strikes twice in the same place. It was discovered, quite by chance, that four grams of meat from every portion went straight into his pocket. And those grams soon mounted up to several thousand roubles. To tell the truth, they only ever found 2,000, but that's not to say that he might not have hidden the remaining thousands somewhere: he might simply have buried them under an apple tree. So that when he has done his time he can return, fit and muscled after years of hard physical labour, and say: "I'm just going to dig some worms to go fishing." And then he will dig up his hoard and embark on a solitary life, soothing his soul with thoughts of greed and stupidity — those twin imperfections of human nature.

Summer came again. The year was 1967. The little town was flooded with greenery and lilac blossoms. The roofs poked out through a sea of lilac, and the people darted about the turbid depths of the cool streets like some mysterious form of marine life.

The windows of the Poddelkovo restaurant at Poddelkovo

station on the line to Moscow were flung wide open. Flung wide open and stretched with muslin to keep out the flies.

The fans whirred and their whirring accompanied endless discussions as to which of the two managers was worse. Mikheev, a railway coupler, stood up for Svidersky. He had become a frequent visitor at the restaurant after he started getting good social security money for breaking his leg at work. His voice would suddenly rise above the noise of the fans, cutting across the hum of conversation:

"The way I see it – Sviderky was shit – if you'll excuse my language, gentlemen! The scum of the earth, and a dog-eater into the bargain – but at least you got a decent meal off him. Generous portions, and tasty. Anyway, who cares whether it's dog or pig?"

"That Zvorikin was a reptile too — and a robber, let's be honest. But he did serve real meat, even if he gave short measure..."

"What do you know about it anyway?"

"I mean..."

Who knows how this absurd argument might have ended, if the fans had not suddenly stopped whirring, for the simple reason that they had been switched off to save a bit of electricity as the temperature in the room dropped. And from the loudspeakers burst the sound of the very latest song, performed by a group of young people in bell-bottomed trousers and collarless jackets, to the accompaniment of various cheerful-sounding electrical instruments. The song which, according to the radio announcer, was the hit of the season, Number One of that bright summer, the summer of youth, the summer of 1967:

"Come back! You've been away so long! Come back! I can't live without your love!"

Etc. etc. You know the song, of course. And if, by some

miracle, you had been in the little restaurant at Poddelkovo station at that moment, you would have immediately started to sing along with the invisible singers on the radio, just like all the other argumentative clients, who instantly forgot about the crimes of the two managers, the two biggest scoundrels of 1967. They all took the singing very seriously, stretching out their necks and holding in their stomachs, forgetting everything else as they concentrated their whole attention on singing. And at this point we must sadly leave the cheerful scene, and move on from the little restaurant to inspect some of the surprising things which are going on in other comers of the country, for example up in the North, in Yakutia, a boiler-man in a brewery fell into a vat of beer, and was there for at least a month before he was found. And when this came to the notice of the population they laid off vodka as well as beer for a whole month, fearing that they might come across a bit of the dead man dissolved in their drink, in which case they would be committing an act of cannibalism. Isn't that a surprising story?

I'd like to write about it properly, but I'm afraid there might be problems getting it published.

Born in 1946 in Krasnoyarsk (Siberia) **Evgeny POPOV** graduated from the Moscow Institute of Geology and spent many years travelling the length and breadth of Russia. He has more than 200 stories and a number of prize-winning novels to his credit and five novels, including *The Soul of the Patriot* published in 20 countries. His stories reverberate with laughter and teasing humor that verges on the lyrical.

Communal
Living

A Crowded Place

by Boris Yampolsky

He met her one autumn evening outside the cinema — a slight figure in a nylon blouse and a high-fitting plaid skirt with a fringe at the hem, and a white funnel shaped hat perched on her head. Her eyes were heavily mascara'd.

There were no tickets, as usual, and it was raining.

He said, "You haven't got a spare ticket?"

She grinned.

"How about you?"

And so they met.

She said her name was Stella, and he made up a name for himself, just in case — Dima.

They chatted about Jean Maurais, and she said she preferred Marc Bernes.

"Shall we go somewhere?" he said.

So they went to the Mars cafe.

They had two big vodkas each, some soup and boiled tongue, which the menu claimed was steak. He had a black coffee, and she asked for the house speciality ice-cream, in the shape of a tower dotted with preserved strawberries and little biscuits.

"Are you really called Stella, or did you just invent a pretty name for yourself?"

"That's a military secret," she said, and he had the impression she was making fun of him.

It got to be midnight. There was a light drizzle, and the leaves were falling along the road.

He walked her home to Taganka Square, to a quiet, deserted side street, into a big courtyard with a lot of staircase entrances veiled in darkness. They went into one of them to say goodnight.

He kissed her, and she responded with some enthusiasm.

"Perhaps I could come in for a minute?" he asked.

He felt strangely unsure of himself.

"For a minute, only a minute," he whispered.

She unlocked the door and said "We've got to be very quiet." She took his hand and led him into darkness down a long corridor. He kept stumbling over boxes and panels on the floor, and getting slapped in the face with wet rags which he realized must be washing dangling from clothes lines. There was a smell of gas and washing powder, the lively, gipsy squalor of a communal apartment.

A door squeaked open, and they went into a dark room. "Don't move," she said, and as he stood there she made a bed on the floor, working by feel alone.

Outside it rained and rained....

"Ciao," she said, as she fell asleep.

In the morning, when he usually woke up for his first cigarette of the day, he opened his eyes and was scared out of his wits. In the grey, lifeless half light of an autumn morning, he discovered he was lying on the floor of a big room crammed with people.

There was one lad squatting in his underpants doing exercises with dumb-bells and behind him another one who could have been his double sitting on a folding chair shaving in a mirror propped up on a stool, and yet another sitting at a table digging in to his breakfast.

Under the window there was a big, old-fashioned wooden bed with an old man lying there reading a paper.

He got the idea that the old man might set the lads on him, and they'd start beating him up with the dumb-bells, maybe even slash him with the razor, and he swiftly closed his eyes again and pretended to be asleep.

Then he thought it must all have been a dream. He cautiously opened his eyelids again and saw, as if it were in a movie, the lad who'd been brandishing the dumb-bells, now fully dressed, sitting on the folding chair shaving.

The one who'd been shaving before was sitting at the table working away with a spoon, and the third, who by this time had finished his breakfast, was standing at the dressing table doing up his tie. The old man was still reading his newspaper.

Last night's Stella was lying beside him, sleeping as peacefully as a child.

He closed his eyes again in feigned sleep, and still couldn't decide whether or not it was all a dream.

After a while he looked warily round him again. This time the lads had gone.

Then a little boy with a skipping rope appeared, a baby in a pram in the corner started to cry until an elderly woman shoved a dummy in his mouth. He started to suck it and stopped bawling.

The old man looked over his newspaper with wide-awake eyes, and he had the impression he'd been sitting there all night like that, staring at him in the darkness.

In the end he thought "Oh, the hell with it," jumped out of bed, and started doing his exercises in his turn. The old man silently observed his performance. The little boy went on skipping. The woman dandled the baby.

It was quite light by now, and sunny. Factory hooters were sounding nearby.

He gently woke the girl.

"I'm on the evening shift," she whispered without opening her eyes. She smiled and went back to sleep.

The old man got out of bed. He was fully dressed in a donkey jacket and white felt boots, and when he stood up he was revealed to be a sturdy big-nosed old chap as bald as a mushroom, with deep-set eagle eyes.

"Well, what about it?" he demanded severely.

The guest produced some money, and the boy was despatched to an Uncle Agafon. He grabbed his scooter and shot off down the corridor, from where he shortly reappeared with a sealed half-liter bottle. The woman produced a pan of fried potatoes and some herring. They sat down to eat.

"Just to keep out the cold," said the old man, knocking out the cork. He ate and drank with gusto and thoroughly enjoyed himself, inhaling the joys of this unexpected feast day.

When they had finished up the bottle and the potatoes, the old man said to the woman, "Well, come on, let's push off. They've got young people's things to do." And he grabbed the newspaper and went off, with the woman and the child in tow.

The girl went on sleeping.

What relation was she to them? Daughter, niece, or just a tenant? That he never found out.

Translated by Gordon Clough

A Marriage of Convenience

by Ksenia Klimova

"A good thing you came," said Sergei, drawing me into the dark depths of a communal apartment cluttered with all sorts of junk. "It's time I had a decent meal, too."

Somehow, Sergei always managed to get the wrong end of the stick. The one good thing about communal apartments, everybody knows, is that they are all situated in the centre of Moscow. But the view from Sergei's window was onto the heavy traffic of the Outer Ring Road, and, moreover, onto that ten-kilometre narrow stretch of it which is notorious for its head-on car crashes and the almost total death-rate of those motorists involved in them. Nor could the window be rightfully called his own: he had got this room out of a complex series of "chain swaps" engineered by some operative who kept saying, "It's just a matter of greasing a few palms, and everybody will be happy."

When the operation was eventually completed, everybody was indeed happy with the exception of Sergei, who found himself sharing this room with an old lady, who, after the proper palm had been greased, was pronounced to be his grandmother. She had been expected to die before the operation was completed, but proved to possess an aristocratically tenacious hold on life. To give her her due, she also possessed an equally aristocratic probity. She apologized to Sergei in French with a shrug, offered him tea, and promised to burden him with her presence as little as possible. She was as good as her word, too, though nobody knew where she spent all those hours when she was away from home, waiting for death to catch up with her.

"What does he mean by a decent meal?" I wondered. I had thought we were going to the tennis court, which Sergei's institute rented for an unknown purpose since Sergei was the only one who ever played tennis there, except for me who tagged along in the hope of learning at least the ABCs of the aristocratic game.

"You could at least have warned me that you expect to be paid for the tennis lessons with food," I grumbled.

"Sorry, no tennis today. I'm thinking of getting married. This evening I'm going to negotiate."

Luckily we had by then reached his room, and I had the old lady's settee to faint on. This bum, this workaholic, for whom any effort outside work was a bother, was thinking of getting married! Unbelievable. OK, I could imagine him bringing a wife into this den of his, but calling the girl on the telephone, taking her out, making a declaration of love — no, he just wouldn't be able to go to all that bother.

I discovered that there actually was something to eat in the place — my function was simply to cook it. Sergei finds cooking an excruciating drudgery. Even boiling noodles is too much for him, involving as it does pouring water into a pan, lighting the gas stove, taking the pan off the heat and then sieving the noodles.

So I decided to cook him lunch just out of curiosity. On a full stomach he was prepared to enlighten me:

"There's nothing for it but to get married," he pronounced in the tone of Gogol's Podkolesin. "It's marry, or die. Earning money is one thing, but standing in food queues, cooking... I made meat aspic once. It's supposed never to go off but after two weeks it acquired the consistency of glue, and began to stink, too. And it's not only the question of cooking either. A married person feels less vulnerable. My foster grandmother, roommate that is, is also thinking of getting married. Another resident in this room. Between them they'll get rid of me in no time. I've met the prospective husband — a racketeer if ever I saw one."

"And does your future wife have somewhere to live then?"

"Absolutely! This very room. She's my former wife, you see. That same Valentina whom I divorced five years ago."

"But why the hell should you marry your own wife all over again?"

"Oh, there are plenty of good reasons. All you women have kinks, but at least I know hers and she knows mine. It costs a lot these days to get a new passport when you take your husband's name, and she's already got mine. And do you know how much wedding rings are? We've still got the ones we bought last time. And generally this is a bad moment to start on any new ventures, plough up the virgin lands, so to speak. There've been all these beauty contests, and women expect a lot. Why, a bunch of roses would leave a horrible gap in my budget. Let alone a honeymoon... Where can you afford to take your young bride to give her something to remember? And my ex may still remember all the good things we had during out first honeymoon. The trip down the Yenisei... Almost a cruise."

"I see. What about love?"

He looked at me commiseratingly, as much as to say: What are you talking about? What love? The main thing is to survive.

"You know my pal Yuri?" he asked. "He's making a lot from his business trips abroad, so he thought he could afford a new wife. And do you know what this new wife has gone and done? After love had paled a little, she invited over some of her burglar pals. They picked the apartment clean. Even carried off the computer he borrowed from the firm. So he lost his job too."

When Sergei left for his "negotiations", I went along, and even made the sign of the cross over him.

And get married they did. When the photographer at the registry office tried to bully them into posing for a "newlyweds" picture, they showed him their old ones, saying they were even better, because they were younger then. Valentina, a thin nervous woman, looked content.

Translated by Raissa Bobrova

Communal Living

by Alexander Terekhov

Basically, I've got to agree that communal living is socialism's harsh legacy and of course, there was nothing like it before the Bolshevik revolution. But the happiest time of my life was when I lived in a communal apartment.

"Why don't you move in tonight?" suggested the man who had the room before me as he tried to avoid looking me in the eye. You've got eight square meters all to yourself and the neighbor's a real cracker. You won't regret it, I can tell you."

I moved in that night, instructions fully memorized: top lock, two turns, bottom lock a bit of a push and then one turn and down to the sixth door on the left. I fumbled my way through the darkness, weighed down by bundles and parcels and then crashed on the bare mattress in my room.

Not that I could sleep in my new surroundings. All through the night I kept waking up. I would wake up, turn over and think "great!" Then I'd be asleep again.

The next minute, I'd wake up thinking about the sort of person who ends up in a communal apartment. They've always come from somewhere much worse, either off the streets, straight out of the army or prison or from a doss house, so you can understand their joy once they get there.

And then I'd go off again only to be woken up once more in the dark with the feeling that I owed all the best in me to communal living. My roots are here and my best roots at that.

It's a source of all the very best in this country: the commune, the communist working weekends, communist awareness... And then I would doze off again.

Next minute I was wide awake. I just lay there scratching my belly, and started to think about the things I would soon need to get — a table, a chair, a wife, a lamp... Then I glanced at my watch and gasped: it was already lunch time. So why the hell was it so dark? Aha, it turned out that my window was completely blocked by the wall of the warehouse next door. So that's why the son-of-a-bitch wanted me to move in at night. Oh, what the hell, anyway.

The post-woman was distributing the mail among the post-boxes, like a poultry maid feeding her chicks. She knew everything about us just by the newspapers and magazines we subscribed to, and the letters and postal orders we received. And we knew each other inside out, right down to the color of each other's underwear and who had what for dinner.

My neighbor was forever just about to get married. Her mute mother was banished to the kitchen each time it seemed like a proposal was in the cards. Her fiancé would sit in the room playing the accordion and singing away to himself, "Oh such brave lads are we, are we, such brave lads are we...!" He cut a lively figure as he sat there stamping his foot in time to the music. The morning after, he would come out of her room, still in his pyjamas, and with an assumed air of importance call his office.

Everyone was listening to his every word. No one missed a thing in that apartment. We could tell who the door was for by the number of rings and all of us knew the long single ring of a stranger — the local policeman or the plumber. Everyone kept a mental register of the others' comings and goings, whether they were trips to the kitchen or the loo. Only the old man who had just moved here from the country couldn't get used to city amenities and would always go behind the nearest fence in the yard where the kids from the nursery had planted some dill. His wife thrived on scandal and whenever she had a chance she would pounce on some poor soul and accuse them:

"Why are you always stealing my papers? What? Me a bitch? That daughter of yours is a bitch!"

Another favorite habit of hers was to wander up and down the corridor late in the evening.

"So whose hair is that in the bath?" she would ask, a hint of a threat in her voice.

Life there was fraught with tragedy, poverty and vileness but it was a great life, the same as life anywhere else in this country. Everyone knew everyone else's business so that only our souls remained undisclosed. There are times when I mourn the passing of this era.

It was the happiest time of our lives because there was always something to look forward to then: everyone dreamed of getting a flat of their own. The time would come... When we have a few more kids... And everyone did leave. Not all at once of course, but one by one, with a sort of shameful pleasure. You would be going off and they would still be there — left behind. There would have been no sense of happiness if everyone had left at the same time, because one person's happiness is always at the expense of another's.

Happiness comes to an end when you get stuck somewhere and, try as you might, you remain stuck there. Then in your defeat you can only become the stain on another's happiness. In these new times there will be more happiness and with this more suffering too. Expectations, tears, applications — they won't get you anywhere, and you will only get whatever you can eke out for yourself. If you're born in a communal flat, you will probably die there. It works the same way if you're born in a palace. Too bad this comes to light much too late when we've all been shaped for a different life.

But on the other hand — what a gift! No one can ever take away the joy of dreams already dreamed.

Even when I'm an old man puffing away like an old steam-engine, I'll never forget the worst horror in my life... It was about one in the morning and I hadn't hung my wash bowl properly on the wall. It came crashing down on top of the toilet, smashing it to pieces. I had a real battle with the water as I first tried to mop it up, then tried to catch it in a bucket and finally sealed the main valve. But I knew that at six in the morning the whole world would wake up and want to know what the hell had been going on. I was just about ready to end it all, but instead spent the night searching the town high and low and finally managed to find myself a plumber who had had more than a skinful.

I hauled him and his toolbox back under one arm and the new cistern under the other with as much love and care as though it were a crystal treasure chest carrying diamond jewels or a prince's crib. I kept lighting the plumber's cigarettes and fussing around him, and he did manage to fix the cistern. When he left I tried it to see if it was working. It was. I went into the kitchen, swigged some water from the kettle and looked out of the window. Suddenly, I just knew that I would never feel this happy ever again. Funny, eh?

Translated by Sandra Stott